SONG OF THE ADOËL

KEVIN KING

SONG OF THE ADOËL BY KEVIN KING

Published by Brimstone Fiction
1440 W. Taylor St. Ste #449
Chicago, IL 60607

ISBN: 978-1-946758-55-2

Library of Congress Cataloging-in-Publication Data
King, Kevin
SONG OF THE ADOËL / Kevin King 1st ed.
Printed in the United States of America

This book is dedicated to my sister, Kristi, and to my heart-sister, Anitra, my co-explorers through many imaginary worlds.

CHAPTER ONE

The ancestral curse weighed heavier on Raendel tonight than usual—not the curse itself, but the way it set him apart. The stares and murmurs from the guests who'd never seen an Adoël before burrowed into his brain, digging up a lifetime of similar experiences.

An Adoël girl stood in the corner, the shining white hair and unnaturally pale skin of her heritage cloaked in shadow. None of the nobles spared any attention for the thousands of flower blossoms that floated in the air around them like glowing snowflakes. If any of them did notice the girl it would be with disgust or fear, not the awe and admiration she deserved for her skills with illusion magic. They hadn't come for the entertainment. They'd come to ogle the young lady who would soon be arriving with her father to be displayed like a side of beef in the marketplace. If they had so little respect for their own kind, how could Raendel expect any better for himself?

Every Adoël served the royal family, a tradition that bound Raendel to his place like shackles. They crafted breathtaking illusions for ungrateful nobility. Raendel's heart burned with the injustice, but what else could they do? The king's favor alone protected them.

"Rae."

He spun to face the prince and bowed. His voice reverberated with an unearthly tone, another distinction that set the Adoël apart. "Yes, Your Highness?"

"Stop that, Rae." Prince Kenan frowned and tugged on the sleeves of his dark blue coat. His tawny hair lay in neatly combed lines except for one stray lock near the back that stood straight up, a rebel soldier at attention. "It's already awkward enough being stuck at this stupid party surrounded by stuffy lords. I don't need that attitude from you too."

Raendel drew in a slow breath, gathering his thoughts before he replied. He didn't want to take out his frustration on his only friend. Prince Kenan appreciated him when others didn't.

"I'm sorry, Kenan," Raendel said. "This is a public function, and you are here representing the royal family. How would it look if your own servant didn't show you proper respect?"

Kenan rolled his eyes and gestured to the open space around them. "There isn't anybody close enough to hear you. Anyway, nobody pays enough attention to me to care how my servants treat me. I'm only here because my mother didn't want to insult an old friend by ignoring his daughter's celebration. Why didn't she send Devin instead? He loves parties."

"You know your brother has other duties."

Kenan gripped the bottom of his coat and pulled down on it hard enough to stretch the seams. "You mean he's doing important things. He's learning to run the kingdom while I get handed around as a party favor to make other people feel important."

Raendel struggled to find an answer. He understood that feeling of insignificance far too well. "This *is* important, Ken. Building good connections to the outer provinces strengthens the kingdom. Showing up at these events is a crucial part of that."

"Well, I hate it." Kenan waved a hand at the clumps of lords scattered around the room. "They all flock to these parties like ravens to a corpse, squawking at each other and puffing out their chests. They want to *look* important. I want to actually *do* something important. Of course, these little court games of attending each other's balls seem important to you. You don't understand how pointless it feels from my position."

Raendel lowered his head. He felt like he should be saying something more, but he couldn't think of anything new to say. They'd repeated this conversation a dozen times and it always ended the same.

After a few moments of awkward silence, Kenan sighed and offered a half-smile. "I suppose if I'm going to hang around here all afternoon I might as well have some wine. It'll help me blend in and make me look like I'm having fun. If I drink enough maybe I'll actually enjoy myself a little. Since you're so concerned about showing me proper respect, you can go and fetch me some."

Raendel bowed with an exaggerated flourish. "At once, Your Highness. To ensure the safety of your Royal Person, I'm afraid I will be forced to taste each glass of wine before I give it to you. In case it is poisoned, you understand. It is my duty to risk my life to protect yours."

Kenan snorted, and a real smile broke through before he smoothed his face into a mock serious expression. "I'm sure you will perform your duty with enthusiasm. Now get to it. I'm thirsty."

Raendel embellished another bow, holding it for several seconds before meandering in the general direction of the refreshment table. The moment he turned his back to the prince he let his face relax into its habitual neutral expression. He joked with Kenan, but he did take his duty seriously. Seriously enough to give his life if required, not from obligation, but for more personal reasons. He didn't think he could live with himself if he failed to protect his only friend.

Raendel wove through the room with practiced ease, gliding between isolated clumps of noblemen scattered across the room, passing the time with idle gossip as they waited for the guest of honor to arrive. His gaze flicked along the way in front of him, choosing the path that would keep him farthest away from the guests. Most of them wore enough perfume to give him a headache from five yards away. The enhanced sense of smell shared by the Adoël only added to Raendel's trepidation. All the nobles stank of pride. The smell of fear drifted in clouds, especially near visitors who had never seen one of the Adoël before. Raendel spent most of his day inside the castle, serving Prince Kenan.

His distinctive features would have drawn stares even without the stories. The name Adoël had been used to frighten children for generations. Mothers would clutch their children as he passed in the street. *Don't go outside at night or the Adoël will get you. Don't wander into the woods, the Adoël will catch you and suck the life out of you.* Each passing generation believed the stories a bit more than their parents. To encounter an Adoël in person resurrected the terrors planted in the hearts of children now grown.

Whispers swirled in his wake. Ghost-child. Cursed. Tainted. Touched by the Necromancer. Raendel had heard them all before, but he still flinched with every sting.

Raendel's nervousness increased in proportion to his distance from Prince Kenan. Connection to the royal family shielded him from overt violence, but accidents could happen. Especially if someone panicked. He hummed to himself to block out the voices.

The flowers in the air around him shimmered, but he wasn't trying to shape them, so they didn't change. The song of the Adoël in the corner maintained the flower illusion. Her voice would be inaudible, even nearby. The songs used to craft illusions fell into a range outside human hearing. He couldn't pick out her unique scent through the stink of the crowd, but he knew it would be Aeriel. Her illusions always displayed a special beauty. Each blossom glowed with different shape and color, showering the walls with rainbows. The candles mounted around the room showed no flame, even though they burned. This grand illusion drew in all their light and reshaped it into dazzling beauty. The guests paid it no more attention than a pack of dogs would to a beautiful painting.

The refreshment table stood in a far corner, out of the way of guests. A few attendants circulated through the crowd with pitchers of wine or bite-size sweetmeats. Raendel plucked a glass from the end of the table and selected a pitcher of red that looked moderately watered. Its floral scent matched the illusory decorations. Raendel poured a mouthful and swirled it before drinking. He tasted a bit of fruit, a touch of oak, and not a hint of poison. After a few moments with no ill effect, he filled the glass and made his way back to Kenan.

He waited until his friend looked at him then lifted the wine to his mouth as if to take a long drink. Kenan stretched out a hand and smirked, one eyebrow arched. Raendel stopped just out of reach and pretended to continue drinking. He made a couple of swallowing sounds and let some trickle down his chin just for effect.

"That's enough!" Kenan laughed as he snatched the glass, sloshing wine onto the floor. A commotion at the front of the room interrupted their exchange. He froze, wine dripping from his upraised hand, eyes locked on the two figures entering the room.

The Baron of Windspire grasped his daughter's arm with both hands. Auburn whiskers sprinkled with gray framed a face softened by the years. Thick fur lined a coat cut in last year's fashion over a freshly pressed shirt that showed a bit of wear around the edges. His voice boomed across the now quiet space.

"Gentlemen, thank you for coming to celebrate the completion of my daughter Peristra's fifteenth year. These last few months she has been accomplishing her lessons with a speed that proves her as clever as she is beautiful. I hope that you all will make her welcome and show her the warm hospitality of your grand city."

Peristra shrank back as far as she could in the Baron's grip. Naturally her father would compliment her looks, but that snub nose covered in freckles didn't strike Raendel as anything more than cute, at best. White lace decorated the edges of her emerald green gown. The folds of her skirt flowed around her like a fountain of silk below a tight bodice and wide lace sleeves. Red hair swept up into braids on each side of her head and joined into a single braid down her back. Her thin lips pressed together; her brow furrowed by a scowl that threatened to burn any man who dared get too close.

The baron lifted her hand and kissed it gently, then leaned down to whisper in her ear. Her features relaxed. She rested her head against his shoulder for a moment then pushed away to face the room full of lords with an expression that, if not warm, at least radiated less hostility than the previous one. Her father backed away far enough that he would not overhear her conversations but close enough to keep an eye on her.

One awkward young lord withdrew toward the refreshment table, blushing. Every other male guest approached Peristra at various speeds depending on each one's rank and boldness. Kenan dragged his feet, showing none of the usual bravado of his youth and rank. Raendel stayed at his friend's side, suppressing the urge to laugh at Kenan's dazed expression.

Before the Prince crossed half the distance, the men at the front began to walk away. A gentleman with graying hair approached Peristra and gestured toward the dance floor.

"Good evening, my lord. You are looking well for your age." Peristra smiled, her face radiating innocence. "Have you come to introduce your grandson to me?"

"I'm only here for the wine. I prefer to keep my family line free of such ill breeding." The man sniffed, then stalked away muttering to himself.

A younger man approached, wearing a coat in the latest fashion, covered in frills and lace.

"A pleasure to meet you, my lord," Peristra said. "What a bold fashion choice. You wear it with such confidence. I do love a man of good taste. I hope to meet one tonight."

His mouth opened to reply before her implications registered. His jaw snapped shut, and he stomped away, red-faced. After several more similar exchanges, the lords began slipping away, even before she turned her attention to them. Some approached the other ladies. Others gathered in small groups, throwing dark looks toward Peristra.

Soon Kenan gazed at her across a few feet of empty space. He didn't retreat, but neither did he advance. His hands trembled as she looked him over like a hunter sizing up her next kill.

"Fetch me a glass of wine." Peristra flicked her hand in the direction of the refreshment table.

Kenan opened his mouth, but only managed a strangled squeak.

"I beg your pardon, my lord," said Peristra, her tone not the least bit sorry. "I mistook you for one of the servants. Forgive the error. I suppose I don't require your assistance after all."

Kenan's face blazed bright red. He spun on his heel and retreated at a pace only slightly slower than a run. Raendel chased him until he stopped near the far wall.

"This is a stupid party." Kenan glared at the wine glass in his hand as if he couldn't quite understand why it was there. "It's boring. And her dress is ugly."

Raendel thought the girl deserved every bit of criticism and more, but duty to keep the prince calm overrode his personal inclinations. "I'm sure she didn't mean it, Ken. She talked that way to everyone. She probably just doesn't want to be here. She doesn't really think of you that way."

Kenan glanced over his shoulder toward Peristra. She stood near the refreshment table, chatting with the awkward young man who'd been hiding there.

Kenan frowned. "I don't care what she thinks about me. I don't know her. And I don't want to. I don't want to be here either. So why are we here? Let's just leave."

Raendel spread his hands, helpless. "The Queen said you must stay until at least half the other guests go home. To leave sooner would be an insult. After the way that girl spoke to everyone, maybe it won't take very long."

Kenan sneered. "An insult? Right. We wouldn't want to insult such a *proper* young lady, would we? That wouldn't be very *gentlemanly* of us."

"You shouldn't let it get to you, Ken. Don't let her rudeness change who you are. You control your own actions."

"Do I? If I really controlled my own actions I wouldn't still be here. You're so worried about my reputation maybe you should disguise yourself as me and stay here in my place."

Kenan stopped; his head tilted as if listening to his own words. "Yes. Why don't you? We can step outside, you could sing an illusion to make yourself look like me, then I could leave, and you could come back as me."

Raendel ducked his head, heartbeat racing in his ears. "I can't do that, Ken. You know I can't. I'm strictly forbidden to disguise myself as any member of the royal family unless your life depends on it."

"But you have to practice, don't you? If you never practice then you won't be very good at it, and then if my life were ever in danger, you would fail, and I would die because you hadn't practiced enough. So, for my own safety, I order you to practice your disguise."

Raendel swallowed. Master Othniel would kill him just for thinking about it. "I'd be caught. The moment I opened my mouth they'd know. My voice would give me away."

Kenan shrugged. "So don't say anything. They're not exactly waiting in line to speak to me. If someone asks you something, just squeak and run away. Apparently, I'm known for that. Come on. Let's get some air."

Kenan headed for the door. Raendel sighed and followed. He caught up to the prince in the foyer. He glanced around to be sure nobody else could see and sang the illusion.

"That's very good." Kenan walked around him to inspect his work. "Just don't speak and you'll be fine. Feel free to have a glass of wine if you think it will help your disguise. I'll hide my coat and slip out the servants' entrance to avoid the guards."

A lifetime of service had taught Raendel the futility of opposing the prince's will. He nodded, drew in a deep breath to calm his stomach, and stepped back into the party. His illusion absorbed relatively little light. It dimmed the flowers near him, but not enough for anyone to notice. The muscles around his stomach clenched just thinking about getting caught. A glass of wine seemed like an excellent idea. The illusion would maintain itself without him singing for long enough to take a drink every minute or two. The cool liquid would calm his stomach and sooth his throat so he could sing longer.

Across the room, the baron towered over his daughter, face flushed. Peristra shrank under her father's angry gestures. She pressed her lips together and marched toward Raendel.

He glanced around, hoping her goal might be something else that just happened to be nearby. Nothing materialized. He'd chosen this spot in the room for its isolation, to avoid interactions exactly like the one bearing down on him now. He scurried toward the farthest corner, fighting the urge to run. Once a wall blocked further retreat, he stopped and wracked his brain for a way out that didn't involve revealing his disguise.

"I owe you an apology, my lord." She stood with her head down, hands clasped in front of her chest. Her breaths came quick and shallow. "My behavior earlier was inexcusable. You didn't deserve that. The truth is, I only spoke that way to push away the less desirable men. So many of them are just hunting for a pretty face to show off to their friends and provide them an heir. I couldn't stand even to talk to them, so I did the only thing I could think of to chase them away. But then I couldn't stop. I went too far. You seem like one of the nice ones and I was awful to you. I'm sorry. Please say you forgive me."

She searched his face. Raendel trembled. His heart felt like a giant hand squeezed it. He couldn't speak. She might not recognize an Adoël voice, but others around certainly would. He nodded, doing his best to make his expression into something he hoped looked benevolent.

She smiled, accepting the wordless gesture. But she didn't stop there.

"What's your name?"

A trickle of sweat ran down his back. He shook his head, grasping for some way to make this end well.

Peristra's smile faltered. "I understand if you don't want to be friends after what I said, but I'm doing my best to offer a truce here. Can we at least go back to being polite strangers? We'll start at the beginning. Hello, I am Lady Peristra of Windspire. I'm pleased to make your acquaintance."

Raendel forced a smile. He could only hope the illusion around his face responded in a natural way. He breathed a silent prayer of thanks for the image of Kenan's clothes covering his own tunic, because the illusion hid growing sweat stains.

"If you want me to leave you alone you could just say so," Peristra said. "Call me names. I've earned it. Tell me you hate me, that you can't forgive me. I'll take it without complaint. Just say *something*. I know you can speak; I saw you talking with your servant earlier."

Her eyes widened. "He looked like one of those special servants. The ones that serve the royal family. I'd heard of them, but I didn't think of it until now. You're the prince, aren't you? The younger one. Prince Kenan? Is that right? I'm terribly sorry if I offended you, Your Highness."

Raendel bit his lip, interrupting his song almost long enough to weaken the illusion. If he remained silent, the queen would hear her son had refused to speak to the person his attendance at the party was meant to honor. If he spoke, his deception would be uncovered. The queen would hear that Kenan had left the party early and that Raendel had helped. His hesitation made the decision for him as Peristra spoke again.

"All right, *Your Highness*. Obviously, you're too good for this poor, uncivilized country girl. Fine. I don't need your condescension, or even your acknowledgement. I did my best. Good day."

She stalked away, leaving Raendel to wrestle with his conscience. Silence had been the right choice. He knew that. Sacrificing himself would have gained nothing and could have gotten the prince in worse trouble. His heart still condemned him as a coward.

CHAPTER TWO

A winding road descended through the foothills to the south, a hard day's journey to the nearest crossroad. Several smooth boulders jutted up through the soil near the castle gates. Snow-capped mountains loomed over the castle to the north, east, and west. Master Jabal's rugged face, capped with snow-white hair, loomed over Kenan.

"I heard how you treated Lady Peristra last night, Kenan. What do you have to say for yourself?"

Kenan lowered his head, his cheeks burning. "Did she tell you how she treated me first? What else could I have done?"

"She didn't tell me anything," Jabal said. "Did you think the other nobles wouldn't be watching you? Several of them spoke to me about your behavior. Regardless, what she said or did is no excuse. You must control your emotions. Never let them control you."

"What difference does it make? I wasn't going to need the Art at that party."

Jabal counted off points on his fingers. "First, the Art of Biomancy is not the only reason to control your emotions. Everything you do reflects on the royal family. Your rudeness yesterday could damage your father's influence tomorrow. Second, don't assume you won't need the Art. You never know when or where assassins may strike. You must always be ready to protect yourself and others. Third, and most important, being a decent human being is everyone's duty. You are no exception. Now sit down and begin meditation."

Kenan swallowed his protest, but it burned in his stomach as he sat cross-legged on the grass. He closed his eyes and tried to clear his mind. Peristra's voice echoed through his head.

"I can see the anger in your face," Jabal said. "Anger clouds your mind and saps your energy. A clouded mind distracts you, and drained energy renders you helpless. Try to use Biomancy even for a few moments while angry and you'll be bedridden for two days after. The Art uses up your reserves quickly enough on its own."

Kenan drew a slow breath. He pressed down against the anger, trying to smother it. It only burned hotter; a live coal buried in his gut.

"Remember the techniques I taught you. Don't fight the anger, distract it. Think of something else, something impersonal. Go over the list of Disciplines you learned last week."

Kenan focused on memory, pulling up the lesson in his mind. He reviewed each power, starting with the ones he knew least about. Six abilities of the Spirit, practiced only by Messengers, those who dedicated their lives to God. The Messengers of the Light currently living in the castle practiced four of those six. The Discipline of Crafting had fallen out of use because of its difficulty, requiring the combination of several skills. No Messenger of the Light would practice Necromancy, long ago banned as blasphemous. He knew most about the physical Art of Biomancy, having studied it for as long as he could remember. In theory anyone could use it, but few could manage the level of training and self-control necessary. To his knowledge, nobody in the kingdom could do it other than himself and Master Jabal. The name of the other physical Discipline escaped him, drifting through the depths of his mind just out of reach. He opened his eyes.

"Master Jabal?"

Jabal sat cross-legged on the other side of the road, eyes closed. He nodded silently.

"Last week you mentioned another Art. One that uses emotions instead of being hindered by them. Tell me about that one."

Jabal's eyes remained closed, and his face barely moved as he spoke. "Pathomancy. Discovered a hundred years ago, at the same time as Biomancy. More deadly. Easy to lose control of. The masters of that time banned it as too dangerous after the deaths of several innocents. No living person knows how to use it, and you wouldn't be able to, even if you found someone to teach you. It is incompatible with Biomancy. I assume you are talking to me because your meditation is complete. Are you ready for the lesson?"

No trace of the burning anger remained. A layer of peace covered Kenan's mind like snow, cooling and quieting his thoughts.

"Yes."

"Good. Pick up the boulder nearest you and throw it at me."

Kenan rubbed his forehead, trying to figure out what Jabal planned to do. He stood and sidled over to the boulder, watching in vain for some further sign from his teacher. Pressing himself against the rough surface, he wedged his fingers into a crevice and used the Art to shift his energy. His vision and hearing dimmed, his mind and reflexes turned sluggish as all the power in his body poured into his muscles. The boulder popped free with a grinding sound. The dullness of Kenan's mind left no room for second thoughts. His body continued to carry out the last imperative of the brain. He lifted the dirt-covered rock over his head and threw it.

Jabal vanished. He didn't turn invisible, he simply moved so fast that Kenan's energy-deprived eyes couldn't track him. Before the boulder reached the peak of its flight path, Jabal had left his seat, run across the road, and stopped with the edge of his hand against Kenan's throat.

"You're dead," Jabal said.

A wave of exhaustion knocked Kenan to his knees. "I'm sorry, Master Jabal. I tried."

Jabal laid a hand on his shoulder. "There's nothing to be sorry for. This wasn't a test. You did nothing wrong. It was a lesson, and I hope you learned it well. Strength is useful, in its place, but your greatest ally is surprise. Speed is often more useful for that purpose."

Kenan still felt like he'd failed somehow. Resentment welled up inside him, instinctively trying to push that feeling of shame onto someone else. "What's the point? We've been at peace my whole life. Father conquered the last of our enemies before he even met my mother. Everything within a week's ride in any direction belongs to us, and every kingdom on our borders is an ally. Why am I working so hard on something I'll never use?"

Master Jabal let the silence stretch. Kenan's words echoed inside his own head, and with each repetition they sounded more petulant. Part of him wanted to take back his hasty words, but another part of him needed an answer. He really did feel that way. Why shouldn't he be honest about it?

Jabal responded in the same level tone he used for all his lessons. "In this world, peace cannot last. Your lifetime is not so long as you feel it is. War could spring up at any moment, and it doesn't always come from the outside. It does no good to post a guard after you've been robbed, or to begin training after you've been attacked. Your brother prepares to lead the army against invasions that may or may not happen, and you to protect the family against assassins that may or may not come. Better to prepare and have no need than to have need and not be prepared."

Kenan nodded; his short burst of resentment burned out for lack of fuel. He couldn't disagree with Master Jabal's logic, and his teacher had shown more respect than his temper deserved. Somehow, a reasonable explanation didn't make that useless feeling go away. He just didn't have the energy to talk about it anymore.

CHAPTER THREE

R aendel trudged down the corridor behind Aeriel. He could have followed her with his eyes closed. Her scent wafted around him, the smell of a rose garden in the early morning sun, covered in dew. He longed to walk closer to her, but he also wanted to delay reaching their destination as long as possible.

"Master Othniel called you in last week," Raendel said, breaking the long silence. "Everyone gets called in, but nobody tells me anything. Once I've done this, we'll be able to talk about it, won't we? Please, Aeriel. I miss talking with you."

She hadn't spoken to him in days, since being called into Master Othniel's chamber. He didn't expect that to change now, but he needed a bit of hope to fortify him against whatever waited in the chamber ahead. She glanced at him over her shoulder. Her eyes expressed deep sorrow, regret, fear, and a single thread of longing. He grasped that thread and clung to it with all his strength.

Aeriel reached the end of the hallway and stepped to one side. She didn't raise her head to meet Raendel's eyes. He shuffled forward a few steps and grasped the handle of the splintered oak door that led into Master Othniel's chambers. He lowered his head and took a couple of deep breaths. His knuckles reddened and he could feel the wood grain digging into his palms. His muscles tensed. The heavy door creaked open.

Inside the chamber, three Adoël in hooded black robes stood around a circle of lighted candles. Raendel pulled the door closed behind him, leaving only the candles' flickering light to illuminate their pale silent faces. His palms dampened when he realized Master Othniel wasn't among them. He pressed his back against the door.

One of the figures spoke. "You will see Master Othniel soon. First, we must prepare you for your Illumination."

Raendel froze. "Prepare? How? What do I have to do?"

"Follow our instructions. Answer a few simple questions. You have come of age, and it is time for you to know the truth. But the truth is not easy to hear. We must be sure you are ready."

"I am ready." Raendel clenched his fists as hard as he could, but still they trembled.

"We shall see. Enough questions now, you have much to learn in little time. Remove your clothes and step into the circle."

The black-robed Adoël withdrew two paces from the circle of candles and bowed their heads. Raendel looked down at his white uniform. *What am I doing here? All my life I've been trained to do what I'm told. To never question. Because that's your place. It's who you are. What would they do to me if I refuse? If they throw me out, where would I go? Does it even matter what I want?*

He unwrapped his robe as slowly as he could, hoping that someone would take pity and explain why he had to undress. No one did. Naked, shivering, hands positioned to attempt some degree of modesty, he stepped into the circle of candles. He closed his eyes and tried to picture himself somewhere else, being someone else. The utter silence pressed down on him, dragging him into the present.

His thoughts kept coming back to those three Adoël in the room with him, and why they hadn't spoken yet. He couldn't stand the pressure any longer. His eyes popped open. A chill ran through him as he looked around and saw no one. Then he realized that with their black robes and bowed heads, the candles' feeble light wouldn't distinguish them from the surrounding darkness. He slowed his breathing, struggling to convince his thumping heart to calm down.

A low hum permeated the room, and the air thickened as if in response. The shadows outside the circle deepened, the glow inside increased. The candles' flames didn't waver, but the light curved inward. Its full intensity focused on Raendel. The smell of burning candles stung his nostrils.

A voice spoke out of the darkness, rough with age and hard use. "Who are you?"

He spun in a circle, searching the darkness. "I am Raendel."

"Who are you?"

Unable to locate the voice, he looked down at himself. The light exposed every blemish, every old scar and fading bruise. His voice shook. "I am Raendel, son of Penuel."

"Who are you?"

He looked down at the floor as he thought. His pasty white legs glowed in the concentrated candlelight. "I am Adoël."

"What is Adoël?" The voice shot back.

It felt obvious. But then, so had the first question. The hum deepened. "Adoël is my people," he said at last.

"What is Adoël?"

"Adoël is my ancestry."

"What is Adoël?"

"Adoël is..." He glanced around as if the answer would be visible in the room. Thick darkness hid everything beyond the candles. He couldn't even see his white robes that must be lying just outside the circle. His white servant robes. "Adoël is a servant."

The silence stretched until Raendel wondered if he'd given the wrong answer again. He took a deep breath, willing his heart to slow. A second voice spoke out of the darkness, higher pitched than the first, hard and cold as iron. "Who do we serve?"

He let out his breath, relieved. He hadn't realized he'd been so tense until his shoulders relaxed. "We serve the king."

"Who do we serve?"

He frowned, tension creeping back into his shoulders. He thought of Prince Kenan, his lifelong friend but also his master. "We serve the royal family."

"Who do we serve?"

He squeezed his eyes shut and prayed for the right answer. The humming pounded in his brain until he could hardly think. The more desperate he grew, the less coherent his thoughts became. He couldn't focus well enough to try to find an answer anymore. Fear left no room for anything but prayers for mercy. *My place here is all I have. Don't let them throw me out. Please, God.*

The words of his prayer rolled around in his mind, and the answer fell into place. "We serve the God of Light."

"Why?" A third voice spoke, so deep and resonant that it seemed to make the air quiver.

"Because." Raendel shook his head. He couldn't think of what to say next. Nobody asked that question. *What reason does anyone need? Why would you not serve the God of Light?*

The silence that followed his half answer convinced him they must be expecting a full answer. He gave them the best one he could think of. "Because he is good."

"Why?"

Raendel thought about every characteristic he could remember about God, everything said in every public prayer, trying to find one that seemed unique and important enough. He wished he'd paid more attention to Master Othniel's prayers. One more idea came to mind. "Because he has all power."

"Why?"

Tears stung his eyes. His chest heaved to bursting. His forehead burned with the effort of thinking. But this time no answer would come. The knowledge of failure weighed against him so he could hardly form the words. "I don't know."

The candlelight vanished. The blackness of the room reflected the darkness that filled his heart, the quiet so thick he thought maybe his wish for death had been granted.

The rough voice broke the silence. "The first judgment is mine. He did not answer the final question. He is not worthy."

Raendel fell to his knees, head bowed over folded hands.

The hard voice spoke. "The second judgment is mine. He doesn't understand his own nature. He is not worthy."

Raendel felt his last threads of hope slipping away. He collapsed full length on the floor, numb with despair, and waited for the final word. At least it would soon be over.

"The third and final judgment is mine," the resonant first voice said. "He is not worthy. None of us are worthy. That's why we serve. Of course, he doesn't understand this yet. That's why we called him here. He has been sufficiently humbled. Stand up, Raendel son of Penuel, and learn who you are. Your Illumination begins."

CHAPTER FOUR

Lord Erick clawed his way back to consciousness. Dark tendrils of nightmare tried to suck him back down into the murky vision. He gasped for air, his heart thudding in his ears like the hoofbeats of a prize stallion at full gallop. His shirt clung to his skin, rank with sweat.

"Well?" Duke Lukas leaned forward in his chair near the bed. "Did it work? Did you find anything?"

Erick ignored his father's questions. He snatched up the pen from the bedside table, dipped it quickly into the inkwell, and started scribbling down everything he could remember from the vision. The dimensions of the altar, the words of the incantation, and a quick sketch of a symbol that felt important even though he couldn't quite remember its significance.

"Don't keep us waiting," the duke said. "What did you learn?"

"Patience, father," Erick's brother, Kris, lounged on a couch across the room. His shirt gaped open at the neck. Condensation glistened around the bottom half of the pitcher next to him.

Duke Lukas growled at his younger son, but said nothing more. His thick fingers whitened from straining against the armrests. A vein in his temple pulsed. The muscles in his jaw stood out like the roots of a tree pushing up under paving stones.

Erick shifted the pen to his left hand long enough to shake the cramps out of his fingers, then dipped it in the ink again and continued writing. He wasn't used to this kind of work. His father had insisted that they couldn't trust any of the scribes, and for once he had agreed to caution. He added a few more notes, vague impressions and unclear memories, any little detail that could possibly help. He read everything he'd written, then dropped the pen into a jar of water and sprinkled sand over the page to dry it.

"I have something," Erick said. "I made contact with a powerful spirit, and it showed me this ritual. If this is correct, I should be able to summon strong allies into the physical world. Shadow-weavers."

Duke Lukas laughed. "Yes! That's perfect. Even if we only get one, our victory would be guaranteed. What does the king have that could stand against a single Shadow-weaver?"

Kris poured himself another glass of wine. "You said 'if this is correct'. What if it's not? What if it does nothing? Or worse, what if it summons a Shadow-weaver but you can't control it? Necromancy can backfire even on masters, and you're a novice. Poison is a much less risky option."

Erick dismissed his brother's objection with a wave of his hand. "Poison is a waste of time. How would you get it past the king's tasters?"

Kris sniffed, leaning away from his brother as if the very smell of the idea offended him. "Poison is an art. I can craft a variety that only kills in large doses, or repeated doses over several days, and shows no symptoms in smaller amounts. The tasters would feel no effects. The king, however, is known for his generous portions. The two princes should cause no difficulty. Young men have healthy appetites."

Erick shook his head. "You risk too much in the delivery. Someone has to add the poison to the food. If that person betrays us to the king, then not only would we fail, but we'd be discovered and charged with treason."

"Better that than to be eaten by a demon because you botched a summoning," Kris said.

"Enough!" The duke held up a hand toward each of his sons. "No victory comes without risk. But we must have safeguards. Erick will set up a secret camp near the city and prepare the summoning. Kris will create his poison. We'll need at least two people on the inside, one to deliver the poison and the other to report to us if anything goes wrong. If the poison succeeds, we will enter the city openly and claim our right as nearest relatives. If it fails, Erick will be in position to strike before they can trace it back to us. Either way, the throne will be ours."

CHAPTER FIVE

Raendel staggered to his feet, then flinched as light flooded back into the room. He blinked until his eyes adjusted to the brightness. Four robed figures emerged from the shadows. Master Othniel stood before him, holding a bowl full of steaming dark liquid. He stretched out the bowl. "You have been judged ready. Take this. Drink it. It is knowledge. Drink deeply and remember."

Raendel took the bowl and raised it to his lips. A raging fire poured into his mouth and stung all the way into his belly. By the time he emptied the bowl, the burning had spread to every part of his body. The world spun and his awareness faded into flashing lights and noise.

A steady red glow radiated from the middle of the chaos. That glow came into focus, followed by the rest of the vision. A fire burned at the heart of a furnace in the back of an otherwise dark room cluttered with hammers hanging from hooks on the wall, barrels full of steel rods, stacks of horseshoes, and tables covered in various metalworking tools. A large leather-clad man crouched in front of the flames examining the glowing shape of a sword. Black eyes glittered beneath his heavy brows. Half a dozen servants performed menial tasks around the room—working the bellows, cleaning up scraps, measuring out salt from rough sacks, and preparing barrels of water and oil for the quenching.

The door crashed open. The servants dove under tables and into corners. A tall man in white robes strode through the open door. The light from the forge cast shadows across his scowling face and made the sword in his right hand glitter like sunlit frost. He stretched the blade out, so the tip pointed toward the fire in the middle of the room. "Ophis! What have you done?"

The man at the forge didn't look away from his work to see who spoke to him. Raendel tried to move around to see the man's face, but he couldn't control the focus of the vision. His viewpoint centered on one of the servants crouched under a table. No amount of effort on his part shifted it.

The robed figure spoke again. "Ophis, answer me! What have you done?"

The blacksmith pulled the glowing red sword out of the fire and lowered it into one of the quenching barrels. "I don't answer to the name Ophis anymore. I used that name when I served you, Arkos. Now I serve none but myself. I have a new name. Call me Morgoth."

Morgoth lifted the blade out of the barrel and examined it. "What have I done; you ask me? I've discovered new Arts, unlocked knowledge, and created a weapon beyond anything you've seen or heard of. I have crafted a defense against the angry mobs on our doorstep. That is what I've done. I will not be a victim."

Arkos trembled. "Where did you find this knowledge? I've heard rumors you've been practicing Necromancy on your servants, stealing their power. Messengers of the Light are forbidden to harm others. You've given yourself to the Dark. What power is worth that cost? Come back to us, Ophis."

The man who called himself Morgoth picked up a strip of leather and began wrapping it around the hilt of his new sword. "I told you, I don't answer to that name. I serve a new master and have a new name. A name I've chosen for myself to represent my new freedom. Morgoth. But you may call me master."

Arkos' face turned as white as his robes, and he stumbled back a step. "Blasphemy! A Messenger of the Light serves only the God of Light. What other master could you have? I will never call another man master. Surrender. I'll kill you if I have to."

Morgoth twisted his sword, so the firelight reflected from a jewel set into the hilt. "You think to fight me? Kill me? This is Anglachel, my newest creation, forged by powers you are too timid to wield. One cut with this blade and your strength will become mine. With Anglachel in my hand, I can use the Art to enhance my strength all day long and never grow tired, so long as I feed it on blood. I'll start with yours."

Morgoth attacked with speed and strength only achievable through Biomancy. His opponent matched every move. The blows fell so fast that, for a long minute, Raendel could distinguish nothing but swirling robes and flashes of steel. The ringing of the blades sounded one continuous note.

The fight edged back toward the middle of the room and slowed until the sound of the individual sword strokes grew distinct. Arkos threw himself forward against his opponent. The two blades locked together. Morgoth fell back against a table next to the forge, straining to hold off the weight of his attacker.

He called to his servants. "Help me! Hurry! His strength is used up fighting me. Throw something at him. Anything. I only have to cut him once to steal his strength and then I can end it."

The servants cringed and looked away. Morgoth's calls grew more strained. "Curse you for cowards! Help me or I'll kill you all myself!"

One of the servants sprinted for the doorway. In his panic he tripped and fell against a barrel of iron rods. The force of the hit knocked the barrel over, spilling metal onto the floor.

Arkos turned toward the sound. Morgoth used the moment of distraction to reach behind him with his left hand and pick up a forging hammer. His blow glanced off Arkos' head and drove into his shoulder, breaking bones with an audible crack. Arkos' sword clattered to the ground as he stumbled back a step and fell to one knee.

Morgoth drew back his sword. His opponent's left hand dipped into his robes and then flung out in a blur of motion. Morgoth doubled over, staring in disbelief at the hilt of the dagger buried in his gut.

Arkos stayed long enough to watch him collapse to the floor before he turned and staggered out the door, dropping a trail of blood behind him from his split scalp and broken shoulder.

Morgoth lay still a few moments longer, then pushed himself to his feet. He pulled the dagger loose and dropped it on the floor, glaring at his servants.

"Now you will pay for your betrayal." One by one he cornered them, cutting them with his sword but leaving them alive. When the blade touched their flesh it pulsed, and Morgoth's movements grew more energetic. Blood seeped from his wound, soaked through his clothes, and ran down his leg. The faster he moved, the faster the blood flowed. When he had finished cutting each of his servants, he raised the sword above his head.

"I will not grant you the release of death. I want you and your children to live with your failure forever. Your descendants will never regain the power of Biomancy."

He chanted in a language Raendel didn't recognize. The servants' hair faded from black to white. Their skin paled, and their eyes lost all color. Cold shock washed over Raendel. For the first time in this vision, he understood better than they did what was happening. They were becoming the Adoël. Just like him.

The vision faded. Raendel found himself once again in the room lit only by candles. "Master Singer, what happened?"

"It was as you saw," Othniel said. "We failed our master. He called on us to help him and we refused to obey. He faced mortal danger, and we failed to protect him."

"But..." Raendel shook his head. "But he was evil. Why should we—?"

"He paid for his own sins!" Othniel said. "We don't get to excuse ourselves based on someone else's guilt or innocence. Each of us must answer for our own actions, or lack of action. We swore to obey, and we broke our oath. If we'd known him to be a Necromancer, then we should have left his service and fought for Arkos. But we neither left him nor obeyed him. We thought only of ourselves and so we condemned ourselves. Because of that failure we must serve now without question. We must not fail our master ever again. But above all, we must protect life, never destroy it. No matter what the cost, even to the point of surrendering our own lives."

Raendel wanted to protest but didn't know how to shape his thoughts into words. His objections spilled out as a string of jumbled questions. "What happened after that? Is Morgoth dead? How long has it been since we...since that happened to our people? Why do we still have to serve?"

"Arkos fled only long enough to find a healer to bind his wounds," Othniel said. "Then he returned to the smithy and found Morgoth dying on the floor. All the energy he gained from the servants could not heal the wound in his gut. Arkos took the sword Anglachel and drove it through Morgoth's heart to finish him off. Then he turned to the servants, our ancestors, and made them swear loyalty to him."

Raendel clenched his teeth against more questions that threatened to interrupt. Othniel nodded approval at his restraint.

"He offered them protection and a place in the castle. In exchange, they swore to keep secret both their own origin and the source of the sword. Arkos used the sword to take the throne, then hid it after rumors of its connection to Necromancy began to spread. Four generations have passed since that time and still we are faithful to his family line. We must serve, as penance for failure to protect our master in his time of great need. Our duty before God is to protect the life of the king and his family. Ultimately our service is not to the king, but to God."

Raendel closed his eyes and tried to make sense of his jumbled thoughts and feelings. Othniel clearly expected him to suffer shame, or at least humility, but he couldn't force himself to feel either. He felt only rebellious anger at being asked to bear the punishment for someone else's mistakes. He looked down at himself, his white skin a shining reminder of why he could never be accepted anywhere but here. His anger melted into a puddle of hopeless resignation. What else could he do? To be Adoël meant to be a servant. For him there could be no other life.

CHAPTER SIX

Queen Havilah picked at the roasted pheasant on her plate. After half an hour she still hadn't eaten as much as the tasters had cut off before serving it to her. She felt sure her appetite would return at a less convenient time, but for now her nerves wouldn't allow her to eat. If she tried, she would only make herself sick. A request to meet with the head of her spy network weighed on her, and she couldn't stop worrying until they met.

Her husband, King Edmond, had no such trouble. He sucked at the bones of his fourth bird, his fingers glistening with fat. Whenever she looked at him, she still saw a young warrior. He'd ridden into her father's tiny Kingdom, slim and rugged in his pristine uniform. The army at his back had won her father's quick surrender. His piercing eyes and warm smile had won her heart. The strong chin and chiseled biceps hadn't hurt any. Now the warrior had run out of battles. Years of peace and of court politics had beaten him down until he retreated into food. The folds of his stomach bulged against the grease-stained shirt. Multiple glasses of wine each day dulled those once-piercing eyes. The man she'd fallen for still lurked in there somewhere, but she rarely caught a glimpse of him anymore.

Their older son, Devin, took after his father. She saw her husband's youthful idealism in his dedication to the kingdom. This evening he'd sent word that he wanted to eat in the barracks so he could get to know the soldiers better.

Kenan took after Havilah. Sensitive, impulsive, prone to getting himself in trouble through misguided sincerity. She'd confined him to his room every evening for the past week as punishment for his behavior at the baron of Windspire's ball. He should be there now, if he hadn't snuck away again.

Havilah sighed. She switched from picking at the pheasant to rearranging the vegetables. The king emptied another glass of wine and waved for more. He didn't even notice his wife's frown. She tried to distract herself by watching the play being performed on one side of the room by the Adoël but couldn't stay focused enough to make any sense of it.

Master Jabal stepped in through a door in the far wall. He looked at Queen Havilah, then withdrew through the same door. She forced herself to swallow a couple of bites before getting up to follow him to the council chamber. She sat to the right of the king's vacant chair and pointed to the smaller one on the other side for Jabal to use.

He shook his head. "Thank you, Your Majesty, but I'll stand."

"As you wish," she said. "Now, what's this about treason? I still don't understand why you haven't yet told the king about it."

"Because it involves *your* family, Your Majesty."

Queen Havilah rose halfway out of her seat. "What? What do you mean?"

Jabal's face remained implacable. "Your Majesty, it grieves me to bring you news of this, but there's little choice. Neither is there any reason to call it something else to spare you. Treason is treason, and I've learned enough to be certain that your nephew Lord Erick is involved."

"It can't be true. How could he?" Havilah drew a hand across her brow as if to wipe away the thought. "My own blood?"

"My informants among the duke's soldiers tell me Erick has been questioning the king's right to rule their lands, threatening and bribing them to join his cause. I'm not sure yet how far the plot goes, or what exactly his plans are. Last week he left your brother's house with no warning." Jabal turned away, pacing a few steps one way and then the other. "My spies haven't been able to learn where he went or why. That is why I chose to inform you first. If rumors of this reach the king, and if it turns out Erick left for the reason I suspect, it could put you in a delicate position. I realize that my highest fealty is to the king, but I wanted you to know this first."

Lightning crashed outside, and Havilah felt as if she'd been hit by it. Once the rumble of thunder subsided, she recovered enough to speak. "My brother. Is Lukas part of this? Does he know?"

"I have no reason to suspect Duke Arnould," Jabal said. "But neither do I have reason to trust him. It is as it always has been throughout history, my dear queen. The title of duke may not be enough for a man who would have been a king. Your father submitted willingly to avoid bloodshed, but he is gone now and with him the counsel of peace that held your brother in check. Please try not to worry yet. Until I know more, my spies will watch Duke Arnould closely. Or, if you think we should tell the king now, I'll go with you."

"No," Havilah said. "Not yet. You were right to tell me first. I can't accuse my own brother of treason until I have clear evidence. If our father hadn't surrendered his kingdom my brother wouldn't have been king. He would've been dead. He knows that. Surely, he wouldn't be working against me this way. Besides, the king will be sleeping off his latest round of drinking soon. He'll be in no condition to hear this kind of news tonight."

Jabal nodded. "I agree there's no reason to tell the king until we can be sure."

Her hands knitted together while she thought. The annual celebration would take place in two days. One hundred years since the founding of the dynasty and the Kingdom of Storvia. This would be the perfect time for an enemy to strike. *What if Jabal is right? And what if they attack during the celebration?*

"Don't let Erick know you suspect him until you find out who else is working with him," Havilah said. "If we expose one without exposing them all, the others will go into hiding and we might never find the truth. I pray he is not but find out for certain whether my brother is involved. Once you have a list of names and clear evidence we will go to the king. Until then, just notify his guards to be on high alert."

"Yes, Your Majesty." Jabal bowed and left the chambers.

Havilah remained for a long time after he was gone, holding her head in her hands and listening to the rain beat against the roof.

CHAPTER SEVEN

K enan stalked through the halls wearing a petulant scowl. The extra lessons with Master Jabal didn't bother him much, but Master Lenore gave him too much memorization work and Master Admah's dull monotone could be used as a sedative for medical procedures. On top of all that, Rae had been avoiding him and he had no idea why. Stuck in his chambers every evening, he had no chance to track down his friend to ask. Another week of this would kill him. His mother would never relent, but maybe he could get a pardon from his father. Despite the late hour, the lamps outside the king's bedchamber still burned. Two guards stood at attention on each side of the door, in place of the usual one.

"Is my father in audience?"

The guard on the left bowed. "He's with Master Jabal now, Your Highness, but I think it's just his daily checkup. He didn't ask me to keep out family."

He knocked twice on the door and pushed it open. Hearing no protest, he stood aside and let Kenan enter the small antechamber.

Kenan slipped through the door, listening for the sound of discussion. The thick rug and heavy tapestries that lined this sitting room dampened the sound of his footsteps. He pictured Master Jabal reporting on how well his lessons were going, and his father praising his good work. He got so caught up in the imaginary conversation taking place in his own head that he forgot to be surprised that he heard no voices at all. Slipping through the door into the king's bedchamber, his daydreams melted into disappointment. His father lay quiet and motionless on the bed. Master Jabal sat by the bedside, holding his hand.

"Is he asleep already?" Kenan whispered.

Jabal didn't respond. He only swayed a bit and moaned.

Confused, Kenan shuffled a few steps closer. "Master Jabal?"

Jabal twitched but still didn't answer. Then his body went rigid, and he gasped. Letting go of the king's hand, he bent forward and pried open the king's eyelids one at a time.

"Master Jabal?" Kenan whispered again. Fear crept in, squeezing out all thoughts of his own petty troubles.

Jabal jumped to his feet and spun around in one quick motion. The muscles in his face drew hard lines under sickly-pale skin. He stared into space over Kenan's shoulder, eyes glazed, for several moments. He shook himself and spoke in a strained voice. "Kenan! Thank God! I was hoping for Master Deborah, but I can't spare the time to send for her. Come here. Quickly!"

Kenan took a half-step forward, his lower lip trembling. "Is father all right?"

"Something has struck at his heart. I was able to stop it, but in doing so I had to drain too much of his strength. I can only transfer energy within others, I can't use my own to help him. I can, however, use yours."

Kenan blinked and rubbed at his eyes. "Mine? What do you mean? How?"

Jabal looked from Kenan to the king and back again. He jerked his hand in a signal for Kenan to move closer. The words spilled out of his mouth in short bursts. "I can connect you to each other. You will become like one person. The energy will balance itself between you. It is difficult and dangerous. It will drain more strength from you than he will receive, but we must try. If we don't, he'll die before morning. Hush now and lie down beside your father."

Kenan climbed onto the bed without further question, fear for his father burying all fear for himself. A random thought that didn't feel like his own popped into his mind. *He's coming.*

He blinked and looked around the room. An old sword over the mantle drew his attention. Nothing about its appearance struck him as unusual, but it dominated his vision. Jabal leaned over him, blocking his view of the sword. Tension he hadn't even been aware of released, like a physical cord had been cut.

At Jabal's instruction, Kenan closed his eyes and worked to clear his mind. Three fingers pressed against his forehead. A burning sensation passed through him, both cold and hot at the same time. Something twisted inside his mind. Strength drained out of him like water from a cracked vase. Nausea churned his stomach and made his head spin. He couldn't remember how long he'd been lying there, but he no longer had the strength to move.

A tingling sensation settled into his fingers and spread with alarming speed. He tried to protest, to tell Jabal to stop, but his body no longer responded to his brain. He threw his last remaining strength at the hole that sucked the life out of him. He used Biomancy to shape the last of his energy into a plug to fill the gap, and then struggled to keep his block in place. Something nagged at his memory, some guilty thought that maybe he shouldn't be fighting this. A sweeping flood of survival instinct washed away any second thoughts.

An unseen force pulled at him with fierce energy, intensifying with every breath. He strained backward against the suction with everything he had left in him but couldn't hold it for long. The edges of his block crumbled, and then it all began to collapse. A moment before his strength failed, the pull began to weaken.

CHAPTER EIGHT

R aendel's knuckles reddened where he clutched the broom handle, his strokes short and hard as he attacked the stable floor with it. Master Othniel had refused to let him have a part in last night's play, saying he needed time to meditate on his ancestral sins and his place as a servant. He didn't want to meditate. He hadn't slept either because his mind wouldn't stop trying to make him feel guilty for a sin that wasn't his.

My great-grandfathers failed their master, why should that make me feel like a failure? No matter how many times he reassured himself, his feelings couldn't be swayed by logic. Nothing worked right for him this morning. Not even the illusion magic.

He held the broom still and pursed his lips. A haunting sound flowed from him, like the wind blowing across the top of an empty jug, a sound unlike any that passed human lips. The air around the broom thickened, and the image of the broom wavered as if seen underwater. The whistle moved into a range inaudible to the human ear. The broom danced in response to the change and for an instant appeared to be a sword. Then it was only a broom again, and Raendel hissed at it. He followed the hiss with a low hum, less musical, but more rhythmic. Interspersed with the hum was an occasional sigh punctuated by more hissing. A pattern wove through it, akin to the wind's moan through a stand of pine. It also held an undertone of anger.

A voice interrupted him. "You know we're not allowed to speak in the old tongue when in the service of the king. Especially the kind of language you were using."

Raendel jumped at the sound, then blushed when he saw who had spoken. Aeriel watched him with a half-smile, one eyebrow arched as she waited for his reply. *Why didn't I smell her coming in?* Her scent washed over him. It carried the fragrance of dew on the petals of a rose, just before the dawn when everything is fresh. He shook his head and reached for a question to cover his embarrassment. "What—why are you—I mean, what did you come for?"

Aeriel smiled but answered in a serious tone. "Two of the cooks went missing after the feast last night, so we're short-handed. We need your help in the kitchen. What are you doing out here? You're not assigned to Prince Kenan anymore."

Raendel leaned the broom in the corner. "I had to get away from people for a while to clear my head. I thought the mindless work of the kitchens would help me, but the noise and the busyness of it drove me crazy. I needed to get out. The horses always help me relax."

Aeriel stepped closer and laid a hand on his arm. "I'm sorry, Raendel. I wish I knew what to do for you. I've been carrying the same burden since my Illumination last week. Now that you've been through it, we're finally free to talk about it. I'll be here for you whenever you're ready to talk."

"No," Raendel said. "We aren't free. We won't ever be free."

Queen Havilah pinched herself to stay awake through the morning service. Master Deborah stood behind the altar reading from one of the books of prophecy. That would have been enough to put her to sleep on a good day. A short, restless night made it worse. The other masters sat in a row behind her, except for Master Othniel who insisted on standing with the servants. Master Admah appeared to be asleep in his seat. Master Jabal's unfocused gaze and worried scowl promised bad news to be delivered at their meeting after the service.

King Edmund slouched next to Havilah; eyes rolled back in his head. He snored steadily but not loud enough to keep her awake, unlike the previous night. The two princes sat on the other side of the king. They at least pretended to pay attention. Kenan fidgeted, tapping his fingers against the leg of his chair. Havilah cleared her throat. He glanced her way then folded his hands in his lap.

The service dragged on for an hour. Queen Havilah didn't hear a word of it, distracted by worries about Master Jabal's news. As the crowd filed out, she dismissed her attendants. Then she pushed her way through the crowds and caught Jabal just outside the chapel door. There was no need to order him to come with her. A simple look was enough to make him offer a bow and follow.

She led him to the first empty room she could find. "I'm worried about the king. If he doesn't stop this endless drinking and feasting, traitors won't have to kill him. He'll do it to himself. He's not as young as he used to be. Every noble in the kingdom will be in attendance at the Anniversary Celebration. It's going to be chaos. We only have two days to prepare for it and still he spends his nights drinking enough to drown a man half his age."

"I'm sorry," Jabal said. "The drinking isn't his only problem. I can't be sure, but I suspect he was poisoned last night."

Havilah's knees trembled. She looked around for a chair to collapse into but didn't find one nearby. Steeling herself, she looked Jabal in the eye. "What happened?"

"Something weakened his heart. It wasn't a poison that I recognize, and I would have dismissed it as natural illness, but two cooks disappeared during the night. None of the tasters showed any ill effects, but the king did eat a large portion. I can't be sure, but the two cooks and the timing of it make me suspicious." Jabal frowned and dropped his eyes. "We can be sure whoever did it will try again. There hasn't been time for any new messages from my informants. Your brother has been on the road for days, he'll arrive tonight and camp outside the city with the others. But I do have word from him."

Havilah reached out and rested a hand on his shoulder, trying to keep her tone soft and her lip from trembling as she spoke. "What is it? What does he want?"

"He demanded we give him a room in the castle tonight. Of course, I insisted that for security reasons we couldn't allow anyone inside early. Not even him. I know you'll support me on that if he questions my authority."

She nodded. "I do support you. He can stay outside the walls with his men tonight and come in with the others tomorrow. Under the circumstances that's a reasonable precaution, even for my own family."

"We can't take any risks," Jabal said. "I'll check everyone at the gate myself. If Lord Erick tries to get in, he'll be arrested on sight. I will make the castle as secure as I know how. After that, the only thing we can do is pray."

"Do that." Havilah twisted her fingers into her hair. "And continue your close watch on the king. I'll keep my brother in hand once the celebration begins."

CHAPTER NINE

Lord Erick studied the village from under cover of the trees. All morning people had scurried back and forth across the open courtyard carrying loads of ribbon and baskets of fruit. The sneer that split his pinched face would have sent most men running in terror if they could have seen it. His lips stretched on the left and his nose bent to the right like someone had gripped his face in their hands and twisted it in opposite directions. The dark shadows under his eyes completed the effect, making his appearance more like a restless ghoul than a living man.

Based on his observation he estimated the village contained fifty people in total. He hadn't seen even ten men of fighting age, and those he'd seen looked like they'd be more comfortable with a plow than a sword. His forty trained soldiers would have no trouble pacifying the place. If they offered any resistance, he could burn it to the ground.

He considered doing it anyway. This village held an important strategic position, a day's journey south of the castle at a key crossroads. The mountains on three sides ensured that all traffic to and from the castle would pass through here. Most of the nobles heading toward the castle for the annual celebration had passed through already. Why wait? He only held back because of the possibility of survivors fleeing into the woods. If he did destroy the village, he had to make sure nobody witnessed the destruction and lived to reach the castle.

The villagers had been dashing about all morning. The women gathered wildflowers into bouquets and set up tables in the town square. The men rolled out barrels of ale, carried in loads of fresh fruit, and gathered wood for a bonfire. They seemed busy enough that they wouldn't notice a group of armed men camped a short walk into the trees. Yes, he would leave them be for now. There would be less risk in leaving them alone until after he completed the ritual. If everything went as he had planned, it would be easier to wipe out the village afterward anyway.

He left the villagers to their preparations and returned to the camp. His guards saluted when he entered the clearing. Most of the men huddled next to the fire, playing dice and drinking. The altar stood alone in an empty space across the clearing from the tents. Erick crossed the camp to examine the altar. The instructions on the scroll described everything with precision. The altar's dimensions, the placement of the candles, and the runes engraved on the blade of the dagger all had to be perfect. The slightest failure or deviation might result in nothing happening at all. Or it might result in his death. In the worst case, it could trap his own soul in the shadow world.

The dangers felt insignificant compared to the prize he sought. Shadow-weavers. Even one Shadow-weaver under his command would guarantee the success of his mission. Forty men would have a hard time reaching the king even in a surprise attack. But with forty men and a Shadow-weaver, they would be unstoppable.

Erick picked up the scroll and read it again to make sure he hadn't forgotten anything. He'd transcribed the frantic scribbles that followed the vision into clear instructions. In that first rush he'd only worried about recording everything, important or not. Later he'd worked to sort through the important parts and add a few illustrations. Some particulars had faded from memory but enough remained intact to fill in the missing pieces. The directions for performing the ritual didn't concern him at all. What worried him was the lack of details about its results. If all went well, a portal would open to the shadow world and one or more Shadow-weavers would cross through. The blood of the caster, in this case himself, would give him control over the demons for a limited time.

Not being sure how long the Shadow-weavers would remain in this world troubled him. He'd received no instructions for how to cast them back into the shadow world should the need come for that. Perhaps the Shadow-weavers would stay for a limited time and then return to the shadow world on their own. All he knew for sure was that the Shadow-weavers would be bound to the caster by his wound, self-inflicted as part of the ritual. It didn't say so explicitly, but the instructions implied the beasts would be released from service once that wound healed. Released to where, he didn't know.

He loathed not being sure, mainly because of the adjustments he'd had to make to accommodate this uncertainty. He hated being forced to wait to perform the ritual close to his target rather than perform it in the security of his own fortified lands. A campsite in the woods would not have been his first choice of locations for summoning a demon, but he had to work with it. If he waited any longer, he wouldn't have time to adjust his plans in case nothing responded to his summoning. Any sooner and he would have risked losing control of the creatures before completing his mission.

The Shadow-weavers had to stay with him for two days to accomplish his task. If he cut himself deeply enough, it would take longer than two days to heal. What would happen if the time passed, and he couldn't banish them back to their world?

Two days. It would have to be long enough. And it couldn't be too long. If they wouldn't return to their world once he was done with them, he would find a way to deal with them somehow. He had enough to worry about for the moment. A glance toward the village showed him nothing but a row of trees and brush. Faint ripples of laughter drifted up through the sound of the wind in the trees like bubbles in a pond.

Erick turned back to his meticulously constructed altar. He lit the candles, picked up the dagger, and closed his eyes. He cleared his thoughts of all else and began to reconstruct in his mind the images necessary for the first step. One part of the picture eluded him, and he drew on Biomancy to supplement his mental energy and probe into his memory's deeper recesses. There he encountered something unexpected. A wall of blackness stretched across his mind like a curtain of tar. It resisted any effort to pierce it, and when he tried to pull away it held him fast.

In a surge of panic, he threw all his strength into the struggle to release his mind from the black wall. Rather than pulling free he sank farther into the black mass. With one last surge of desperate energy, he broke loose and rose into the air. His body lay on the ground below. Despair sapped his will to resist.

It's no use fighting anymore, he thought, *fighting won't bring me back from death. I wonder what hell will be like. For some reason I always thought it was underground, but I seem to be rising. How odd.*

His vision blurred, and when it cleared a massive bedchamber lay before him. He judged it fifty paces to a wall. Satin sheets wide enough to build a ten-man tent stretched across a massive bed. A more reasonably sized desk and chair stood to one side, built of thick dark wood and covered in elaborate carvings. Richly embroidered banners covered every part of the wall except just above the marble fireplace. Above the mantle hung a sword. Its classic style matched the suits of antique armor in each corner, but it showed no other sign of age. The sheath, crafted of fine-tooled leather set with golden runes, glowed with the shine of new material. Before he could decipher the runes, they faded, eclipsed by another glow that encompassed the entire sword.

For the first time in this strange dream, a voice broke the silence. It whispered in his mind like an echo down a long hallway. The voice pulled at him, but a greater force gripped him and drew him out of the room. He emerged from a dark corridor and floated above a large courtyard. A crowd occupied the southern end, some seated on wooden benches and others on the ground. Those on the benches wore the silken garb of nobles. Among them sat the king. Erick wanted to examine the king, but he couldn't control his movements. Instead, he found himself looking over the shoulder of the elderly priestess who faced the crowd. A book of prophecy lay open on a small stand in front of her.

His view shifted again. He faced the old woman and watched her lips form the words to the ceremony of Blessing. Yet instead of the familiar words of Blessing, a strange and distorted sound reached him. The voice he'd heard from the sword spoke from the old woman. Erick recognized the spell of summoning that he had been attempting, with slight variations. The harsh metallic voice sounded unlike any human tongue, and it pierced him like a dagger. He wanted to cover his ears, but in this vision, he had no ears to cover. The voice reverberated through him until his soul twisted in time to each syllable. The reading ended, and the scene faded.

He struggled awake, gasping for air. For a long time, he couldn't remember what happened. Pain radiated from his chest. He pulled himself into a seated position and stared at the sacrificial dagger gripped in his right hand. The blade dripped red. Erick looked down at his chest and saw several deep cuts, slashes that formed the rune of summoning described in the ritual. Sprinkles of blood covered the altar. He knew somehow that the blood had come from him.

Frost spread across the top of the altar, solidifying the blood-drops. A dark figure stepped out of the air above it like a black smudge on the face of reality.

Good. A voice echoed in his head. *A Shadow-weaver has answered our call already. That will make things easier.*

Erick dropped the knife and slapped himself in the face. The thought had been inside his head, but it felt different from his own thoughts. It sounded like a stranger speaking directly into his mind.

Disconcerted, he answered the voice aloud. "Who are you? Why am I hearing you in my head?"

You are hearing me in your head because that's where I am, the voice replied. *Do you remember the sword you saw in your vision?*

"The sword?" Erick rubbed his forehead. "Yes, I remember it. What does that have to do with anything? Who are you? And how did you get in my head?"

You opened the door. I came through it. I heard the sword calling me. We must acquire that sword. It will be a powerful tool for you. I can teach you how to use it.

"That's great," Erick said. "But who are you?"

You are my new apprentice, and I am your master. You may call me Morgoth.

"The famous Necromancer!" Erick smiled and rubbed his hands together. "You did great things while you lived. But now you answer my call. You'll have to do more than just talk in my head before I'm ready to call you master. But perhaps you can be useful to me. Tell me more about this sword."

CHAPTER TEN

S eriam floated up out of sleep and inhaled the gentle sunlight that flowed in through the window. The last rains of spring had dried up, and everyone expected relatively clear and warm weather for the next three or four days. She saw this as God's way of giving them a chance before the rains came to patch up leaky roofs, plant fields and gardens, and have outdoor celebrations. Like weddings. Tomorrow the realm would celebrate the founding of a Kingdom, but today belonged to Seriam.

This morning will be the last time I wake up in this bed. While the notion thrilled her, at the same time it made her savor every moment wrapped in the warm comfort of familiar blankets. *Perhaps mother and father will let me take these blankets as a wedding present.*

The door creaked open. A stern face peered around it, with dark brown skin, high cheekbones, and black hair streaked with gray. "About time you woke up. I can't believe you slept past sunrise on your wedding day! How late did you stay up last night?"

Her mother's round form followed her face into the room. Seriam stretched and rolled over. "I've been up for hours. I hardly slept at all last night. I've been sitting in bed daydreaming. Oh mother, today is like a holiday. I just want to make it last forever."

Her mother smiled. "A holiday for you maybe, and for all those fool men downstairs. But you've got every woman in the village baking and sewing and cleaning just for you, and it's time you came down to get ready."

Seriam groaned and rolled the rest of the way out of bed. "The men have started their party already? What time is it?"

"Men will get up earlier to drink and play games than they will to work, but it's not early anymore. It's nearing mid-morning. I only let you stay in bed so long because you stayed up late, and because you won't be getting much sleep tonight either."

Seriam's mother laid a bundle of clothes on the foot of the bed while she talked. "We already moved most of your things out for you. You can wear this for now. We'll have to sneak you out the back door to keep the men from seeing you before you're ready."

Seriam leaned forward and picked a veil out of the pile of clothes. She held it up to her face, trying out the feeling. "How long do we have until the procession?"

"Not enough time for you to dawdle. Meli will help you with your bath, and then you'll need to come straight back to the house to get dressed. Make sure to keep your hair up, we'll never have it dry in time if you let it get wet."

The instruction continued, but it all passed through Seriam's head like wind through a spiderweb. All the daydreams, the plans, the work, the joy of years all rested on this day, and her mind had grown numb from the weight of it.

She allowed herself to be led outside and into the river, bathed, and then back inside to be dressed by someone else as if she were a small child. Her head jerked in time with the brush strokes as they pulled the tangles out of her curly black hair, but she didn't make a sound. Nothing mattered enough to draw her out of her dream world. They scrubbed her face raw, painted her lips with crushed berries. She didn't even blink when they plucked at her eyebrows. The time passed without her taking notice. Before she knew it, she stood outside the church waiting for her betrothed to appear for the first stage of the traditional prelude to marriage.

The men tumbled out into the main street in a rambling procession, with Ephron at its head. Seeing his broad shoulders and warm smile made her heart pick up its cadence and her blood roar in her ears. The group turned west into the afternoon sunlight, toward the end of the street where Seriam stood watching. Ephron approached and knelt before her, his soft brown eyes caressing her like a gentle kiss. When the men had settled themselves into something resembling order, she held out the traditional white arrow to her betrothed and forced her trembling lips to speak the opening words of the ceremony. "Who is this who comes before me?"

Ephron lifted his rough hunter's hands, palms up. "One who seeks your hand in marriage."

"What do you give as a token of your love?"

"I have nothing that is worthy of you. All I can give is myself."

"Then what will I gain by accepting this gift?"

"My undying love, for as long as I live."

"What do you ask in return for your love?"

"Only as much as your heart would give."

Her heart screamed at her to say yes, but she knew that wasn't allowed. Not yet. Tradition ruled this village like a tyrant. To break it would be to break her ties to family, to life, to everything she knew. So, she swallowed her rebellious heart, held out the arrow, and spoke the words prescribed for her. "Take this arrow, to seal your love. Bring back to me whatever mark it finds. If I deem it worthy, I will accept your offer."

Ephron lifted the arrow out of her hands as he spoke the words that marked the end of this phase of the wedding ceremony. "May the God who gives life, the God of love, grant me what I seek tonight."

He rose, kissed each of her hands, and turned to walk out of the village. Biting her lip to keep tears at bay, Seriam watched him walk into the forest. Tradition gave him until sunset to return with wild game for the wedding feast. Most men bent the traditions a little by hunting the day before so that all they had to do was walk to their house and pick up the animal they already had prepared. A man less confident in his hunting skill might even hire someone else to do it for him. But her beloved Ephron, a hunter by trade, took pride in his ability and insisted on doing things the proper way. In fact, often other prospective grooms would hire him to do their hunting for them.

Seriam's thoughts drifted back to her childhood, growing up with the woods as her back yard. While the other boys did everything they could to frighten her with snakes or disgust her with dead things, Ephron had treated her with tenderness and respect from the start.

"The animals are scared of you," he'd said. "But if you're gentle with them they will learn to trust you."

With her father always busy managing his inn, Ephron had taught her to sit quietly near a pond in the evening to watch the animals coming for a drink. He'd shown her which plants she could eat, which snakes to stay far away from and which to ignore.

He had made the forest feel like home to her, and her love for the forest grew so naturally alongside her love for him that for a long time she couldn't separate the two feelings. He belonged to the forest, as much at home there as the wild foxes.

Though confident in Ephron's ability, Seriam couldn't suppress the nervous worries that welled up in her heart. The slightest mishap —a broken bowstring, a sudden change in the weather—could ruin an entire week of preparation. If the groom didn't return by sundown, it would invalidate the whole ceremony, and they'd have to reschedule it for at least a month later. Having poured a month's wages into preparing this one, her father would be furious. She tugged anxiously at her skirt; eyes locked on the tree line.

Her thoughts and dreams absorbed her so completely that she didn't feel the time passing. Eventually someone brought a chair and pushed her down into it. Refusing to hear the hushed whispers around her, she sat with her hands clamped on the sides of the chair and her back rigid until sunset faded into full dark.

The bowls of soup lining the tables grew cold. The plates of vegetables began to wilt. They had begun preparations for the feast almost before Ephron walked into the trees, confident that he would return well before dark. As the sun sank below the horizon, the men's lighthearted jokes about Ephron enjoying his last day of freedom shifted to more serious discussions about search parties. Seriam could no longer ignore them. She twisted the material of her dress, then smoothed it out again. Nobody knew these woods like Ephron. What could possibly have happened to him?

She glared at the trees that had been her childhood playground. They had swallowed her beloved, and she now felt as if she'd been betrayed by her dearest friend. Her anger grew until it drove her to her feet and into the forest. The men, busy trying to organize their search party, failed to notice the forsaken bride walking into the forest alone.

The outline of a boulder loomed ahead, shrouded with a darkness thicker than the darkness of a clear night. A raindrop splashed against her forehead and evaporated into steam from the heat of her skin. The dozen raindrops that followed had no greater impact than the first. A rumbling like thunder pounded the inside of her skull. Her anger focused on the boulder, making it the personification of whatever had taken Ephron from her. She lashed out with her mind, screaming at it in rage. "What have you done with him?"

Light flashed around her. A shockwave of sound lifted her off her feet and flung her against a tree. She didn't even realize she was in the air before she hit the ground again, blacking out from the pain.

She awoke confused, unable to remember why she'd slept outside or why her head ached. She could think of no reason why she would be waking up on the ground outside at sunrise. Water dripped from the trees into puddles too wide to step across, and her clothes held more moisture than dew alone could account for. It must have rained during the night, which made her presence here an even greater mystery. She looked down at her ruined wedding clothes and remembered Ephron. A tremor passed through her. She gripped a tree branch and pulled herself to her feet, brushing ineffectively at the worst of the stains.

I'll have to get a new dress before Ephron sees me, she thought. *Father will throw a fit over the wasted money.*

She looked around to find her bearings, but only saw trees and two boulders—no, just one boulder that had been broken in two and burned along one side. The scene felt familiar. She stared for several seconds trying to recall why she thought she'd seen it before, and why that odd burning smell would come from a rock after a rainstorm.

Caught up in trying to remember the night's events, it took her a moment to realize the burning smell came from somewhere behind her, not from the boulder in front. She turned around. A tendril of smoke coiled above the trees. Heart racing, she pushed through the underbrush toward the rising smoke. *They must be roasting the deer already. Everyone will be wondering where I've been. Ephron will wonder—Ephron!*

The thought made her snatch up her tattered skirt and run. Her eyes burned, watering until she had to stop and wipe them. This much smoke wouldn't come from just a cooking fire, or even a bonfire. It drifted in the air all around her like a light blue fog.

Maybe the wood is so wet from the rain... She stumbled out of the forest into the silent clearing that had once been her village. The silhouettes of trees showed through the blackened shell of her father's inn. Her chest squeezed, forcing the air out of her lungs. She fell to her knees, retching, fighting to draw a breath.

Crows circled overhead. Seriam shrank into herself, crawling back under the shadow of the trees, whimpering. The few smoldering posts that still stood couldn't have hidden a child. Nothing rose out of the ash to threaten her, yet the early morning light combined with the haze of smoke and absolute silence sent a shiver down her spine. Even the crows worked in dead silence, landing for only moments at a time as if they also feared to linger.

"Help." She couldn't raise her voice above a pitiful squeak. "Somebody."

No answer came. She had to go and see for herself, to find out what might have caused such a fire. She pulled herself to her feet and shuffled forward through the ash, trying to spot signs of life without looking too closely at the bodies scattered around. Bodies. Though her mind tried not to acknowledge them as such at first, after passing the third or fourth prone figure she had to stop and look at each one. She had to acknowledge that she recognized the person.

Near the entrance of the ruined inn sprawled a familiar body. She flinched away and pretended not to have seen it. Shock covered her again with its numbing force, sparing her a complete breakdown among the smoldering ashes. Her mind refused to accept what her eyes had seen.

"Is anyone still here?" Only silence answered her. She forced her feet to move on.

The feast tables lay on their sides near one side of the clearing. Most of them lay end to end in a tight ring, their tops facing outward. One table lay in the center, legs in the air, with several bodies crushed underneath it. She jerked her eyes away and forced herself to move on. She got only as far as the next house before her legs gave way. Her hands reached up and rubbed ashes into her hair, adding streaks of gray to her black locks. Numbness settled over her mind, smothering her thoughts. Her lips formed the names of each member of the village in turn, a private funeral dirge. When she got to Ephron's name, she stopped. *He can't be dead. He simply can't! We're going to be married.*

Whispering his name, she sat up and forced her eyes to look directly at the bodies. She shouted his name, again and again, louder each time. A few of the crows ruffled their wings and squawked at her, then turned back to their grisly meal. She leaped to her feet and ran from body to body, matching a name with each face she found. Each one stabbed her heart with new pain. She forced herself to look at her father's body, and her friend Meli. Everyone she'd ever known sprawled on the cold ground, even the children.

She shoved the thought firmly to the back of her mind. She couldn't deal with it now. She only had to find Ephron, to know if he still lived.

She didn't know how many times she looked at each body before the light grew too dim to recognize their faces. Yet she'd found no sign of Ephron. She collapsed to the ground, shoulders heaving with sobs. Her eyes burned from smoke and from crying. She gazed into the forest, willing her beloved to come walking out of the trees. Had he ever returned from his hunting trip?

As darkness cast its shadows among the bodies, she couldn't bring herself to remain in the village any longer. She yearned to stay and wait for Ephron, but she had to find someplace safe. She needed food and a place where she could sleep without fear that whoever had done this would return in the night. Most of all, she needed to be surrounded by the living. The king would know what to do. She followed the road toward the castle, guided by the light of the first stars.

CHAPTER ELEVEN

Kenan looked over his shoulder again. The feeling of being stalked had been growing on him all morning. Everyone else in the castle scurried around setting up for the kingdom's anniversary celebration, and he worried that if anyone caught him lingering, they would recruit him to help with something. None of the servants would approach him on their own of course, but the preparations today fell under the direct supervision of his mother. She seemed to believe work is good for idle young men. Kenan disagreed. He'd tried to visit his father, but the guard wouldn't let him in. The king needed to rest in preparation for tonight.

Devin was in the kitchen drinking wine with some of the soldiers of the Royal Guard. He still couldn't find Raendel. That left him nothing to do but go outside the castle walls. Extra guards manned the exits, but exceptionally large crowds flowed through them. With the help of a simple cloak, he kept on hand for exactly such occasions, Kenan managed to slip out.

People of every description packed the streets for the holiday, pressing against one another as they strained to see the envoys who had come from all across the kingdom. Soldiers dressed in the exotic uniforms of distant lands pushed with the bruising end of their spears to clear paths through hordes of tattered peasants, shouting in thick accents for them to make way for the lord and lady. Proud stallions, their saddles resplendent with silver embroidery and tinkling golden bells, pranced through the openings cleared by their escorts. Gold-plated carriages flashed in the sunlight, and from time to time the crowds were blessed to see velvet curtains part to unveil glimpses of painted faces and flowing silk.

Kenan wandered at random for a while, gaping at the feather-adorned costumes and muddy accents of the newcomers. When he grew tired of watching people, he headed for the market square to see what entertainment had been set up for the festival. Harps and flutes battled with each other and with the lowing of nearby cattle. Vendors stood at their booths crying out for those passing by to come and see the best, the most delicious, the most beautiful treasures in all the world. A juggler flung hoops into the air between a man polishing boots and a display of sweets.

Kenan stopped to buy some taffy. The woman selling the candy stared at the gold coin he handed her, then looked up and blanched when she recognized the prince. "Your Highness!" she stammered, fumbling to find enough change. Her mouth worked as if she wanted to say more, but no further sound came out. She set his change down on the table, stepped back, and dropped to her knees.

"Thank you," Kenan said. The woman didn't respond or even look up, so he shrugged and went on his way.

He meandered in the general direction of the city gates. *Maybe I can catch a glimpse of the tents being set up outside the city. Devin said it's like an entire town of bright-colored miniature cloth mansions.* Streams of people flowed around him, trying to drag him in the opposite direction. For once he was glad to be thin, otherwise he never would have found a path through the crowds.

He stopped in front of the city gates where a line of people stretched back past the inner gate, out of sight down the tunnel to the outer gates. Guards stopped each person coming in and checked their name against a list. They tagged any weapons people might be carrying and stored them in the guard tower. Master Jabal stood near the gate, scanning the crowd. Kenan backed away in alarm, keeping his eyes locked on Jabal. He edged back toward the side of the street until he found an empty doorway where he could observe without being seen.

A row of twenty wagons pulled up to the gate, the first one driven by a figure wearing monk-like robes with the hood pulled over his head. Two more dressed exactly the same way sat beside him with their arms folded into their robes. Large casks filled the wagons, most likely wine for the celebration.

One of the black-robed figures climbed down from the first wagon and stood with his head bowed while Jabal searched the lists. A man passed through the gate without stopping to be checked, taking advantage of Jabal's distraction. A large hunting bow hung on his back in clear view, and a hunting knife big enough to skin a boar hung on his belt. Jabal shouted after the man. Two guards moved to flank the intruder, each of them grabbing one of his arms.

Kenan's moment of pride in the quick reflexes of his kingdom's military vaporized when the man threw both guards down on the ground in front of him, drew his knife, and killed them both with one efficient slice of his blade. A guard at the gate raised his bow, but the attacker pushed his way into the throng of people, using them as shields to cover his escape.

Jabal stood frozen for a moment, staring. He dropped his list on the ground and ran after the man. His current path would lead too close to Kenan's hiding place for comfort.

The prince ducked his head and sprinted down a side street in a different direction, hoping Jabal would be too busy chasing the intruder to worry about him. Angry yells pursued him through the mob as his elbows and knees jammed into ribs to help clear a path. At every step he dodged and twisted to find openings. After a few paces he risked stopping to look behind him. Jabal pushed through the crowds on a parallel street. He sighed with relief and continued through the crowds at a less desperate pace until he reached the market square. Just as he arrived, Jabal entered from the other side.

"Rotten luck," Kenan muttered to himself. He ducked into the entryway of the nearest building, which happened to be the library. He turned around under the shadow of an arch and scanned the crowds. Jabal examined each face in the crowd, turning to look in every direction. Some of the tension drained out of Kenan's shoulders. His tutor hadn't noticed him. At least not yet. He stayed to watch from the shadows for a moment longer just to be sure.

Jabal stopped a pair of soldiers and appeared to be questioning them. Kenan leaned forward, ready to run again if they pointed in his direction. The soldiers shrugged and shook their heads, and Jabal turned back toward the gates. He couldn't believe Jabal would give up that easily. The open streets didn't quite feel safe yet. He retreated into the silence of the library and hid himself among the piles of books. The library seemed like the last place Jabal would look for his wayward pupil.

CHAPTER TWELVE

Raendel leaned against the wall of the dining hall, watching the crowded tables and hoping the tension would ease soon. Two hundred nobles packed the hall today, every one of them expecting to be waited on as if they were the most important guest. Master Othniel had ordered him to remain near the high table, ready to step in the moment any of the royal family showed signs of wanting something. Several times already the king had sent Raendel with messages asking where the two princes were and why they were late. The nobles shifted in their seats, and the murmuring grew louder with every minute they spent waiting for the king to signal the start of the feast. The king leaned over and whispered to Master Lenore, who sat at his left hand.

Master Lenore answered in a louder voice. "Master Jabal hasn't returned from the city gates either, and the last groups of nobles to come through didn't see him there. We must wait for him at least. It would be unseemly if we began without him."

King Edmund waved a hand. Raendel jumped forward to kneel beside him. The king leaned over him to speak, his towering bulk making Raendel flinch. The lights in the hall were already fairly dim, and the king's shadow seemed to darken the whole room even further. He thought this must be what it feels like to be a sapling watching an avalanche descend on it. The king's breath reeked of sour wine.

"Go and find Masser Jabal," King Edmund slurred. "Tell him to hurry, we're all waiting for him to shtart the ceremony. And find my sons, too. My sons should be here. Devin..."

The king blinked and peered around with bloodshot eyes, then turned back to the table and gazed silently into his empty wine glass.

Raendel waited for more, but His Majesty seemed to have forgotten him already. So, he bowed his head and then stood and backed up two steps before turning around to hurry toward the main entrance. Messengers ran between there and the city gate at regular intervals.

He approached the nearest guard and dipped his head, forgoing the greater formality of a full bow for the sake of speed. "I have an urgent message from the King for Master Jabal. Is there a messenger near?"

The guard didn't turn his head when he replied, and only glanced at Raendel before turning his attention back toward the street outside. "A messenger came just moments ago to report that Master Jabal left the gate in pursuit of somebody. I can send that one back with your message, but I don't know how long it might be until Master Jabal returns and hears it." He turned slightly to one side and shouted. "Messenger!"

A young boy jumped up from where he'd been leaning in the shadow of the doorway and ran over to the guard. The guard gestured toward Raendel, and the errand boy turned to him.

Raendel relayed the king's message to Jabal. When he finished the boy repeated it back to him to be sure he had it right. As soon as Raendel nodded approval the messenger turned around and sprinted in the direction of the city gate.

Turning back to the guard, Raendel asked. "Is there any word of the two princes?"

The guard's previously blank expression tightened a little around his mouth and eyes, and Raendel smelled a hint of bitterness in his reply. "His Highness Prince Devin is in the kitchen playing dice with several of the other guards. Messages have been sent to him, but he refuses to leave before his game is finished. He's also keeping all the free guards busy with games when it's past time for the shift change."

The corner of his mouth twisted, and he pursed his lips as if to spit, then glanced at Raendel and swallowed instead. "Her Majesty the queen has been searching for Prince Kenan all morning. We had word to stop him if he tried to leave but none of us has seen him at all. An hour ago, she decided he must have gotten out somehow anyway, so she sent a dozen men out to scour the city looking for him. From the look on her face, he'd better hope one of us finds him before she does."

He's probably wandering the streets enjoying himself while I'm stuck here waiting tables and delivering messages. It must be nice to be so carefree. Some of us have work to do.

He stood there for a bit longer considering his options. He didn't think he could find Master Jabal or Prince Kenan any faster than anyone else, nor was he likely to have any more luck convincing Prince Devin to leave his game early without a direct order from the king. He'd delivered the king's message, or at least passed it on to another messenger who would deliver it as soon as possible. With nothing more useful to do, returning to his post at the high table seemed his best option.

He didn't run back to his post, but he didn't drag his feet either. He moved at the speed of a servant who knows he must go quickly but really doesn't want to go. The queen had joined her husband at the table.

Queen Havilah sat on the king's right side; her eyes fixed on the door. She nodded politely to anyone who spoke to her, no matter what they said, without shifting her gaze. Master Deborah looked toward the king every few minutes, waiting for the signal to begin. Nobody could begin eating until she started the celebration with a benediction, and it was clear to Raendel that even the even-tempered Deborah grew impatient at the delay.

The king coughed into his sleeve with a rattling sound, then motioned for Raendel to kneel beside his chair. "Go tell Prince Devin to come at once. I don't care if his game is finished or not. We have more important things—"

A loud crash reverberated through the hall as the doors burst open and at least two dozen armed men charged into the room. The nobles knocked over chairs and tripped over each other in their panic to get away from the attackers. The men nearest the door fell, wounded or dead, before they had time to stand. More attackers flooded through the doors every moment, spreading death across the hall. Raendel fell back against the wall and covered himself in the illusion of blood. Other Adoël did the same, blending their illusions of death with the reality that filled the hall.

Master Lenore yelled to the guards. "To the high table! Protect the king!"

The dozen guards scattered throughout the room pushed their way through frantic nobles to reach the high table. The invaders outnumbered the guards four to one.

"Where are Prince Devin and the rest of the castle guard?" Lenore shouted. "Come this way, Your Majesty. We must get you out of here."

The attackers carved a path halfway to the high table. Some of the guests tried to fight them off with knives and chairs but proved ineffective against their well-armed assailants. A shadow drifted among the combatants like a black cloud, hints of a humanoid shape cloaked in darkness. One of the braver nobles stabbed at it with a long carving knife. The knife struck something solid through the black cloud. The nobleman screamed. His muscles convulsed while he dangled from the knife handle, thrashing wildly, until he rattled out a wordless cry and fell limp. Raendel uttered a quick prayer and concentrated all his efforts on maintaining his self-protective illusion.

The king didn't respond to Lenore's shouts, or to the bloody melee around him. His glazed eyes stood out from a face as white as the Adoël as he watched the attackers draw closer to him. Duty pulled at Raendel, demanding action, but in his panic, he couldn't think of anything to do that would help. He maintained his illusion and watched as Lenore and Deborah took the king by the arms and dragged him out of his chair toward the small door behind them.

Urgent shouts of "Protect the king!" echoed in Raendel's head while flashbacks of the vision from Master Othniel's chamber pricked his conscience. He covered his ears with his hands, but he couldn't block out Othniel's voice that spoke inside his own mind. *We failed our master. We must never fail him again.*

Raendel argued back against his conscience. *What can I do? I don't know how to fight! The king has Master Lenore and Master Deborah to protect him. I would only get in the way.*

The shadow creature knocked aside nobles and soldiers alike, advancing to within a few yards of the high table. Lenore and Deborah pulled the king through a door that opened into a passage ending at the king's chambers. He considered the advancing enemy and then the door where the king had gone. He didn't know what he could do, but his conscience wouldn't let him just lie there and do nothing. With one last glance at the attackers, he leaped up and ran after the king.

Inside the hallway he used the dim lighting to his advantage, darting from shadow to shadow and covering himself with illusion at each stop. He glanced over his shoulder to make sure no one spotted him moving from one hiding place to the next.

Even with this sporadic movement Raendel advanced faster than the king and caught up with them quickly. The sounds of fighting behind them drew nearer. The king stumbled again, and this time he struggled to rise on his own. Lenore lifted the king and carried him down the hall, shouting for Deborah to cover them from behind.

Raendel picked out his next hiding place, looked back, and froze. The shadow creature floated into view like a patch of night. Even the light of the brightest torch couldn't penetrate that darkness. The entire hallway dimmed as it approached.

Master Deborah slowed to a walk, allowing Master Lenore and the king to get ahead of her. She glanced over her shoulder and turned to face the creature.

Fangs gleamed through the unnatural darkness, and dark spectral arms rose from the cloud to point toward the king. Its fingers lengthened into rays of darkness that stretched out toward Master Deborah. Throwing up one hand as a shield, Deborah raised her other hand and responded by sending rays of light to stab into the darkness. Back and forth they struggled, alternately fading and brightening. The shadow wavered, but while the battle of energy raged it didn't stop moving forward. Raendel struggled against the instinct to hold his breath as the thing passed inches in front of him. The song maintaining his illusion wavered, but not enough to reveal his position. He had no way to know whether his illusion would deceive this unnatural creature, but he had nothing else to try.

The beast reached Master Deborah and opened its twisted fingers to physically grapple with her. At the shadow's touch, the light around Deborah vanished, and she crumpled. Another ray of light shot out from behind Deborah to strike the shadow creature. Master Lenore stood near the end of the hall, with the king slumped at her feet. She waited just long enough to see the effect of her attack, then dragged the king through a doorway.

Raendel held his breath, ready to surrender his hidden position and run. But this time, when the ray of light struck it, the creature collapsed.

Deborah struggled to her knees, stunned by the attack. Before she could recover a man stepped into view. His clothes looked like they had been expensive once, now destroyed by rips and stains. A beard matted with dirt framed an ugly, twisted face. His eyes flickered back and forth in apparently random patterns, like the eyes of a man who dreamed even while awake. A strange and sickening invisible energy radiated from the man like rays from a dark sun. He smelled like the den of a wild predator, full of bones and death.

Master Deborah's hands dropped to her sides. She staggered, weakened by her struggle against the shadow. The newcomer made a throwing motion, and a spike of pale fire shot from his hand to bury itself in Deborah's forehead. She fell backward without a sound and lay still. Raendel choked back a scream. He barely resisted the urge to flee, even knowing that the slightest movement or sound would sign his death sentence. He could smell his own fear so strongly he wondered how it wasn't making the enemy gag.

The man stalked past him without a glance, intent on the doorway Master Lenore and the king had fled through. Raendel's heart felt squeezed by two compelling forces. His fear urged him to flee, his conscience compelled him to follow. Guilt dragged him as far as the king's chamber door before fear paralyzed him again.

The attacker opened his mouth and spewed out a blast of energy that billowed like steam toward Lenore. It wailed with the sound of a lost soul as it raced forward.

Lenore's response appeared too weak to hold against the attack - a feeble curtain of light between her and destruction. At the last moment her shield changed into a wedge pointed toward the energy cloud. The raging torrent didn't stop but split on a razor edge to pass harmlessly on each side of her.

The enemy stretched out his hand. A cloud of tiny daggers flew from it. Lenore's wedge melted into a dome surrounding her. The daggers swirled around the shield for a few moments then faded away.

Raendel's mind had been able to connect some sort of image with the tests of strength that had preceded this. Now, having failed with simpler strikes, the attacks shifted to a deeper level. Raendel offered a prayer of thanks that he hadn't been noticed yet, just being near the flow of power nearly overwhelmed him. Lights and colors assaulted his senses, blended with voices whispering corruption. The smell of decay permeated every-thing as light and darkness collided in a struggle for dominance. Yet it seemed that more was going on than what could merely be sensed by physical means, that what he was experiencing with his eyes and ears was only the backwash of a raging flood. The intensity of the battle locked the two combatants together more strongly than iron chains.

Motion on the other side of the room drew Raendel's attention. The king dragged himself across the floor to the fireplace in the far wall. He gripped the stones of the fireplace and used them to pull himself upright. Once he'd gained his feet, he held himself up with his left hand while with his right hand he drew the sword that hung above the mantle.

The sword flickered with a pale greenish glow. A sound radiated from it, like a whispering or a murmuring, sounds that felt like words even though Raendel couldn't understand them. The glow and the sounds flowed like a kind of energy, holding the king up and drawing him toward his attacker. With tremendous power the sword moved the king like a puppet, pulling him across the room to where Lenore and her assailant struggled.

The enemy forced his way past the last of Lenore's spiritual defenses, drew a dagger, and buried it in her chest. The king gasped and clutched his own chest as if he were the one who had been stabbed. He collapsed on the floor. The enemy snatched the sword from the king's lifeless hand and stabbed him in the chest with it. He stood for a moment as if waiting for something, then shook his head. "Dead already? Curse your weak heart, I needed you alive! My Shadow-weaver is destroyed, and my soldiers outnumbered. I don't have time to hunt down your sons. At least now I have the sword. They will come to me."

Raendel waited until the man turned and strode out of the cham-bers before he crawled over to the king's body, too weighed down by guilt to stand. *Please let it be a mistake. He can't be dead. How can I face Kenan after this?*

He checked for signs of life but found none. He knelt beside the body and wept, this time not for the failures of his ancestors, but for his own.

CHAPTER THIRTEEN

K enan crouched inside the library doors, wondering how long he should wait for Master Jabal to stop looking for him. He'd rarely visited this place. Servants would bring any books he needed for his studies to the castle.

The vastness of the library felt intimidating in the dark. Dim corridors of books stretched out into infinity. The nearest wall faded into shadows in both directions, and the other three couldn't be seen at all. The blackness above could have been the emptiness of space with all the stars burned out. Dead silence filled the building, lacking those small life-sounds produced by the very existence of people within a closed space.

This expanse of the unknown weighed on Kenan almost as much as the thought of Jabal searching for him. Once his heartbeat slowed, he mustered the courage to move farther in. A light flickered near the back of the library, like the guttering of a candle that had burned down to a stub. *Surely it wouldn't be someone studying today. Not on a celebration day—*

A movement in the shadows made him duck behind a pile of books. Someone crept through the aisles without a light, obviously trying to make no sound. Kenan shifted his nervous energy with the Art, using it to enhance his perception, but still heard nothing more than a faint impression of somebody breathing nearby. The one movement he'd seen must have been a shadow cast by the person moving between him and the candlelight. A pile of books fell over. He looked toward the noise automatically. The shadow of a man faded from view as the outside door closed it off at the source.

Kenan wondered who it might have been and why they had run out so quickly, but his curiosity about the candle at the back of the library pushed those other questions out of his mind. He tiptoed toward the flickering light, wanting to see who else might be hiding in the library today, and why. He found an opening on the shelf beside him that seemed at the right angle and peered through. That cloud of white hair could only belong to Master Admah. Kenan breathed easier. Master Admah practically lived in the library. He should have expected to find him here.

The old man sat at a small desk with his head slumped forward to rest on the large open book. Kenan struggled over what he should do. Admah seemed to have fallen asleep. He would be missed if he didn't show up for the celebration. But if Kenan woke him, he would demand to know what his pupil was doing here. He could lie and say he'd been sent to find his teacher, but such a lie could easily be discovered and then he would get in worse trouble.

Help me. A voice in his head interrupted his internal debate.

The voice didn't come from anyone in the library. For a moment his mind buzzed with noise and other people's thoughts, not quite clear enough to understand but just clear enough to leave the impression of panic and suffering. A heavy foreboding pressed down on him. The urge to return to the castle multiplied, so strong that he took a step toward the door before he stopped himself.

He glanced at Master Admah's sleeping form. The strange sensations in his head made the decision easier. He would awaken Admah, endure the old man's scolding, and return to the castle with him. It was simply the right thing to do. Besides, it seemed safer with all the crazy things happening. He shuffled his feet as he approached, hoping to avoid startling the old man. Admah didn't stir. One hand hung loose at his side, and the other rested on the desk. A pool of ink seeped across the pages of the book, obscuring most of it. Chuckling at how deep his teacher slept, he came within reach and laid two fingers on Admah's back. Getting no response, he edged closer and softly shook the old man's shoulder.

Something crunched under his feet. He looked down. An empty ink bottle lay in a puddle of drying ink. So much ink had spilled on the floor he wondered how there could possibly be so much on the table. Suddenly uneasy, he shook the old man harder and called his name. "Master Admah!"

He still got no response. He touched the old man's forehead. It felt like a tallow candle, cool and greasy. He reached out a trembling hand and lifted his teacher's face toward the light. Master Admah's unblinking eyes stared straight ahead, but they didn't see. Blood dribbled from a slash across his throat.

Kenan jumped backward against one of the bookshelves. His feet kept trying to back away but the sturdy shelves behind him kept him in place. A distant voice called his name, but he couldn't take his eyes off Admah. His vision grew red around the edges and the world slipped out of focus. He closed his eyes. Panic and shock swirled in his head, scrambling his thoughts. He focused on breathing, rehearsing his lessons to calm himself. Master Jabal's face materialized in his mind. His eyes popped open.

Someone had murdered Master Admah. Master Jabal had run off after an armed intruder and could be anywhere in the city by now. Who else could he go to for help? Father would know what to do. He sprinted for the door, no longer caring whether Jabal caught him. He would have welcomed that now. Stacks of books exploded in every direction as he plowed through them and he hit the door without slowing, flew over the steps without touching them, and landed on the street running at full speed toward the castle.

Dodging through the crowded streets, he rounded a corner and had to throw himself to the side to avoid a line of wagons that thundered through the narrow streets at a suicidal gallop. Eight wagons flew past in a blur of foaming horses and spraying mud. Devin and a group of castle guards ran after the wagons waving bloody swords. Too intent on his own purpose to wonder what his brother was doing, Kenan picked himself up and continued his mad dash to the castle.

Inside the castle people ran in every direction, calling for help and for healers. Most gripped some makeshift weapon. Many of them bled from fresh wounds. None of them paid any attention to Kenan. The blood and the chaos broke through Kenan's haze of panic, slowing his steps as he tried to figure out what had happened.

The litter of bodies inside the Great Hall slowed his progress further. The confusion centered here, although fewer living people milled around this room than in the other sections he'd run through. Wounded men groaned and cried out for help as he passed by. The sounds of weeping echoed through the room until it seemed like the stone walls cried out.

His feet crunched on broken glass and slid on grease from spilled food. Fewer bodies cluttered the floor around the high table, which did little to ease Kenan's worries. The nobles on this end of the room must have seen the attack coming and had more time to get ready.

Farther in toward the king's chambers a somber procession brought him to a halt. His mother wept next to a pallet being carried by six servants. None of them spoke as the prince approached. The body stretched out on the pallet made words of explanation or comfort seem pointless. Soon the sound of Kenan's weeping mingled with his mother's.

CHAPTER FOURTEEN

Torches along the walls shone light on the backs of heads, throwing shadows on the table that twitched and flickered with a hypnotic rhythm. Queen Havilah's eyes wandered among those unstable silhouettes; her mind lost in the shadows of memory. Twenty years ago, when King Edward's army had swept across her father's tiny kingdom, her father had met him under a flag of truce. He'd been wise enough to know that fighting would only destroy the crops they needed to get them through the winter without the slightest hope of driving the invaders away.

Her father offered unconditional surrender, and tribute. The marriage of his daughter to a powerful and ambitious king secured his position as duke in the new-formed kingdom and saved his family from death or exile. Havilah, barely sixteen and stuck in a political marriage to a man thirty years her elder, had resigned herself to a life without love. She consoled herself with the thought that love was a luxury rarely offered to the daughters of nobility.

Now, after years of quiet evening talks beside the fire, the constant struggle of balancing personal life with political facade, she couldn't point out the moment or the day when she first realized she loved her husband. Even before drink and age began to overtake him, love had been putting down roots deep in her heart. Now those roots had been ripped out, leaving a numb emptiness behind. All she wanted to do was crawl back into her memories and hide there forever.

She couldn't, of course. Not until Devin assumed leadership of the kingdom. Once he was crowned, she could enter a period of mourning that she hoped would last until her death. She never wanted to have to face people again.

A touch on her shoulder pulled her back into the present. Master Lenore's eyes had always struck her as kind, but now a deep sorrow overshadowed that kindness. Havilah found it hard to even look at her as she leaned over and whispered, "Everyone is here, Your Majesty. We are ready to begin."

Havilah nodded and motioned for her to proceed.

Master Lenore levered herself out of her chair, favoring her bandaged left shoulder, and addressed the assembly.

"The queen has asked me to speak to you as acting regent until Prince Devin's coronation. Yesterday we suffered terrible loss. Treacherous assailants struck down many of our nobles from across the kingdom, as well as the king himself. The attackers fled after killing the king, but we have to assume they'll be back. We must not let the next attack destroy everything that King Edward worked so hard to build. We meet today to discuss how we might respond to this pending attack, and to offer our counsel to the new king-to-be. I invited Master Othniel to join us for reasons I will explain later. Master Jabal is busy investigating the events around Master Admah's death. He has been gathering information from his own private sources and asked to be excused from this meeting."

Master Lenore nodded to Prince Devin, who failed to respond. His dazed expression never changed. Lenore's sigh ended in a wince, and her hand reached up to touch the bandages around her chest.

"We identified the man who led the attack as Lord Erick, the queen's nephew and Duke Arnould's son. Master Jabal suspected Erick of treason but he disappeared several days ago before we could arrest him. As soon as Duke Arnould learned of his son's treachery he came to us eager to help. We thank him for his presence here today."

She nodded toward the somber Duke Arnould, who nodded back, then cast his eyes downward. Havilah lifted her gaze from the table and let it rest on the duke for a minute. Her brother's thick black beard was sprinkled with a bit more gray than last time she'd seen him, and he'd gained a few pounds. Otherwise, he appeared unchanged. Years of moderate drinking had touched his nose and cheeks with red. His face showed no reaction to Lenore's words, only the same concerned interest as all the others at the table, but there was something in his look that stirred a moment of suspicion in Havilah's heart. Before that suspicion could take root, her sorrow rose up again and drowned it in a sea of fog.

Lenore's words continued to buzz in her ears like a fly that wouldn't leave her alone. "Through our own sources and information from the duke, we expected Erick to make a move of some kind. We didn't expect this kind of strike, for several reasons."

Master Lenore leaned against the table, resting her weight on her good hand. "First, the attack happened on far too small a scale for him to seize control of the kingdom by force. If he meant to take the castle, why didn't he attack with greater numbers? Either he never planned that to begin with, or he failed. I find it hard to believe he could have been so foolish. Second, Lord Erick killed the king, stole an old sword, and then left without killing King Edward's sons. If he wanted to leave the throne empty, he should have killed both princes as well. But he doesn't seem to have even tried to do that. In spite of these issues, he does seem to have planned his attack well, if his goal is what we suspect."

Havilah's mind wandered. She barely heard Lenore describing how Master Jabal had been led away from the gate just as the wagons entered. They'd been full of soldiers hidden inside large barrels, delivered to the castle on the pretext of bringing wine for the celebration. The increasing intensity in Lenore's voice caught the queen's attention again as she built up to her conclusion.

"The assassin who led Master Jabal away from the gate escaped before we could identify him. We believe he is the one who killed Master Admah in the library. Such a well-organized attack could hardly have overlooked the two princes. Either Lord Erick never planned to kill them, or he failed. I don't believe he failed. I think he had a different mission, and he succeeded."

Devin cleared his throat, and the group seated around the table turned to him. "What do you think he planned to do, Master Lenore?"

"Exactly what he accomplished," Lenore said. "To steal the sword—"

Duke Arnould slapped a meaty hand down on the table. "Ha! My son is arrogant and rash, but not a total fool. Why would anyone, especially my son, risk his life just to steal a sword?"

Lenore answered calmly. "The sword that hung in King Edward's chambers is not an ordinary sword. It is Anglachel, forged by Arkos and used by him to establish the Kingdom of Storvia."

Arnould snorted. "Do you not hear yourself? You're talking about a sword that you claim hung above King Edward's mantle! You mean the legendary Anglachel has been hanging in plain sight since the death of Arkos a hundred years ago? If it's so powerful, why was it hung on the wall to collect dust for generations? I don't believe that old sword holds any power. Arkos had a good weapon, I won't deny that. But if there was any magic involved, it was his own. And I doubt that any magic could win a war by itself."

Lenore sighed. "Has all knowledge of history and of the Art been lost? Young Prince Kenan could easily wrestle you or any of your best men to the ground in less time than it would take you to stand up out of your chair. With a little more training and a good spear, he could pierce a breastplate at a hundred yards. The Art of Biomancy by itself is powerful and can be learned by any person who has the time and discipline to study it. But the Art alone only makes use of a person's own power. Anyone using it will tire quickly. Anglachel is a tool designed to make the Art limitless. You only have to cut someone with it to soak up all of their energy, so your strength is constantly renewed. It grants terrifying power to its wielder, but only for fighting. That is why, after the Great War, Arkos hung it on the wall and left it to collect dust. After several generations in obscurity, people began to forget."

Master Lenore paused to take a drink. She looked around at a circle of skeptical faces. "Most people forgot, I should say. The king and two Messengers have kept the chain of knowledge alive, passed on to each new king after his coronation. The common people have legends, and a person could still find documents that speak of the sword. An intelligent enemy might have learned of it and decided to use it for himself."

Duke Arnould grunted and shifted in his seat. "Maybe. But that's a terrible risk to take based on fairy stories. How would he know where to find a sword that has been kept such a close secret for nearly a hundred years? I still say he came to kill the king. He probably would've killed the two princes if he'd had the opportunity before we chased him away." He looked around at the others and received several nods of agreement.

The tone of his voice roused Havilah far enough to put a little fire back in her own voice. "Hold your peace for a moment, Lukas, and let Master Lenore finish. She's been gathering information from several reliable sources and knows more about the situation than anyone else here."

Duke Arnould surged to his feet. His chair scraped backward across the floor, hung up on a crack between two stones, and toppled over with a crash. He clenched both his hands into fists and beat against the table hard enough to rattle it and spill a few drinks. "It's my son we're talking about here. I think I have a right—"

Prince Devin sprang to his feet. "Hold your tongue! You forget your place, uncle. You're not the only one here who has suffered loss. I know this is hard for you, but you will show proper respect, or I'll call the guards and have you removed."

Arnould stared at Devin. His fists hovered in the air over the table and his mouth locked open, but he remained silent. His teeth came together with an audible click, and he gave Devin a glare that had withered many men. Devin's face remained implacable, his lips silent, waiting for the duke's reply.

Arnould's face flushed red, then purple, then faded to its normal color. One by one his fingers uncurled, and he turned to pick up his chair with only a few barely audible grumbles.

"You may continue, Master Lenore," Devin sat down, still keeping his eyes on Duke Arnould.

Lenore looked from Lukas to Devin, then continued as if she hadn't been interrupted. "A man with enough knowledge of our city to plan that kind of strike could hardly overlook the two princes if that were his main goal. It's not as if we kept them hidden. He planned the details of his attack with precision, timing it perfectly and knowing exactly where to strike. He doesn't seem the kind to leave anything to chance."

Havilah turned her face away from her brother. His outburst had pulled her out of her daze momentarily, but she didn't feel up to an argument yet. "I feel you are right, Master Lenore. Why would he take the sword unless he knew it was valuable in some way? If he wanted a sword, he could have brought his own. Even so, what can we do about it other than gather our strength for a fight? Either way we must be prepared for his return, this time perhaps with a full army behind him. Whether Erick's immediate goal was to take the sword or kill the king, his ultimate goal seems to be power. That means he's likely to come back."

Lenore shook her head, face clouded with worry. "If we are right, if he's gained knowledge of how to use the sword, then he has the means to obtain the kingdom. Anglachel will only work for the man it

is bound to, but if he has learned how to bind the sword to himself —
we must get it back before he has the chance. We know the sword is
bound by blood, but we're not sure exactly how that works. The
descendants of the king would be able to use it. For anyone outside
the family, we believe that he would have to use the sword to kill one
of the family in order to transfer the bond to himself. Yet we do have
some encouraging news. Lord Erick escaped with less than a third of
his men still alive, according to the guards who finally chased him out
of the castle. We should pursue him immediately to catch him before
he gets back to his main army, if he has one."

Murmurs buzzed around the table. Duke Arnould leaned over to
the man next to him and whispered in his ear. The man nodded, then
rose to his feet. "Begging your pardon Master Lenore, Your Majesty,
but in my homeland, we have a saying. 'Never chase a snake through
tall grass.' What I mean to say is, we have no idea where he might be
hiding an army ready to ambush us. If we go running after him in our
underclothes, so to speak, we might get ourselves in worse trouble no
matter what his purpose was. So, he has a new sword. That's just one
more reason to have an army behind us before we go chasing him. I
say we stay here and gather our strength."

Duke Arnould winked and clapped him on the shoulder as he sat
down again. "Well said. Couldn't have said it better myself."

Again, Devin questioned Lenore. "Do you really believe Erick
could have learned about Anglachel and planned to steal it? If so,
what are the chances he knows how to bind it to himself? I don't even
know how it works."

"You will know soon. I will relay the knowledge to you in private
later. I know you can see the wisdom of keeping it secret. I do not
know how Erick learned of the sword, and that disturbs me. I'm
afraid there is more going on here than we can see. There is a
prophecy that might help us understand. Or might have helped us. I
need Master Admah to help decode it, and I'm sure that's why they
killed him—to prevent us from fully understanding the situation. But

perhaps you can help me, Master Othniel, for I believe it refers to the Adoël. This is why I called you to the meeting."

Othniel bowed his head and said nothing.

Lenore began to chant.

"When that which was sleeping is wakened
When the king in his own house doth fall
When beasts long unseen rise to battle
Then doom is near to us all.
The old ones must go into battle
The young ones go seeking the lost
The least of the least must then save us
For his people's sins pay the cost."

Duke Arnould chuckled. "A typical prophecy. It says nothing specific and could mean anything at all. The only thing it says for sure is that we must fight, and we all agree with that already."

Lenore ignored him, speaking to Othniel. "Othniel, my friend. The sword is awake. The king has fallen in his own house. Shadow-weavers have shed blood inside the castle walls. There is more going on here than we know. You must agree. The time has come for war, Othniel. Who is the one who must save us? Surely the 'Least of the Least' is the kind of title used only by your people. What does it mean? You speak of sins. Now might well be the time to pay for them at last. What will you do?"

Othniel answered without raising his head. "I am sorry, I don't know what it means. My people have no business in wars. We failed our master once before and we are still paying for it. I will not risk failure again. I can do nothing."

Lenore gazed at Othniel. Othniel gazed at the table. The silence stretched out. Lenore shook her head and turned to the royal family. "Queen Havilah, Prince Devin, the decision must be made by one of you. I know it will be hard, but there's no time for public mourning. Prince Devin, your official coronation will be one week from today, but you must begin to act as king now. We cannot afford to lose any time. You have heard my advice, and at least one opposing view. What will you do?"

Havilah dropped her head, letting her hair fall in front of her face like a curtain. What she wanted to do was get away from everybody. No. Not yet. First, she wanted to hunt down Erick and kill him with her own hands. But she knew her emotions clouded her judgment, so she would bite her tongue and leave the decision to Devin.

Prince Devin's gaze shifted to each council member in turn. They met his look with steady eyes and closed mouths, indicating with their silence that he had heard their advice and the decision rested on him. His voice trembled. "Must I lead the army when it goes out?"

Lenore nodded. "Yes. It is the duty of the king in times of war. The queen must stay and look after affairs of state, so the king is free to do battle. I know it is sudden, but this is what you have been trained for. You must be seen to act, to keep the people's confidence."

Duke Arnould waved a hand at those gathered around the table. "Don't worry, young prince. You have the training, and you will have advisers with you always. Some here have experience in war."

Devin looked around at the nobles. "How many men can each of you bring here, and how soon?"

Figures passed around the table—numbers of infantry and knights, transport and supply issues. Once everyone had given their best estimate, Devin did some calculations on his fingers. "We have three thousand here already. If all of you send your armies here, we could gather a force of eleven thousand in two or three weeks. Add an extra week for the farthest southeastern provinces. But perhaps we can meet them partway."

Duke Arnould looked at Devin, and his eyes glittered. "I can see you're considering a more defensive approach. Allow me to make a suggestion. Why do we need to bring the armies here? This valley makes a perfect trap. Only two passes cut through the mountains to the west and two to the east, which you can seal up with only a handful of men. We have outposts at each. The soldiers coming from the southeastern provinces can sweep up from the south end of the valley, leaving them no place to go except back toward us. Most likely our men will run them down shortly, and you'll save yourself a great deal of trouble. Even if they slip past somehow, we will at least have all the approaches to the castle guarded, with armies ready to move on a moment's notice. Meanwhile we will be gathering strength and setting things in order here. What do you think?"

Devin rubbed his chin. He looked at his mother, then at each noble in turn. "What if Erick wants us to react by chasing him? What if he was only baiting us to draw us out of the city?"

His eyes stopped on Master Lenore. "I'm sorry, but we must protect what we have left. Duke Arnould, your idea is good. It would be rash to run after them from here when we can block the way ahead of them. Each noble should arm those who came with him to defend the castle and send a few men quickly to guard the passes. Once our position is secure, then we can take our time gathering armies if there's any need."

Havilah watched all the nobles nodding in agreement. Lenore's face fell. She shook her head but didn't object. She looked at Queen Havilah as if searching for support. Havilah shrugged and lowered her eyes. It was as good a plan as any. Even if she had the will to disagree, she wouldn't challenge her son in public.

Duke Arnould caught the Queen's attention with a wave. "Dear sister, my heart grieves that my own flesh and blood has caused you such pain. I will send for my younger son, Kris. I know it's been years since you saw him, but he can help."

"I remember my nephew, of course," Havilah said. "But why would you send for him? What can he do?"

Duke Arnould smiled. "He came with me for the festival, and he's camped just outside the city. He's a better politician than he is a commander, but he follows directions well. He can stay here as my spokesman while I return to lead my army. I prefer to be with my men rather than sitting here in court, waiting. Kris will be outraged to hear what his brother did. With your nephew— forgive me, with your *loyal* nephew here to act as a personal bodyguard, we can be sure no harm will come to you while I'm gone."

Havilah nodded absently, barely hearing the end of her brother's speech. She looked for Devin's reaction, but her son and his council were already busy planning strategy and hadn't been listening to the duke. While they discussed tactical details and prepared messages, she let her mind slip back into the shelter of more pleasant memories from her childhood.

CHAPTER FIFTEEN

K enan studied the guard walking beside him. He had the look of a man who took his job far too seriously, eyeing the doors they passed as if he expected to find enemies hidden in every closet.

This is stupid, Kenan thought. *The attackers took what they wanted, killed my father and left—*

The thought of his father's death made him stumble, and he turned his head so the guard wouldn't see his tears. *They aren't still hiding in the castle waiting for the chance to jump on me the moment I'm alone! Besides, using the Art I could strip this guard with my bare hands and beat him to death with his own armor.*

He pressed his lips together, frowning. *Of course, then I'd have to sleep for a day to recover. But that's beside the point. Why are we hiding in the castle anyway? Devin made the wrong choice. A whole week wasted with meetings and talk. We can't let this assassin get away. If they won't go after him, I'll have to do it myself.*

First, he needed to get away from these guards. He staged a dramatic yawn, then casually turned and walked toward his bedchambers. He dragged his feet just enough to make a scraping sound against the flagstones as he walked.

"I'm exhausted. I think I'll skip supper tonight and go to sleep early."

He glanced at the guard. The man's expression never changed. He still followed a step behind, eyes darting nervously at every shadow. Two more guards stood posted outside the door of the prince's bedchambers. Kenan made some mental adjustments to his plan as he approached. He dismissed his escort, then approached the door guards.

"Are you going to be here all night?"

The guard on the left nodded. "There will be a watch at your door all night, Your Highness, but we won't stand here that whole time ourselves. Someone will come to relieve us at midnight."

"Oh, that's good," Kenan rubbed his stomach and looked down the hall. The other guard had walked about halfway to the nearest corner. "I guess I am a little bit hungry after all. I'll just run and catch my escort and have him take me to the kitchens. Don't worry if I'm out late, I might ask my brother if I can stay with him in his room tonight."

One of the guards asked a question but Kenan ignored it. He took off in the direction his escort had gone using the slow, loping run he'd perfected as a way of sneaking up behind Devin. It covered the ground quickly enough to make him look like he was hurrying, but he landed so lightly on his feet that he made no sound at all. He timed it perfectly, rounding the corner a few seconds behind his escort, then slipped into a side room to wait. The guard he'd been supposedly catching up with never noticed him.

He stopped by the kitchens long enough to pilfer some extra food, then headed for the stables. If anyone saw him going that direction, they would assume he was looking for Raendel. He could hide out there until dark.

Several piles of hay filled the back half of an empty stall, thick enough to hide him from casual observers. He buried himself in one of those piles, shifting until he found a position where nothing poked him too much. Daydreaming of a way to get past the guards stationed at the city gates, he drifted into sleep.

He woke confused. An odd sound, similar to laughter but not exactly the same, approached until it seemed to be in the stall with him. He held his breath and did his best to shrink farther out of sight without moving too much.

For a moment he worried that evading the guard Devin assigned hadn't been such a good idea. The stables were near the castle walls. What if the enemy had come back to finish what he'd started? What if he'd seen Kenan's hiding place? Worry pressed on him, making him feel trapped.

He distracted himself using techniques learned from Master Jabal. The muscles in his shoulders relaxed. Having cleared his mind, he talked himself through his options. Even if this were an armed assassin, he wouldn't go running back to his mother. He would find a way to handle it himself.

He shifted his head slowly until he could see the person who had interrupted his nap. A young woman leaned against the door with her face in her hands. Definitely not an enemy. Her muffled sobs echoed through the stable.

Her hands dropped away from her face, and he recognized Peristra. She stared into the straw near Kenan's hiding place. He felt sure he'd been caught. He almost decided to reveal himself and try to pass it off as a joke, but her expression changed his mind. Swollen red eyes blazed at him out of a flushed face. Her features knotted like someone fighting tears, or fury. She showed no sign of having seen Kenan. Her eyes focused on something far away, something she didn't like, at a spot just above Kenan's head.

"Father, why?" Her voice came out harsh, raw from crying. "I didn't want this. Why did I ever come here with you? We should have stayed home. I could have taken care of you. Now you're gone and I have nothing left."

Kenan's face burned. He obviously wasn't intended to hear this, but he couldn't do anything about it now. He decided to wait and hope she left without noticing him. Once he decided to stay hidden, his discomfort multiplied. The hay pressed down on him, growing hotter by the second, making it difficult to breathe.

Peristra continued to mutter under her breath. Tears fell in a steady trickle down both cheeks. She seemed to be trying to stare a hole straight through the pile of hay. "I will avenge you father, I swear!"

The heat grew painful. Kenan bit his lip to keep from making noise. The stalks in front of his face twisted, changing from yellow to brown to black. The heat concentrated on one spot, and fire burst out in front of his eyes. He flailed his arms and legs, rolling out of the hay toward Peristra, bellowing in pain as she screamed in surprise. He rolled until he knocked her down on top of him. Arms and legs flew in every direction as Kenan struck at the flames and Peristra pummeled Kenan. He smothered every flame he could see, then gave the straw one last buffeting for good measure. Peristra landed on top of him, sitting on his chest and pelting him with her fists with no sign of slowing down.

"Wait. Stop. Peristra, it's me Prince Kenan," He grabbed at her wrists.

She struggled for a moment longer, then her eyes came back into focus, and she looked at his face for the first time. "Prince Kenan? What are you doing here?"

He looked around for more flames. Finding none, he turned back to her. "What happened? Did you do that?"

She shook her head. "I—don't think so. I don't know. I felt like I was burning up inside, I was so angry about father. Then there was fire, and you thrashing around screaming."

He let go of her wrists and wiggled experimentally. "Uh, could you let me up now?"

She blushed and scooted to one side. "Sorry, you just scared me. What were you doing under there anyway?"

He chuckled. "*I* scared *you*? Imagine my fright when the hay caught on fire. I wish I'd seen how you did that."

She narrowed her eyes. "I told you I have no idea what happened. And if you don't answer my question, I'm going to sit on you again. You must have hidden there long before you even saw me coming in. What were you doing there?"

He laughed nervously and edged toward the door. "I don't know what you're talking about. I was getting my eyebrows burnt off. I'd better go see if they need treatment."

Peristra moved faster than Kenan thought possible without Biomancy. She dropped into a crouch, and his feet flew out from under him. His back hit the floor, knocking the air out of his lungs. Peristra settled back into her previous position on his chest and glared at him. "You had better answer me when I ask you a question, boy, or I'm going to have to whip you. I gave you fair warning."

He grinned sheepishly and did his best to sound humble. "Promise not to tell anyone?"

She bounced lightly, forcing the air out of his lungs again. "You're in no position to bargain. I could tell on you now if I wanted to."

He tried to shift his strength with the Art, but he couldn't concentrate well enough with someone sitting on him. He worked harder at it, trying to clear his mind.

She recognized the look in his eyes and twisted his nose until he gave up. "No, you don't. I see what you're trying to do and it's not going to work. I can sit here and distract you all day if I have to."

He thought about it, then decided he didn't really want to hide it from her anyway. "I was going to hide until dark, then sneak out of the castle to go after the man who murdered my father. I'm going to kill him."

Peristra looked away, wiping her eyes. "I'm sorry, Kenan. I know how you feel. He killed my father too. I won't tell anyone what you're doing, on one condition. Let me go with you to help. I want to avenge my father."

He tried to think of some way to change her mind. He couldn't even convince himself that he didn't want her to go. "All right, but hurry and get ready. We want to ride as far as possible by dawn. The longer we wait, the harder those filthy dogs will be to track."

She walked over to the stable door and picked up a pack that had been leaning against it. "I'm ready. Was that fast enough for you?"

Kenan noticed her outfit for the first time. She wore a traditional lady's riding jacket, ankle length, almost like a dress but split down the front. Loose-fitting pants narrowed at the bottom so they could be tucked inside sturdy boots. "Good," he said. "Now we just have to saddle some horses and we can be on our way."

Peristra wrinkled her nose. "No, we only need to saddle one horse. Yours. I finished my preparations while you were in here hiding. You're the slow one."

"Well, then get your horse and wait for me beside the south entrance. I'll be there in a moment."

She grinned and made a mock curtsy. "Yes, Your Highness. I live to serve you, Your Highness. I run to obey your every whim, Your Highness. Are you sure you don't need help with the saddle? I would be ever so honored to be allowed to assist Your Greatness."

She whirled around and sauntered out the door. He opened his mouth to yell after her, then stopped. There might be others around who would hear. Hopefully they hadn't already heard him flailing around putting out the fire.

Chagrined, he went to pick out a horse. Thankfully he'd insisted that Raendel teach him to saddle his own horse. With everyone else in his life either bowing every time he looked at them or telling him how to behave 'properly' he needed at least one friend who treated him like a person. Raendel still had to serve him, of course, but when they spent time alone together sometimes, they could forget all that and just be two boys hanging out. It wasn't much, but at least now it spared him the embarrassment of asking Peristra's help.

Thinking of Peristra made him blush, but he couldn't figure out why. He felt like he should be angry at her. She'd certainly earned it. She treated him with less respect than his brother did, and she didn't have the excuse of being a sibling. When he focused on what she'd said to him anger warmed his gut, but it vaporized faster than water drops on a hot stove. He hated the way she talked to him, but it felt good at the same time.

He picked out a tall thoroughbred, one of his father's best horses. Frustrated as much with himself as with Peristra, he slapped the saddle down on the horse's back and jerked on the straps so hard the poor beast rolled its eyes at him and pushed up against the corner of the stall. By the time he finally got it saddled, he had to nearly drag the animal all the way to the south entrance.

He found Peristra reclined against the door dramatically, as if she'd been waiting for days. She pulled the door open and walked out without saying anything.

Kenan led his horse through the doors after her. "How are we going to get through the castle gate? The guards aren't going to let me out at night with no escort."

She rolled her eyes at him. "That's why we waited for it to get dark. They're guarding against people trying to get in, not people getting out. Just keep your hood up and let me do the talking if they ask us any questions. I'll tell them you're my mute servant."

"All right, I guess that should work. I think we should ride as long as night holds, making camp during the day. The trail will be clear enough for a while, and there's only one road anyway. We don't want to risk being seen by daylight. Hey!"

Peristra, already riding away, called over her shoulder, "Don't lag too far behind me."

He galloped until he caught up with her, then pulled up next to her and glared as hard as he could. She ignored him.

"Peristra." Kenan made his voice as deep as he could, projecting forcefully. "I'm not going to put up with this. If you keep up this attitude, I'm going to send you home. Now, stop!"

She kept a steady pace, with her eyes fixed on the churned mud and deep ruts that marked the trail of the enemy through the muddy street. Kenan ground his teeth together.

"All right." Kenan lifted his hand toward Peristra in a gesture he'd seen his father use toward petitioners when he granted them favors. "We've both suffered a lot in this last week. I can forgive you for lashing out at me this time — as soon as you're ready to apologize — take all the time you need."

Peristra snorted. She kept her face directly forward, riding as if she were on the road alone. Finally, he gave up and they rode in silence for the rest of the night.

CHAPTER SIXTEEN

R aendel brushed the tips of his fingers over Master Deborah's forehead. They tingled faintly when they passed over the spot the fiery spike had pierced. It had struck Deborah in the center of the forehead, going in at least six inches, yet it had left no physical mark. None that Raendel could see, anyway. Her body appeared healthy, but she didn't respond to anything. The door creaked open, and Master Lenore entered. Raendel jumped to his feet, knocking over the stool he'd been sitting on.

"Has there been any change in her condition?" Lenore asked.

Raendel shook his head. "No, Master Lenore, no change."

"How long have you been here?"

"Since just before full dark. I was told to help with the wounded. But I don't know what I can do for this case."

Master Lenore walked over and stood next to him, looking down at the quiet figure on the bed. "There's nothing you can do. Her wound is not physical. I don't know whether I can do anything for her either. Master Jabal is the best healer I know, and even he could find nothing wrong."

The sorrow that creased Master Lenore's face made Raendel

uncomfortable. It reminded him too much of his own feelings of fail-ure. Except that Lenore's feeling was undeserved. She had done everything she could. Raendel motioned toward the heavy ceramic bowl on the table beside the bed. A napkin lay across the top to keep the contents warm. "I brought soup in case she woke up. Can I get anything else for you, Master Lenore?"

She stood looking down at Master Deborah in silence for so long Raendel thought she hadn't heard. He was about to repeat his ques-tion when she answered. "Jabal is busy with the other wounded, helping those he can. I don't know what else to try. I know Prince Kenan helped with his father sometimes. Perhaps he could do the same for us now. Find him and send him to me."

"Yes, my lady." Raendel bowed and set off to find Kenan.

ERICK GLOWERED AT THE SOLDIER COMING OUT OF THE TREES. "I told you to stay out of sight! That means out of *my* sight as well!"

The man stumbled to a halt, glanced back toward his compan-ions, then bowed to Erick. "Yes, m-milord. But it's gonna be dark soon, and me and the others was wonderin' if maybe we should—"

"Go! Now!"

The burly soldier scooted back a few steps, tripped over a tree root and scrambled into the tree line on his hands and knees.

Erick returned his attention to the charred remnants of the village, and the instructions he waited for. So many unknowns weighed on his patience, a virtue he'd never had much of to begin with. This constant waiting and guessing had made him more irri-table than usual. The fact that he shared many of his soldiers' doubts didn't make it any better.

He still had seen no physical evidence of his new master. Only the voice in his thoughts gave him guidance. He needed that guid-ance now. Foggy areas blotted out patches of his recent memory. Things had happened that he couldn't recall directly, yet he knew everything about them. He remembered parts of his own life as if they were stories told by someone else. The stories must be true, for at his side hung the sword he couldn't remember taking. The voice had told him about the sword, that it would be a powerful tool for him, but that he couldn't use it yet. Something still needed to be done, and the details hadn't yet been given to him. He had nothing left to do but wait for those instructions. That alone would have been enough to make his temper flare. Waiting for orders from someone who lived inside his own head pushed him over the edge.

The ruins around him left by his first victory bore evidence of how easily they could be taken by surprise. They'd won the first fight easily, even with most of the men grouped in the center of the town behind makeshift barriers. It would have been harder, but the one he'd taken captive in the woods had given him a victory with almost no losses. They had let the spy right into the center of their strongest defense, unaware that he was under Erick's control right up to the moment they felt their friend's knife in their backs. The horrified looks on their faces had been quite satisfying.

The castle assault had gone well also, judging by the evidence he could see and the little he could recall. He'd acquired the sword and lost few men. Still, he had the nagging feeling he'd missed something. He consoled himself with the thought that it couldn't be anything important. He just wished he could remember the actual battle. It would have been nice to watch the king die, to witness his revenge on the man who'd pillaged his birthright and destroyed his own father's will to rule.

The sun sank behind the mountains, and still he waited. He knew his followers wanted to set up camp for the night, but he couldn't allow that. Not yet. His greatest victory lay before him still. He felt it. As soon as the voice spoke again, he would know what to do.

Something moved along the north road, visible through the broken walls of the former inn. Erick shifted his position to get a better view, every muscle tense. If a scouting party had come from the city already there would be trouble close behind. The village ruins made a comfortable camp, but comfort must take a secondary spot to safety. Best to ambush this group, then move farther south.

A solitary man walked into view along the trail. Erick smiled confidently into the darkness. Either the man was a not terribly bright and soon-to-be-dead foe, or he was one of Erick's own scouts bringing a report. A steady rain of leaves and twigs dropped from a bush of curly black hair as the man turned his head from side to side, examining the trees along the road. His broad chest strained the seams of a simple cotton shirt. The rough leather of his leggings scraped with every step. The village spy had returned from his mission.

The scraping sounds stopped. The man's nostrils expanded to suck in the night air. Dead brown eyes showed neither surprise nor fear when Erick stepped out of the darkness. The spy shuffled closer. His lips parted as if to speak. No sound issued from his mouth, but something like a wisp of smoke. A long tendril drifted on the night air, sliding toward Erick, twining itself into his hair. Erick tilted his head to one side for a moment as if to listen. Instead of words, images flashed through his mind, memories from the spy transferred directly into his head.

"Well done, my pet," Erick whispered. "Let them whimper behind locked doors. Let them seal the passes and hope we are stupid enough to walk into their arms. We move south tonight, into the swamp. You remain here to make sure nobody sees the way we've gone. If anyone follows, kill them."

The scout withdrew into the trees, where the shadows cast by the last glimmer of the setting sun swallowed him. The moon would rise soon, and Erick wanted to move on before dawn the next morning. He turned back toward the place where his followers waited. A wave of dizziness crashed over him, and a black veil dropped across his vision. A presence rose up in his mind, more familiar than he would have liked. Uncertain whether this person could read his thoughts, he spoke them aloud.

"I'm impressed with our new spy. It turns out he's a pretty good assassin too. Can we make more like him?"

I will certainly make more like him. He had talent when we took him, and the body remembers it for a while. Over time his reflexes will slow. In a few weeks his mind will die, and his body will follow. I need fresh prisoners, as many as I can get, to build a usable army. Soldiers work best. They have the necessary skills, and if they have trained properly their bodies will remember how to fight long after they've lost everything else.

Erick had waited a long time to hear that voice, and yet he trembled when it touched his mind. "Very well. Where do we get soldiers? Should we go back to my father's lands? We have some men there who are dedicated to our cause. The rest we could control with those lesser spirits you summon, like we did with this man."

No. Your father will have to manage his own troops and pursue his own little plans. I have different goals. I will lead our ragged band back to the swamps and replenish our numbers by ambushing the enemy's reinforcements. Then I wait. The key to unlock Anglachel will come to me. It is bound to the line of the man who killed me with it. The blood of his descendants will bind it to me again.

Erick clenched his teeth. Sweat trickled down onto the small of his back. "How are you going to lead anything? You don't even have a body. That's why you need me."

That's why I needed you. But now I do have a body. Yours.

Erick's muscles spasmed. His eyes rolled back in his head. Someone else's thoughts flowed through his brain, over and around him, pressing him down into a small corner of his own mind. He still felt connected to his body, but it refused to respond to his instructions. Thoughts flashed around him but didn't touch him. Cold bars of despair closed around him, a prisoner in his own head.

CHAPTER SEVENTEEN

Queen Havilah rubbed her swollen eyes and blinked at the papers scattered in front of her, trying to bring them into focus. "I'm worried about Kenan. He never skips supper."

"I spoke to his bodyguard," Jabal said. "he told me Prince Kenan went to bed early. He's upset of course, but he's tough. I worry more about you."

"I'm fine." She put on what she hoped was a reassuring smile. "Have you learned anything new about the attack?"

"I've identified the creature with them as a Shadow-weaver, but I'm not sure where it came from or why it was helping Lord Erick. There've been no reports of those demonic things in generations. If he had one helping him, he might have more. We must be prepared to face them. I'd like to spend some time searching the library for information on them, with your permission."

"Yes of course, if you think it's important," Havilah said. "I'll send for you if I need anything."

She held on to her smile until Jabal left the room, then let it collapse back into the blank stare that had become her habitual expression. Her head ached, and she couldn't bring herself to care enough about bureaucratic paperwork to get anything done. The papers on her desk had been important two days ago. Today nothing felt important. She rested her head in her hands and closed her eyes. A knock on the door made her jump. She rubbed her eyes and wondered whether her hands had left red marks on her face. "Enter."

A smiling young man came in carrying a tray with a tea pot and cups. His blond hair gleamed with grease, and the gold jewelry dangling from his neck clicked against the tray with every step.

"Kris," Havilah said. "What are you doing here?"

"I heard you were having trouble getting to sleep, dear aunt, so I brought you some tea." Kris set the tray down and poured a cup. "Do you take sugar?"

"Just one spoonful," she replied. "Kris, I have handmaidens waiting in the next room who could do that if I wanted it. I sent them away because I didn't want to be bothered. Why are you here?"

Kris's teeth glittered like the massive gemstones that weighed down his fingers. "You're under a lot of stress, my queen. I am here to serve you any way I can. All I have to offer is my humble advice, and some small skill in medicine. This tea is a special blend that I made myself, it will help you relax."

She shook herself. "Thank you again, Kris, but I don't need to relax. I need to clear my head so I can do something. Do you have any medicine that will snap me out of this daze? Everything feels so distant."

Kris's brow furrowed. "No, my queen. Your feelings are natural, caused by grief. I have no medicine for sadness. Only time will heal that. Meanwhile your stress is making you tired, and your fatigue is clouding your thoughts. You should rest and recover. When you have rested you will feel alert again."

She took the cup he offered, her will to resist exhausted already. She sipped it, careful not to burn her tongue. Her mouth twisted. "It's a bit strong. Whatever you added to it has a nasty aftertaste. Pass me another spoon of sugar."

The warmth of the tea soaked into her muscles and eased the

knots in her shoulders. By the time she finished the first cup her head wanted to sink back down into her hands. After the second cup she had trouble lifting her hand to her mouth. "I think I should sleep now. That tea really does seem to work."

She tried to stand but didn't manage to lift herself off the chair. Her mind felt like a glass room in a rainstorm—she could sense her thoughts and feelings beating against it from the outside, but nothing touched her. Peace wrapped around her like a thick winter coat. A knock on the door didn't make her lift her head.

Kris called out. "Come in."

A boy entered and bowed to the queen. "Your Majesty, Prince Devin sends word that the passes have been closed and armies are on their way. Master Lenore still searches for news by her own methods. She says the commanders here have the armies well in hand and asks if you need assistance with internal matters."

Havilah didn't reply. She thought maybe she ought to but couldn't make herself care.

Kris stepped up to stand between her and the messenger. "The queen is tired and cannot be bothered now. Tell Prince Devin that we thank him for his concern, but she already has all the help she needs. Everything is taken care of here, you may go."

The bang of the door closing jolted Havilah out of her daze. "Who was that? What did they want?"

Kris patted her shoulder. "It was nothing, Your Majesty. Don't worry yourself. Have some more tea."

"Thank you, Kris." She put a hand to her forehead. "There is so much to do now, with all the wounded and the preparations for war. I should check on... something. Shouldn't I?"

"You are tired. Rest is what you really need. Drink your tea and relax. You can deal with those things later when your mind is clear."

"Of course, I couldn't accomplish anything in this condition. You're right. I'll deal with it later. You are good to me, Kris."

Raendel closed his eyes and inhaled the smells of the stable. The scent of horses hit him hardest, but underneath that heavy aroma hid a fainter one. He would never have been able to distinguish it if he didn't know it so well. Kenan had been here recently. The empty stall that normally housed the prince's favorite horse confirmed Raendel's suspicion.

Raendel struggled with this dilemma. On one hand, his duty demanded that he immediately report this information to Master Lenore. On the other hand, that would lead to lengthy questioning, debate about what to do, and then time to organize a search party. Meanwhile the prince would be getting farther away every minute. Raendel knew his friend and understood his motivation. Kenan would not return willingly. If guards were sent to retrieve him, he would do everything he could to avoid them. He would put himself in more danger to avoid being found by those sent to protect him. The duty to protect the prince outweighed the duty to report his discovery. They would learn what happened soon enough on their own. Until then, Raendel decided, his best option was to follow Kenan on his own and protect him. The prince couldn't have been gone more than a few hours. If he left now, he might be able to catch up in a day or two.

CHAPTER EIGHTEEN

Kenan swayed in his saddle and covered a yawn with the back of his hand. He must have slept during the ride, because his memory of the trip was patchy. Fortunately, his horse had enough sense to follow Peristra without too much encouragement from its rider. He shifted his backside into the least painful position he could manage and wondered whether he'd be able to sleep on the hard ground later. The path ahead had grown noticeably easier to see. He kicked his horse into a trot and pulled up beside Peristra.

"Shouldn't we think about stopping soon? We don't want to be seen traveling in the daylight."

She shook her head. "There's a village nearby. I can get us a room, and then you can slip in the back. We can get food there, too."

Kenan bit his lip. "Um, Peristra? I think that village was destroyed."

Peristra's nose wrinkled. "What? What do you mean, destroyed?"

"Devin told me about the reports he's been getting. He said a woman had just arrived from the village, that she had escaped and was the only survivor. He said it sounded like the same force that attacked the castle. They destroyed the village the night before."

Peristra rode in silence for a moment. "Well, maybe there'll be something we can use. At least some shelter to camp in for the day. A barn or stable or something. It'll be better than camping on the open road."

He yawned again and rubbed his stomach. "Hmmm, food. I could use some breakfast about now."

"I hope you brought enough for yourself, because you're not getting any of mine." Peristra patted the saddlebags hanging next to her. "I've heard stories of how much you eat."

He straightened in his saddle. "Fine, then I won't share any of what I get from hunting. You can scrounge for yourself."

"Oh? Did you hide a bow and arrows in that little bag of yours? Or are you going hunting with your bare hands?"

He hoped the red light of the dawn disguised the blush he felt rising in his face. "I'll manage. Anyway, I thought we were partners in this."

"I never asked for a partner. If you can't carry your own weight, I don't plan to suffer for it. I brought my own supplies. Oh, looks like this is the village."

Kenan stopped his horse and looked around the clearing in front of them. The first rays of the rising sun cast light on the smoldering ruins of a village. A few charred walls still stood, but not a single roof remained. He looked over at Peristra and raised his eyebrows.

She looked back evenly. "Well don't expect any feather beds, Your Highness. We should split up and look around for some reasonable shelter. There might be houses farther out with less damage. Maybe something in those woods over there."

He dropped his eyes and turned his head. "All right, I guess that's a good idea. We need a signal for when we find something. Can you whistle?"

"Yes, I can. You go around on the left side; I'll go around the right. If neither of us finds anything, we'll meet on the other end of the village and decide what to do from there. Don't take too long, it'll be full daylight soon and people will be traveling on this road."

He watched her ride away until he lost sight of her in the trees, then slowly turned his horse and rode off to the other side. He let the horse plod along at its own pace and even stop to graze or nibble on the bushes. Some part of his mind kept a lookout for shelter, but most of it was preoccupied with thoughts of Peristra. He'd mostly gotten over her words at the party. Like Raendel said, she probably hadn't wanted to be there either and she hadn't known who he was. But now, with what had happened, and both their fathers so cruelly taken from them, why was she still being so rude to him?

And why does it irritate you so much? He rolled the thoughts around, poking at them as he would at a sore lip to see exactly where it hurt, and how much. The words he could handle. Raendel teased him constantly, and that didn't bother him at all. He knew what Raendel thought of him. They understood each other. The teasing between them rested on a firm layer of respect and friendship. Peristra's jabs felt cold. Kenan had no idea what lay underneath, but it certainly wasn't friendship, and it didn't feel like respect.

The sun set the upper branches of the trees alight, and the birds had built up to a full chorus. Peristra's whistle cut through the birdcalls, loud enough to wake him out of his reverie. He turned his horse in the direction of the sound and kicked it into a trot. The thought of cutting through the devastated village made him nervous but going around would take too long. He would have to whistle for Peristra if he lost track of the direction her signal had come from, and she already had enough ammunition to use against him without getting himself lost enough to call for help.

He picked his way around the burned-out shells of buildings and bodies almost hidden under flocks of crows. The crows' harsh calls stood in sharp contrast to the sweeter tunes of the songbirds. Kenan shuddered and dug his heels into his horse's ribs. He swung in a wide arc around the central square, where most of the bodies lay. The stench made his eyes water even after he covered his face with his shirt.

Peristra stood waiting for him at the edge of the trees, holding her horse's reins. She looked a little paler than usual and her lips had a greenish tinge to them. "I looked at a few of the buildings. It's worse up close. I don't think I can stay in the village."

"Are they all too damaged?" he asked. "Surely one of them—"

"No!" She put a hand on her stomach and looked away. "I just can't. I found another place, a clearing near a stream. We can stay there."

An image of the bodies he'd passed rose up in Kenan's mind, making him shudder. "You're right. That's probably a better idea. Show me that clearing."

They made their way to the clearing, tied off their horses, and started unloading the saddlebags. Peristra jumped and let out a squeak, looking past Kenan into the trees. Kenan followed her gaze. A scrawny figure in a dark green tunic stepped out of the woods from the direction of the road. The last of the sunlight touched his face, which Kenan recognized as the awkward young noble hiding near the refreshment table at Peristra's ball.

The young man stopped and blushed, twitching nervously. "Sorry, I didn't mean to startle you. I tracked you from the castle."

"Timothy!" Peristra said. "You didn't tell anyone you saw us, did you?"

Timothy shook his head fervently. "No, of course not. But I heard about your father—about the attacks. So, I had an idea of what you were doing. You're following the raiding party, aren't you? I can help."

Kenan groaned. "You want to help? You can go back to the castle and forget you saw us, that's how you can help."

"Hush, Kenan," Peristra held up one finger in his direction. "You don't speak for both of us. Timothy, you're welcome to stay. We need all the help we can get."

Kenan glared at Peristra. Timothy looked back and forth between them, then his eyes settled on Kenan. "Look, I know I was kind of awkward around the castle. I spent the first half of my life in a village like the one that was here. Being around royalty makes me nervous.

I'm not that good in my lessons or with courtly things. But I can track and hunt and cook for you."

Kenan opened his mouth to protest, but his stomach interrupted him with a loud rumble.

Peristra looked at him with raised eyebrows. "Sounds like your stomach votes with me. Timothy stays with us. Besides, how else are we going to know which way they went at the crossroads? Would you be able to track them from there?"

Kenan pressed his lips together and tried to think of a good reason to send him away.

Timothy filled the silence. "I brought lots of supplies with me. I didn't have to sneak out, nobody cared if I left. I can cook us a good breakfast before we start for the day."

"Today?" Kenan let out the yawn that had been trying to escape all night and emphasized it with an exaggerated stretch. "I'm not going anywhere today. Besides, we planned to stay out of sight."

"You can't expect him to track in the dark, can you?" Peristra said. "We assumed they would follow the road this far because there's no place else to go. But there's a crossroads here with each path leading to a different mountain pass. They could've gone any direction. We should eat a little and maybe get a bit of sleep, but we'll have to travel by day from here on out."

"All right. At least we'll have had a good meal." Kenan dug in his bags to find his meager supply of bread and dried fruit. The cured meat he left for later. It would keep a long time. They didn't have much variety, but they had plenty of food.

Peristra produced several kinds of bread, and she even unwrapped a small package of butter and a ceramic jar of honey.

Timothy unpacked some bags of herbs and a small skillet.

Kenan busied himself collecting wood for the fire until the cooking was done. He glared at Timothy over his plate while his tongue pushed a lump of food around his mouth. He shifted in his seat, trying to find an angle where he wouldn't see Peristra's smile floating in the corner of his vision—a smile not for him, but for Timothy, along with plenty of compliments for Timothy's ingenuity and ease in this forest setting. He wiped his plate clean with a piece of bread, then sucked on his teeth and looked to see if there was any more.

Timothy offered him the skillet.

Kenan looked from the skillet to Timothy and back again. Something in Timothy's eyes made him pause. The young man's posture and movements displayed new confidence, as if some other person had come and taken over Timothy's body. The awkward youth hiding at the back of the ballroom had found his own kingdom here in nature, and for the first time he looked like a noble.

Kenan took another helping of food and then withdrew into himself, unwilling to join the talk. His teeth ground together at each bite. Timothy and Peristra ignored his looks as they discussed the food and the fire and their plans for the day. His stomach heavy with food, Kenan's eyelids drooped, and his head started to nod. He tossed his empty plate to the side, walked several paces away from the fire, pulled a blanket out of his bags, and let the sound of Peristra's voice carry him into sleep.

"KENAN!"

His eyes popped open. Peristra knelt on the ground next to him. The fear in her voice sliced through the blanket of sleep that had settled over his mind. He sat up and looked around, seeking the source of her panic.

Someone stumbled toward them out of the trees. Sticks and leaves covered the figure so completely, it could have been a piece of the forest that had come alive and dragged itself into their campsite. Dead, unfocused eyes stared out of a vaguely human face. The creature's right hand held a long hunting knife.

Years of training rose up in Kenan's mind. He heard the voice of his tutor in his head, telling him to focus. Think, and then act. Thinking only takes a moment, and it could save your life.

The knife. I have to stop him, but first I have to handle the knife. He's heading toward—what? The man's eyes focused on nothing. They gave no sign of his purpose. Kenan imagined a straight line from the figure ahead of him. Its path lead toward a rumpled blanket on the other side of the fire. Peristra figured it out the instant he did and started to rise. He brought her back to her knees with a firm hand on her shoulder. She looked at him questioningly, but he only shook his head. He couldn't spare the time or energy to explain.

Timothy hasn't seen him yet, maybe isn't even awake. Too late to warn him. Speed to catch the man, then strength to stop him.

Kenan shifted his energy, a little for speed and a little for strength. He rolled just far enough to get clear of Peristra and his blankets, jumped to his feet and sprinted headlong into the approaching figure. He ran at an angle across the clearing to get between the stranger and Timothy, who had wakened but still fought to get free of his bedding.

Kenan grabbed the man's knife hand and twisted. His extra strength had no effect. A normal man would either have dropped the knife and fallen back or suffered a broken arm. The knife arm barely turned at all, and the man didn't stop moving forward in his vacant-eyed march toward Timothy.

More strength, Kenan thought. The Art would allow that. But at what cost? He would either have to give up his speed or drain his mental energy, and there wasn't time to think about the utter exhaustion that would result. He had to act now.

Again, Master Jabal's training saved him. He left one small part of his brain to handle automatic bodily functions and focused the rest of his energy into strength. At last, the attacker responded, turning the knife toward Kenan and grabbing at him with his free arm. Kenan's arms flexed and stopped the knife inches from impact with his chest.

Arms locked, they stepped forward and back, to the side, and around in circles like dancers at a grand ball. Sharp pains shot through Kenan's arms, his bones informing him they were never meant to endure this kind of stress.

Kenan hooked his leg around his attacker's knee and shifted his weight to the side. Both of them crashed to the ground, with Kenan on top. He managed to aim his opponent's hand so that it hit a rock when he fell, and most of his weight come down on that side as they landed. He felt the man's hand bend and crack. For the second time he fought shock. The attacker's hand must have shattered, but still, he didn't drop the blade.

Kenan grasped the knife with both hands, hoping to pry it loose with a combination of strength and body weight. As he grabbed for it, a knee hit him in the groin, and the body under him rolled. Now their positions were reversed, with Kenan trapped under a man twice his size who matched him in strength even with the extra power of Biomancy. The attacker shifted the knife to his left hand. He leaned his right forearm against the knife's pommel, with the full weight of his body on top of it.

Kenan focused his energy one last time, throwing every last bit of his reserves into strength. The tip of the knife touched his chest and stopped. Both combatants trembled and dripped sweat. Kenan's arms screamed in agony; his bones bent to the limit of their endurance.

A metallic crack jolted him, and the weight lifted. The trickle of energy remaining reverted to its natural state. Exhaustion dragged him down into darkness.

CHAPTER NINETEEN

P eristra raised the skillet over her head, but after a moment she lowered it again. Their attacker lay still, his body now as lifeless as his eyes had been. Timothy finally struggled clear of his blankets and stood next to Peristra, looking down at Kenan's unmoving form. Peristra knelt to search for wounds.

At her touch Kenan's eyes fluttered open. "I'm fine. Jus' the Art. Never used it like that before. Used up all my energy. Have to sleep...."

His eyes closed and his breathing deepened. She stayed beside him long enough to finish checking for injury. Once satisfied, she looked up at Timothy. "What *was* that thing? It was like a walking dead person."

He shook his head. "I don't know. I've never seen anyone acting like that before."

She looked around, then toward the ruins. "We can't stay here, with all those bodies in the village. What if there are more like that one? If we get attacked again with Kenan helpless, we'll be in trouble. We have to leave. Now."

Timothy nodded. "Help me lift Kenan. We'll have to tie him to his saddle. Then we'll pack up everything else. That way if something happens, we can run on a moment's notice. We might lose a few things, but we can't lose him."

Peristra saddled Kenan's horse while Timothy dragged him over close to it. With a bit of hoisting and pulling they managed to get him in position, and Timothy lashed him in place.

Timothy grabbed his pack. "I'll get the food; you take the skillet." He grinned at her. "You're better with it than I am."

She couldn't suppress a chuckle. "Thanks, I'll keep it handy. At least now I know you won't ever try to cross me."

"If I do, I'll hide my cookware first."

The rest of the packing went quickly. Timothy looked down at the body of the man who had attacked them. "I don't think he's dead. You just knocked him out. What should we do with him?"

Peristra rolled the question around in her mind. "Maybe we should kill him, but I'm not sure. The way he acted, it's like something possessed him. He didn't seem to have conscious control of his own actions. It's like the stories my nanny used to tell me to keep me from walking in the woods."

"I heard those too," Timothy shivered. "Spirits and ghosts. Do you actually believe any of that was real?"

"Shadow-weavers were a big part of those stories," Peristra said. "I didn't think those were real either until one attacked the castle. If that part was true, why not the rest?"

He frowned. "Maybe so. Besides, if he is possessed by something, what would happen if we killed him? In the stories I heard, when you kill a possessed body, the spirit breaks free to possess something else. Like one of us. Better leave it trapped in an unconscious body."

She shuddered. "All right, then we can't kill him. But how long will he stay unconscious? We should at least tie him up."

She glanced toward Kenan, lashed to his horse. "Do we have any rope left?"

"I don't know. If we leave him tied up out here, wouldn't that be the same as killing him?"

She raised her hands and tightened the leather tie holding back her hair, which did little to subdue the bright red tendrils that trailed down her nape and forehead. "Would you rather him follow us and kill us? It's not exactly the same thing as killing him. We can leave him some water in a bowl, and if you just tie his wrists and ankles maybe he can work himself loose after a while. I'm sure someone will eventually come by and find him."

"Well, all right, if you really think so." Timothy dug through one of his bags. "We have one more rope. Good thing we each thought to bring a piece. It took two just to get Kenan secured. I can cut this one in half and tie his hands and feet with it."

He flipped the man over onto his back and started tying his hands together. "How tight should I make it? He seemed pretty strong."

Peristra shrugged. "We only need him secure enough to give us a head start in case he wakes up too soon, what happens to him after that is in God's hands."

Timothy nodded. "Nothing we can do about it, anyway. Now with the prince in this condition, the question is which way are we going?"

The look on her face didn't need to be put into words. They headed south, following the trail of the enemy.

CHAPTER TWENTY

"Just a bit farther," Havilah whispered to herself. "I know you can do this."

She stumbled down the hallway, trailing one hand along the wall. Her knuckles dragged lightly and then heavily as waves of dizziness swept through her. Every time she passed a doorway, where she had to lift her hand for a moment, she had to hold out both arms as if balancing on a tightrope. Occasional thunder from the approaching storm vibrated in her bones. After one closer rumble she stopped walking and lowered her head, willing herself to keep moving.

Her legs threatened mutiny. She thought of the wounded that lay in beds all over the castle, unable to stand, and glared at her legs. They creaked back into motion. She knew she'd seen Kris pass this way, probably going to take care of his pigeons. He'd carried their cages to the castle himself rather than trust a servant to do it.

Kris used the birds to keep in touch with the family back home, sending private notes to supplement the official communication. Of course, they kept an official flock of birds in the castle for important communications, but those were for emergency use only. Now that

Kris had his own private means of sending messages home, the thought crossed Havilah's mind that perhaps she could add a line to the end of one of his notes. With the loss of her husband and their son gone missing, her need for some family connection multiplied each day. Kris himself had turned out to be such a welcome blessing, she could barely recall what she'd done before he came.

She reached the pigeon room and had to stop again. Her head spun so fast she had to close her eyes and lean her whole weight against the wall. She rested her forehead against the cool stones, drawing deep breaths and admonishing herself to hurry. Devin would be waiting on her to meet with him, but she couldn't go in this condition. She needed something for this sickness. Or at least, that's all she could think to call it. It couldn't be just depression as Kris insisted. She could deal with the sorrow. That part had improved over the last couple of days. But this malaise that tormented her night and day had only grown worse since then.

When she managed to open her eyes again, she leaned on the door latch and tapped twice as the door swung open. This was a public room, but Kris had asked her to knock first to keep from startling the birds. The door stayed closed to lessen drafts from the windows where the pigeons were released. She'd kept her knock deliberately soft. Even so, Kris started when the door opened. The look on his face reminded Havilah of the time she caught Kenan sampling the good wine. A look gone so quickly she wondered if she had imagined it. Now his face showed only a warm smile.

He gave her a wave, then a small bow of respect. "Hello, dear aunt. I was just preparing a message to send home to let our family know how everything is going. I'll be sending it as soon as the storm passes."

Thoughts of home distracted her from the queasiness in her stomach. "That's nice. I'd like to send a little note too, if you have room for it."

Kris glanced at the scrap of parchment in his left hand. "Of course, there's room to add a few words if you write small enough."

She took the message and stumbled over to the writing desk, settled into the chair and thought about what she wanted to send. Sitting helped her feel more stable. While she considered what to write she glanced over the message Kris had written. The tiny lines of text refused to come into focus. She recognized her own name, and Devin's, but couldn't quite make out the rest. The effort brought back her nausea stronger than before.

She pressed her fingers against her temples and squeezed her eyes shut. "Kris, there's really something wrong. This can't be just depression. I'm really sick, and I'm supposed to meet with Devin soon. The nausea is still so terrible, my head feels like it's going to fall off. If you can't make this stop, I'll ask Jabal—"

"Certainly, you should ask him for help if it's that bad," Kris said, concern oozing between every syllable. "But I think you must be having a reaction to the medicine you're taking for depression."

He reached in his pocket. "Here, take a sip of this and it should clear up your symptoms."

Havilah looked askance at her nephew. "Do you always walk around with medicine in your pocket?"

That caught-with-the-wine look flashed across his face again. "I suffer from nausea too, especially when I travel by wagon. I keep a small bottle on hand for myself. Don't worry, I have extra."

Thunder rumbled, closer now, and a wave of sickness washed away Havilah's suspicion. She pried open the bottle and took a sip. As soon as it hit her stomach the world around her settled back into a familiar pattern. The spinning of the room slowed to a manageable pace, and her belly no longer threatened to empty itself with every breath.

"Thank you, Kris. That is better. Amazing how fast it worked." She handed the bottle back, picked up the parchment and returned it to him. "I can send a message another time. I need to meet with my son now. If you have time you should come with me. In case the sickness comes back."

Kris bared his teeth in something close to a smile. "Of course, I always have time for you when you need me."

She hurried to the meeting place and found Devin slouched in a chair waiting for her, watching the stormy sky outside the window. He stood when the Adoël serving him announced her approach. His face brightened when she entered, then darkened again when Kris came in behind her.

"I wanted to meet with you alone, mother," Devin said.

Havilah put a hand on his arm. "Kris is family. He's here to help, and I'm grateful for it."

Devin scowled at Kris, then turned back to his mother with a concerned look. "How are you feeling? Better today?"

"Much better," she said. "Kris thinks I was just having a reaction to the medicine I was taking. He gave me something that really helped. I'd rather have him around than those silly girls who usually wait on me."

"That's good to hear, mother, I'm glad you're feeling better." He shot Kris a sharp look. "All right, you can stay if the queen wishes it. But these reports are confidential. If anyone hears this from you, I'll have you executed for treason, family or no."

"Of course," Kris said, his face smooth. "You must be king first, cousin second. I would expect no less from a wise ruler."

"King first, son and brother second," Devin replied. "Cousin takes a distant third at best. Do not presume on your family connections. Might I remind you it is your own brother who has caused this calamity?"

Kris answered with a bow and a look of humility that looked quite practiced.

Devin turned back to Havilah. "Master Jabal and Master Lenore somehow managed to contact the outposts by dreams. I don't know how it works, but at night, when they can find someone sleeping, they send messages faster even than the pigeons. The passes have been secured. The first soldiers have reached the northeastern pass. There are enough men to blockade it, with Uncle Lukas only days behind them. Our outposts at the other three passes sent word too. They are sealed, with more men arriving to reinforce them. Trackers have found no sign of the enemy passing in either the east or the west. Everything we can find indicates they fled south."

Havilah clasped her hands together and tried to focus on what Devin said. She longed to ask about Kenan but was afraid of the answer. If he had good news Devin would have told her right away. She bit her tongue and nodded for him to go on.

"Our southern provinces responded quickly," he said. "Their men entered the bottom end of the valley before anyone could possibly have reached it from this end. The valley is wide at the southern end—our scouts are spread thin there. But they're making their way north and have found nothing yet."

Thunder rolled outside, and Devin paused to shoot Kris another warning look.

Havilah laid a hand on his arm. "Go on."

"Scouts followed Erick's trail south. They'll be trapped in the valley, and our net is closing. Our only disadvantage is not yet knowing the size of the enemy's forces, whether he has reinforcements nearby. With all the roads blocked I'm confident that if I lead our army south from the castle, we can smash them between us, and the city will be safe. At the first hint of trouble, we could fall back here with enough men to hold the fortress. We would have reinforcements at hand from any of the passes. No besieger would stand a chance of success. They would be foolish to even try with the first snowfall possible in mere weeks. I plan to ride out in two days. Master Lenore would have us move faster, even tonight, but I want to take at least a week of supplies with us, and we'll need that much time to gather them."

Havilah couldn't hold back her question any longer. "And Kenan?"

A shadow crossed Devin's face as he shook his head. "Nothing certain. He might have ridden south. His Adoël friend Raendel disappeared the same night after being sent to find him. We've found evidence that two or three riders have been tracking the enemy ahead of our scouts. We encountered someone we assume is an enemy spy, bound and left in the ruins of the village. We might learn something from him. Master Lenore is examining him now. I'm going to get a report from her as soon as our meeting here is over."

Havilah's heart raced. "Those trackers? It's Kenan, I know it is. He's always been headstrong. He probably rode off with Raendel, trying to track down Erick on their own. When I get my hands on that boy, he won't leave his room for a year."

Devin put a hand on her shoulder. "He's all right, mother. We'll find him soon."

Havilah wrapped her arms around him and squeezed. Devin held her gently and stroked her back, whispering soft assurances in her ear while she smothered her sobs against his shoulder. Outside, a crash of thunder answered her cries.

CHAPTER TWENTY-ONE

Master Lenore watched the rain come down in the courtyard outside the window. Storms always formed quickly here in the mountains. She knew that, but sometimes it still surprised her. Minutes ago, the sky had been clear and bright. Lightning flashed, and a moment later clouds covered the sky. The storm reflected her mood rather well. She felt like a woman searching in the dark, grasping at shapes that seemed almost familiar, but she couldn't quite put a name to them. Things were blowing wildly out of control, and it scared her. Queen Havilah behaved as if living in a dream, keeping everyone at a distance. Prince Devin threw armies around without a thought, letting his uncle talk him into taking dangerous risks. She felt as if the weight of the whole kingdom had fallen on her shoulders as the king's adviser.

The candles on the table burned down to the first hour mark. They'd been new when she lit them. *What is taking Prince Devin so long?*

As if the thought had summoned him, the door opened, and Devin strode in. For all the time he'd taken to get there, he wasted none once he arrived. He spoke before the door closed. "Is there any word yet of Kenan? Has Master Jabal found anything? How is Master Deborah? Is there any change?"

Lenore shook her head in answer to all the questions. "Prince Kenan does seem to have ridden south. His favorite horse is missing from the stable, and the kitchen staff admitted that he took more food than usual the night he vanished. I've heard nothing directly from him, nor from the young Adoël I sent to look for him. Master Jabal has found nothing yet. He tells me that, without Master Admah to help him research, it could take weeks to find anything useful."

Lenore fell silent and looked out the window again. Devin prodded her with a question. "And Master Deborah? What of her?"

The weight in her heart pressed down on her words. "It's not good. I almost sensed something yesterday, but it's like her mind is sleeping. It's more than a sleep of the body. I can't even touch dreams or subconscious thoughts. I will keep trying."

"Even while we travel with the army?"

Lenore nodded. "If necessary, yes. I'll save her some space in a supply wagon, and make sure she's well cushioned for the journey. She won't be feeling any bumps in the road. And if the jolting of the wagon awakens her, all the better."

Lenore smiled as she said it, trying to make it a joke. She could see in Devin's face that he wasn't fooled, but that he played along with it.

Perhaps the boy has some discretion after all. That kind of restraint will serve him well in court someday.

"I won't have time to meet again in person until we leave," Devin said. "If anything changes, let me know."

The prince hurried away, and Lenore rushed to Deborah's sick-room. Even Master Jabal had given up trying to heal her, saying he could find nothing wrong physically. If Jabal, the Master of Healing, couldn't think of a way to help, Lenore knew her own efforts were likely wasted. Yet she couldn't stop trying to help her friend.

She stood next to the bed and placed her hands on either side of Deborah's head, as she'd done many nights before. Pushing back her fears, she closed her eyes and traveled through her hands into the darkness that filled Deborah's mind. She didn't dare move farther into that emptiness. She simply stayed on the edges of it and strained her senses to detect any sign of life. So far, she'd only found more darkness and more cold, until her own mind grew numb with it. She had no better success today.

A knock on the chamber door pulled her back to the living world. One of the Adoël stood in the doorway, already beginning to deliver a message.

"...prisoner is secured and ready for examination. His eyes are open, but he is unresponsive. He appears to be in some kind of trance, and you are needed to come examine him."

Lenore nodded and motioned for the servant to lead the way. While her body walked through the halls, thoughts of Master Deborah filled her mind. When the Adoël stopped and indicated one door on the long hallway, Lenore paused outside the room to collect herself before she opened the door and entered.

The prisoner lay on a long wooden table wrapped in so many chains that only his head could be seen sticking out from under the pile. The guard standing next to him, hand on his scabbard, seemed superfluous. The prisoner's eyes pointed up toward the ceiling, unmoving and unblinking, pupils so wide that no color showed around them. The guard confirmed that the man had uttered no sound since they found him in the ruined village.

Lenore motioned to the guard. "He cannot be made to speak, but there are other ways of gaining knowledge. Step back."

The guard nodded and obeyed. Lenore placed her hands on each side of the prisoner's head, just as she'd done with Deborah. She had the same immediate goal—to make contact. Only her reasons for making contact differed.

The cold black void she found there nearly swallowed her, but she'd expected this. She managed to hold on to a thin connection back to her own body and the world of light. The dark and stillness filling the man's mind felt familiar. It matched almost exactly the feeling she'd encountered in Deborah's mind. Similar, yet different. In Deborah the chill radiated from one location, as though a block of ice deep inside sucked up all the warmth. Here the cold rose in waves and spun in ribbons that curled and twisted from all directions. The sensation unsettled her. It felt like standing at the bottom of a well full of icy snakes.

One of the ribbons of cold brushed her arm, and she swatted at it instinctively. Several more grazed her, swarming around her as if curious about this intruder. She snatched at one, gripping it tight in spite of the painful chill in her fingers. She focused energy on it, generating heat to drive back the cold.

The living ribbon writhed and twisted, trying to escape her grasp. It twitched a few more times, then fell limp and faded away. As if the death of the thing had summoned them, a dozen more ribbons of cold struck at her. Stings like the bite of tiny fangs hit her from all sides. She writhed and twisted, slapping at invisible attackers. One by one she grabbed them and squeezed the life out of them until only a few remained. They fled into the darkness with Lenore close behind. They dodged and turned like rabbits with a fox on their heels, but everywhere they went they left an easily followed trail of cold.

One at a time, she chased them down and extinguished them, until, at last, she stood alone in the dark. She made an effort to calm her thoughts. In her relentless pursuit she'd lost her bearings. Panic threatened to swallow her. She acknowledged it, allowed herself to feel it for a moment, then pushed it aside. The darkness pressed in, the same on all sides. The chill had vanished, and in its absence a faint warmth spread from one direction. She made her way toward that warmth, and as she moved the darkness grew lighter. No images immerged. The area just took on a lighter shade of black.

A shape coalesced in the darkness. The figure of a man crouched, looking around with the intensity of a night watchman who heard a threatening noise. This must be the true owner of the body in which Lenore was lost, or at least an image that represented him. The man would experience this encounter as a dream, so his mind would generate images for it.

Lenore eased her mind closer. "What is your name?"

The man crouched and spun to face Lenore's voice. He peered into the darkness around him, fists clenched.

"Stay calm, I'm not here to hurt you," Lenore said. "My name is Master Lenore. I came here to find out who you are, and if you mean no harm then I will try to help you. Those things that tormented you have been destroyed. Your mind should be your own again. So, tell me, who are you and what happened to you?"

At the sound of her voice, the man's posture straightened, and his hands unclenched. "My name is Ephron. I don't know what happened to me. I was hunting, and I stumbled into an encampment of armed men. Next thing I knew, I woke up in this darkness. I haven't been able to find my way out. I don't even know how long I've been here. Where are we, anyway?"

"Physically we are in the castle" Lenore kept her voice calm, but eagerness made her speak quickly. "This conversation is happening inside your mind, in a kind of dream. Those things I destroyed had taken over, but you should have control again. Try to remember what happened to you."

Ephron closed his spectral eyes and remembered. The memory called up images in Ephron's mind, and those memories took shape around them. Lenore found herself standing in the woods outside Ephron's village, looking through his eyes at the enemy camp. This view lasted less than a second. Something struck from behind, and the vision spun and grew dark.

The next memory started inside a tent. Before them stood Lord Erick, who had invaded the castle and attacked Master Deborah. The man leaned in with a knife and cut loose the ropes that had bound Ephron's arms and legs.

Ephron left the tent and walked to the city, where he killed a guard at the gate before escaping into the crowds. He slipped into the library and cut Admah's throat, then hid in the alley until dark. He returned to the village and received his new orders to watch for pursuit and ambush any who came that way.

This confirmed Lenore's suspicion that they would flee south toward the swamps. The knowledge thrilled her but worried her at the same time. If they moved quickly, they might slip past the search parties while they're spread thin across the southern end of the valley.

She needed to inform Devin of this. But Ephron's memory continued, and Lenore wanted to see how it ended. A night passed without incident, hiding in the trees and watching the empty road. The memory blurred and jumped through that time. At sunrise, activity in the woods attracted Ephron's attention. Noise and woodsmoke led to a camp with three people, two of them asleep. A young red-haired girl stood watch.

Ephron stumbled toward the sleeping figure directly in front of him. The girl yelled in alarm and ran to the second sleeping person, the one Ephron had not focused on. Lenore wondered why she went first to the one in less immediate danger.

In a blur of motion, the person wakened by the girl threw off his blanket and grappled with Ephron so quickly Lenore hardly saw him move. She would have recognized him even without such a close-up view of his face. Other than Master Jabal she only knew of one person who could use Biomancy to move like that.

Prince Kenan did *go south to follow the enemy. At least he's not alone.*

The combatants rolled on the ground. Lenore's pulse quickened —Kenan struggled for his life. He wouldn't last much longer. Darkness fell across the scene. Ephron woke on the ground, tied at the wrists and ankles. Memories blurred together, lying on the ground in light and then darkness and then light again. Devin's scouts found him. They picked him up and brought him back to the castle to be examined.

The memory caught up to the present and faded away. With Ephron's mind alert and active, Lenore found her bearings and withdrew back to her own body. Ephron remained asleep. Lenore motioned to the guard. "Take these chains off and bring him to the sick rooms. This man is not our enemy, and whatever controlled him is gone."

She hesitated in the doorway. Queen Havilah and Prince Devin would want to hear the news of Kenan right away, no matter what. They should be made aware of the enemy's plan to go south as soon as possible. Yet she couldn't stop thinking about Master Deborah, and how her mental condition mirrored Ephron's.

Messages can be delivered by anyone, but Deborah depends on my help alone.

Three long strides carried her back to the desk next to the bed. Finding two pieces of parchment, a quill, and ink, she scribbled two copies of a note and sealed them with the signet ring she wore. She handed the notes to a guard with instructions to deliver them to Queen Havilah and Prince Devin. That duty out of the way, she raced through the halls to the room where Deborah lay. Sitting by the bed, she placed her hands on her friend's head and entered her mind again.

The familiar darkness surrounded her, but this time Lenore focused on the chill. Hoping to imitate her success with Ephron, she glided farther in toward the source of the cold. Something like a giant icicle floated in the darkness. The pointed end sank deeper into Deborah's mind in a way that reminded Lenore of the spike of pale fire flung by the enemy into her friend's forehead. She set the force of her will against it and pushed gently, trying not to cause any more damage. The chill seeped into her as she pushed, numbing and painful at the same time. The spike slid back an inch at a time, moving more easily the farther it went, until finally it slid free. With the source of the cold gone, Lenore focused on the slight warmth that would lead her to the center of Deborah's consciousness. Fainter than what she'd felt with Ephron, still it gave her a direction. Unbroken darkness surrounded her on all sides. She sensed a presence, subdued as if in a deep sleep. She probed a little farther and called out. "Deborah. Deborah, it's me, Lenore. Wake up. Come back to us. The kingdom is in trouble, and we need you. Come back to us."

She heard no response, not even a flicker, not after multiple repetitions. Lenore felt as if the cold spike she'd removed from Deborah's mind had buried itself in her heart. She withdrew into her own body, then slumped by the bedside and stroked Deborah's lifeless hand.

All right, my friend. Rest for a while, I'll come back and try again. We have to travel soon. I'll make sure you are comfortable.

She kept vigil at Deborah's bedside for the rest of the night.

CHAPTER TWENTY-TWO

K enan stood in an open field. Grass stretched all the way to the horizon in every direction. The sky shone bright and cloudless, but without a sun. The light emanated from everywhere at once.

A familiar voice murmured in his ears. He spun in a circle and called out, "Jabal?"

Kenan? the voice responded. *Kenan, is that you?*

"Yes Jabal, it's me Kenan. I'm following Erick. I had to, nobody else was doing anything. Where are you?"

More important, where are you? Are you alright? You're not chasing them alone, are you? Be careful Kenan, there are things out there even your Art won't defend you against.

"I'm not alone, Peristra and Timothy are with me," Kenan said. "We followed the enemy as far as the village, then we were attacked by—I still don't know what it was. It had the body of a man, but it seemed mindless. And it had strength beyond anything I could match, even with the Art."

Are you alright?

"Yes, I'm fine. I fought with him, and that's the last thing I

remember. He had me pinned on the ground, and then I was here—
Oh no. I'm not dead, am I?"

*No, this is a dream. Your mother and brother are very worried
about you. Nothing you can do will bring your father back. We don't
want to lose you as well— Kenan? You're fading. I think you're
waking up...*

The world around him dissolved. Jabal's voice faded, and Peristra's voice took its place. "...no choice but to load him up again. We
can't sit here waiting for him to wake up. We don't know how long he
might sleep."

Kenan stirred and cracked his eyes open, giving them time to
adjust to the light. His muscles sent him strong signals that they
weren't going to be moving quickly anyway. "I'm awake, Peristra. Just
give me a moment. How long did I sleep? Is there daylight left?"

Timothy jumped in before Peristra could answer. "There's plenty
left today, but you've missed about two days of being tied to your
saddle."

Kenan pushed himself up to a seated position and opened his
eyes. "What? Two days? Have we been moving that whole time with
me asleep?"

Peristra laughed. "No, we just tied you to your saddle to keep you
from sleepwalking. Of *course*, we've been traveling. Didn't you even
notice?"

He shook his head. "I don't remember a thing. Jabal told me this
would happen if I ever used the Art for very long. It really drains
your energy. Where are my saddlebags? I'm starving."

She rolled her eyes. "Well, I guess you have an excuse this time.
We poured some water down your throat, but I wasn't about to shove
food into your mouth for you one bite at a time. We haven't put away
breakfast yet, you can have some of this."

He let her sarcasm roll off him. Hunger and lingering fatigue left
him little energy to waste on caring about her jibes. It took all his
concentration just to reach up and take the bread she offered.

"Thanks," he mumbled, tearing into the bread so fast he didn't even taste it.

Timothy looked up from packing. "I'll saddle your horse for you today, but don't think I'm going to keep doing it. And try not to fall off or I'll have to tie you to it again. Hurry up, the trail's getting cold."

Kenan didn't need to be told to hurry; he was already stuffing food into his mouth with both hands. Almost two days of rations disappeared down his throat before he licked his fingers clean and rubbed his swollen belly. "That's much better," he sighed. "Now I'm ready to go."

Timothy finished cinching up his saddle. "Good. Let's get moving."

Kenan mounted, then turned to look back along the road. Even using a touch of Biomancy to enhance his vision he couldn't see the ruins of the village from here. He next looked at the road ahead of them, trying to gauge how far they were from the south end of the valley. Movement caught his attention, and he bit his lip in excitement. *Could it be the enemy? Are we really that close? No, that can't be right. It looks like they're moving toward us. And those are uniforms.*

"Are you going to sit here staring all day?" Peristra said. "Come on, we—"

"Wait!" Kenan hissed. "There are soldiers coming this way."

"Soldiers?" Timothy's voice squeaked. "Is it the enemy?"

"I don't think so," Kenan said, "they look like ours. They're spread across the valley, moving slow, like they're searching for something."

"Oh," Timothy said, sounding relieved. "That's good—"

"No, it's not," Kenan said. "I'm not supposed to be out here. If they find us, I'll be in trouble, and probably you too for helping me. They'll take us straight back to the castle. Mother would skin me alive and then put me under guard for a month. We have to find some place to hide, quick!"

"Where? It's no good trying to hide in there." Peristra waved her hand at the scattering of trees on the right side of the road, then up at the hills on their left. "And there's nothing but bare rocks—wait—is that a cave?"

Kenan followed her gaze up to a dark slash in the hillside. "It is, and it looks big enough for the horses, too. Good thing we brought oats for them, enough to hide for several days before they get hungry. Come on!" He turned his horse and rode up the slope toward the cave with Peristra and Timothy close behind.

"Can we make it inside before they're close enough to see us?" Timothy called out as he followed Kenan up the side of the hill. "And even if we do, if they're looking for someone wouldn't that cave be an obvious place to look?"

"Do you have a better idea?" Kenan growled.

"Well, no, but still."

"Then be quiet. And hurry!"

RAENDEL SUCKED IN A COUPLE OF QUICK BREATHS, THEN WENT back to maintaining the illusion of boulders in front of the cave and over himself. The illusions held steady just long enough to let him breathe but wouldn't last more than a minute if he didn't keep them up. He stopped long enough to take a drink of water between one wave of soldiers and the next. It helped that military patrols tended to be predictable. He always knew exactly how much time he had before the next wave. Two days of singing had left his throat raw, even with the short breaks. He looked forward to nightfall when he would be able to get some rest.

He didn't know what he might do if any of them happened to camp for the night in sight of the cave. Hiding the cave from outside viewers while letting those inside the cave see a normal view of the valley stretched the limits of his skill. Sometimes they used that technique for plays, to create scenery for the audience and not block their own view. But never for so long.

He'd considered joining their group openly. Two things had stopped him. First, he didn't know Kenan's traveling companions well enough to trust them. He preferred to watch them a while unobserved. Second, he needed to save all his breath for maintaining the illusion. He couldn't stop to explain himself.

Assuming that Kenan still followed the enemy's trail, then it must continue beyond this place. The patrols coming up from the south continued searching, which meant they had not found anything. So, the assassin must have slipped past them already.

A figure moved in the distance. Raendel resumed his song, and the illusion of boulders covered the mouth of the cave again. A few moments later the next wave of soldiers came into view, straggling up the valley in a thin line.

Maybe I should come out and let them know they missed their quarry. As he considered it, the next wave of searchers passed. His throat stung. Not quite enough to hinder his voice yet, but close. He hoped it would hold out until nightfall. With the cover of night and the small chance of night patrols, he could rest.

Better just to let them go by, he decided. *They'll figure it out eventually. If I reveal myself now, they'll find Prince Kenan, and his mission will fail because of me.*

The current wave of searchers trooped by, and he took another drink of water. The tenderness in his throat had grown worse. He would wait as long as he dared before he began to sing again.

A long time passed, and no more soldiers came into view. Raendel let the illusions fade but stayed ready to call them back at any instant. After a long time, he began to relax. Fatigue crept into his muscles and weighed him down, making it hard to focus.

Movement near the cave mouth caught his attention. The young man traveling with Kenan had left his lookout post and moved farther into the cave. *They'll be on their way again soon, but I'll never be able to keep up with them when I'm so tired. I don't think I could even stand up on my own. I'll just rest a little while and catch up with them tomorrow.*

He dragged himself behind a boulder to a crevice where he'd been sleeping at night, out of sight of the road, and covered himself with loose brush. *Still some daylight left,* he thought, *but not much. They won't have time to get too far ahead.*

CHAPTER TWENTY-THREE

Seriam caught her lip between her teeth as Ephron's eyes fluttered open. She'd waited for this moment for what felt like ages. She'd wanted to tell him so many things. Most of all she wanted to tell him how grateful she was that he lived. Every second had been excruciating since he left to hunt and didn't return that day. His disappearance had nearly crushed her, and then to return and find their whole village slaughtered had been unbearable. She'd lost herself that day. But now that she had the chance to tell him these things, her mind had gone infuriatingly blank. She could only squeeze his hand and sink into his deep brown eyes.

"Seri," Ephron whispered. "Are you really here?"

She ran her fingers through his hair, brushing a few loose strands away from his face. "I'm here," she said, then fell silent again.

He caught her hand and kissed it. "The village? What about the others?"

Images flashed through her mind of burned buildings and lifeless bodies. She looked away and shook her head.

"The whole village? Our families? Gone?"

She nodded, then lowered her head to compose herself before she answered, "They were on their way to attack the castle. They must have destroyed our village to stop any of us from warning the king. I only survived because I left the village before it happened."

She looked up at him, her eyes wet with tears. "But I didn't get here in time to warn anyone. They killed the king. Prince Devin will be crowned today. Then he's going to lead the army out to pursue the attackers. Ephron, dearest, I'm going with them as a nurse. I gave my vow before I knew you were still alive. I've promised, and I have to go."

Ephron closed his eyes for a moment, then opened them and pushed himself up to a sitting position.

Seriam stopped him with a hand on his shoulder. "I'm so sorry. Please lie down—"

He pushed her hand away gently. "If you go, I go with you."

"But you're not well—"

"No, actually I feel fine," he said. "What happened to me felt like a terrible dream, but it didn't hurt me. Well, to be honest my hand was a bit sore, but they have a healer here who works wonders. I'm fine now. I'm pretty good with a bow. I know the army will take me."

Seriam shook her head. It thrilled her that he felt well and terrified her that he wanted to run straight back into danger. She wanted to hold on to him and never let him leave. But he would be miserable if she tried. She wanted to support him, to tell him he could go. But she couldn't make her mouth say the words.

Ephron reached out and took her in his arms. "Seri, I want a chance to strike back at the ones who did this to us. I deserve that. We deserve that. So, you want to be a nurse? All right. Nurse, hand me my shirt. We're going to the coronation."

She searched his eyes, accepted that his words weren't bravado, but truth, and handed him his shirt.

Throngs of people crowded every side of the courtyard, and more leaned down from surrounding balconies and windows. Seriam and Ephron couldn't get any closer than a doorway on the far side of the courtyard, doing their best to peer over the heads of the crowd. Music floated down from a balcony overhead. A choir of Adoël enhanced the decorations with illusions so smooth Seriam couldn't tell where the real flowers ended, and the illusion began. Queen Havilah watched from a balcony across the courtyard next to her brother, Duke Arnould, who had just returned with his army. Her smile shone like the beams of sunlight that filled the air. Prince Devin knelt before Master Lenore, who held a golden crown that flashed brighter than sunlight alone could account for.

The music stopped. Master Lenore spoke the words of the ceremony. "We meet here today on the verge of great events. It is a time of tragedies, a time of struggles. It is a time of change and new beginnings. Many lives hang in the balance, as the world holds its breath to see what its fate will be. This is a time when above all else we must remember the things worth fighting for, things worth living for, and things worth dying for. We are all here to begin a journey, a quest to recover what was lost, to restore peace and unity to the land."

The swearing of oaths and ritual questions and answers followed, interspersed with cheering. Seriam lost interest, distracted by other thoughts. Ephron had chosen his course, and she would do whatever she could to support him. She scanned the crowds, searching for the officer who had signed her on as a nurse.

"The man across the courtyard there," she said, pointing. "The one with the red stripe across his breastplate. That's the one we need to talk to if you want to join the army."

Rather than trying to fight through the crowd, they waited for the end of the ceremony. Lenore spoke a final blessing, rested the crown on Devin's head, and raised him by the hand to face the crowd. "Lords and ladies, I present to you your sovereign, King Devin! Long live the king!"

The crowd echoed, "Long live the king!" Cheers broke out on all sides, and in the midst of the chaos it took a while for Seriam and Ephron to reach the officer they'd come to see. They caught up to him as he left the courtyard, and Ephron fell in beside him.

"Sir," Ephron said. "I'd like to join the army."

The man stopped and looked Ephron up and down. "We leave this morning, so we've no time to train new recruits. Do you have any skill at all?"

"Yes sir. I'm an excellent shot with the longbow. Used to hunt for my whole village."

"Longbow, eh?" The officer scratched his head and looked at the ceiling. "I don't think we have any longbows left, but we might have some crossbows. Ever shoot one of those?"

"No sir," Ephron admitted. "But I've always taken right to any new weapon I try. If it shoots, I can shoot it."

"All right then, if you really can shoot worth anything then we can use you. If you want to stay in the castle, you can join Duke Arnould's men. They came in just this morning. They'll be staying here as a garrison until the rest of the army returns. Or you can join the main body of the army if you're ready to leave today. I guess I'll give you the choice, since you're a volunteer."

Ephron looked at Seriam as he answered. "I'll be going with the main army."

The officer reached in his belt pouch and handed Ephron a coin engraved with crossed spears. "Take this to the supply tent just outside the gates. Tell them the man who gave it to you said you need a crossbow and whatever light armor they can find that fits you. They'll direct you to the officer in charge of crossbows. He'll test you and tell you everything else you need to know."

CHAPTER TWENTY-FOUR

Peristra sat and watched the mouth of the cave like a cat watches a bird flying overhead. Kenan sat and watched Peristra like a dreamer watches the moon. His eyes rested on her, but his mind drifted far away. Not counting the days he'd spent unconscious and tied to his saddle, he hadn't spent this much time sitting in one place doing nothing since his father died. His thoughts ran in circles, debating whether he should continue this crazy journey or just give up and go home.

Why am I hiding in this stupid cave? What do I think I'm going to accomplish? Master Lenore or Master Deborah either one could tie me in knots without even trying, and both of them together couldn't defeat this man I'm chasing.

He recognized it as true, but still couldn't convince himself to give up. *Maybe I can sneak in while he sleeps, take the sword, and kill him with it. But he doesn't sleep alone. He could have more of those shadow creatures with him, maybe other things. Maybe some that never sleep.*

He imagined the look on his mother's face if he came back with nothing to show for his time away on what was looking more and more like a grand but not well-thought-out scheme. Then he pictured the look on her face if he were brought back dead.

How can I go back now and face her? But how can I leave her there wondering where I am and whether I'm alive or dead?

"Stop staring at me."

It took him a moment to realize the voice was speaking to him, and that the voice was coming from the face of Peristra. It wasn't a happy face.

"Stop staring," she said again. "It's making my skin crawl."

Her words finally connected in his mind, and the heat of embarrassment rose from his neck all the way into his hair. He jerked his head away to face the wall instead. "I'm sorry Peristra, I really wasn't staring at you. I mean, I didn't know I was staring. I didn't mean to look at you at all."

"Kenan, you were looking straight at me. I don't care if you meant to or not, just don't do it again."

"Really," said Kenan. "I didn't even know what my eyes were looking at. My brain was totally on something else. When I'm thinking like that, you could pass a whole herd of elephants two inches in front of my face, and I'd never see it."

She wrinkled her nose at him and turned to look back toward the cave's entrance. "Well, I'm not a herd of elephants, and comparing me to one won't make me feel any better. Just leave me alone."

"I'm sorry." He whispered it under his breath, so low he didn't even hear it himself. He wasn't sorry for staring, because he honestly hadn't meant to. But he was sorry that she was angry, and sorry they were stuck here, and sorry for all the things that had brought them to this point.

Timothy slipped into the cave, low and quiet. Kenan jumped to his feet. He had the next watch, and at least he would be alone outside under the open sky. Whether he could keep his mind focused on what his eyes were looking at remained to be seen, but at least a tree won't take offense to being stared at. Smiling to himself, he brushed past Timothy without sparing him a glance, focused on the mouth of the cave and freedom.

Timothy grabbed his arm as he passed. "Wait. I'm not here to switch for the next watch. I'm here because the last of the soldiers have gone. It's clear for us to leave now."

Peristra glanced toward the opening and then back to Timothy. "Are you sure?"

Timothy nodded. "They kept a very regular search pattern, always staying in sight of each other. The last soldier left my line of sight several minutes ago, and I haven't seen another one since."

She chewed her lip. "There could be stragglers. Maybe we should wait a while longer to be sure."

Kenan grabbed his pack and walked over to the horses. "No. We've lost two days already. If I stay in here any longer, I'll go mad. I almost don't even care anymore if we get caught. The worst that could happen is we would be sent home, and home is looking better all the time."

Peristra crossed her arms. "I don't know. When I saw the search party, I was sure we'd be caught. They weren't looking for us, but they were searching for someone. I don't understand how they missed this cave. It should've been an obvious place to look. How did none of them think to look here in two days of passing by it?"

Kenan finished strapping his pack in place and untied his horse from the jagged rock at the back of the cave. "I don't know how they missed it either. But they did, and we can go now. So why are you still sitting there?"

Timothy looked back and forth between them; his lips pressed together. Kenan pushed past him toward the front of the cave, glaring at the ground in front of his feet. Timothy shrugged and began to pack his own things.

Kenan didn't look at Peristra as he walked by her. But he couldn't resist making one more jab. "You do what you want. I'm leaving now. And when I leave, you won't have the Art to protect you. If you're still here when I come back this way, maybe I'll let you travel home with me."

She sprang to her feet, eyes blazing. "You bullheaded, pompous, self-centered—boy! Fine! You want to go back to playing the prince? That's great! You'll get us caught, but you don't care as long as you're the one giving the orders. I won't say I told you so, just remember when it happens that I told you so. And you stay out of it!"

She directed that last comment at Timothy, who'd just finished loading his horse and was doing his best to disappear behind it. He didn't bother trying to respond. He ducked his head and made his way out of the cave after Kenan.

Kenan led his horse down to the place they'd last seen the enemy's trail. He studied the ground for a moment, then looked up at Timothy. "Which way do we go now? Can you pick the trail back up from here?"

Timothy shrugged and looked around. "I don't know. It had already faded before and now it's been two days. I can track game in the woods, but I usually follow trails that are less than a day old. I'll try."

He bent down until his nose almost touched the grass and inched his way around in a spiral pattern. Kenan watched him, pulling at his bottom lip. He wanted to help, but knew he was more likely to get in the way. Peristra stood a few feet away watching both of them, arms crossed.

Timothy straightened up and shook his head. "It's no good. I can't find the trail. They left the castle in a hurry, and that made them sloppy. They didn't care about leaving a trail, only about getting away quickly. The farther they went the more careful they became. Now that patrol has trampled all over whatever was left. I can't track them any farther. I'm sorry Kenan, they've gotten away."

Kenan shook his head, partly in denial and partly to clear his thoughts. It's true that he'd considered going home but faced with the choice he didn't really want to. And if he did, what would Peristra, and Timothy think of him? He was the prince. He was supposed to lead them.

Peristra's arms clenched more tightly against her chest. A tear filled up the corner of her eye and slid down her cheek. "All this way for nothing."

The tone of her voice wrenched Kenan's heart, and her words echoed his thoughts. He lowered his head. "That's it, then. We're done. The mission's over, and we failed. All we can do is go home."

Kenan turned to face north. His feet refused to move. His horse didn't mind the delay. It tore up mouthfuls faster than it could chew and swallow them, half of the grass falling out the sides of its mouth.

Despair weighed on Kenan's heart. He'd started so confident, sure he'd find the enemy quickly and bring him to justice single-handed. His first experience with a real fight had shaken his belief that he could defeat the enemy, but at least he still knew he could find the man and try something. Now the trail had vanished, and with it, Kenan's last hope.

"Kenan." Peristra's voice trembled. "I can't go back. I have nothing. I'm not old enough to inherit and I have no family to hold it for me until I can. With my father dead, our estate will revert to the crown. I'm too old to apprentice myself to a trade. I would have to marry whoever would take me, and I refuse to settle for that. I'm going on. I will not stop until I find my father's killer. I don't know what I can do, but I have to try. If you turn back, I understand, but I'm going on."

Her words stirred something in Kenan. She had less reason for hope than he did, but she hadn't given up. She had saved his life back at the village. He couldn't leave her to go on alone. So, he did the only thing he knew to do. He made a decision and threw himself into it with all the strength left in him.

"All right." Kenan said. "We go south. The trail still led that way when we last saw it, so that's the way we go. We can move faster now that we don't have to watch every step. If we go fast enough maybe, we can gain on them and pick the trail up again. Timothy, you've been helpful. You can stay with us if you like."

He mounted and turned his horse south along the path, not looking back so see whether the others followed. Moments later they rode up on each side of him, lips pressed together, eyes locked on the road ahead.

CHAPTER TWENTY-FIVE

A tall man in leather armor sprinted across the road into the trees where Morgoth stood waiting. Once he'd caught his breath, he reported. "The archers are in position, my lord."

Erick stirred in the back of his mind, struggling to regain control of his body. Morgoth suppressed him firmly. The pathways of this body had become familiar enough to give him confidence in his control. He'd squeezed Lord Erick into an area full of childhood memories, where he wouldn't be able to interfere with anything important. In the beginning the man had struggled to break free almost every minute. Since then, the frequency had dwindled to one feeble attempt every couple of days.

A dark face glowered at him from under a horned helmet. The leader of some local band of thugs, with enough leadership experience to make a useful field commander. The man's nose had been broken so many times it looked more like a random lump of skin than a nose, and a jagged scar stood out just below his right eye. That face could give lesser men nightmares, but Morgoth had seen his kind before. Bullies as long as they knew they had the upper hand, but cowards the moment they met their match. They wore a thin layer of bravado over their fear, a scab on top of a festering wound. It poisoned their minds and made them easy to control. He made no attempt to hide the disdain in his voice when he spoke.

"Very good, Commander Brach. The Shadow-weavers and their escorts are ready. The last of Devin's reinforcements from the south-eastern provinces will pass through soon, and we will have our chance at them."

Brach shifted his feet and glanced along the road to the east.

Morgoth lifted an eyebrow at him. "If you have doubts, speak now."

"My Lord, they still outnumber us four to one. They are trained soldiers, while our men are a ragged lot of thieves and deserters with hardly a decent weapon or a full set of armor among them." Brach waved a hand at the hills across the road. "The archers might kill a few by chance and perhaps cause some confusion, but a counterattack by disciplined infantry will break them to pieces. Not to mention what a single division of knights in full plate mail will do to us."

The man had a basic grasp of tactics, but his ignorance and cowardice tested Morgoth's patience. He pointed into the trees behind them. "You see that patch of blackness? One of those Shadow-weavers alone can take down hundreds of men. We have a dozen of them, with a band of guards for each one to protect their backs. A single cry from them will make men tremble in fear and most horses flee in terror. We have a few crossbows that can knock down the ones who don't run away. It will be enough."

Brach fingered his sword and looked down the road again. "It will be close even so, I think. I wish you'd reconsider your order to take as many live prisoners as possible. A man will fight better if he's not trying to avoid killing his enemy. It's a distraction we can't afford."

Morgoth sneered. "Cowardice is not a good quality for a commander. If you want to run home to your wet nurse, go ahead. I can replace you, along with the rest of these scrawny rabbits you call soldiers. Every soldier taken alive can be made to fight for us, each of them with the strength of three men and not hindered by pain. We cannot miss this opportunity to weaken Devin while he's still foolishly overconfident. We will teach them caution here and multiply our own strength at the same time. Prove yourself a man today or risk my displeasure. There is no place in my army for cowards."

Brach's face turned white, and he bowed. "Yes, my lord."

A bird call echoed through the trees. His scouts had sighted something. Morgoth looked toward the road, and then turned to his commander. "They're coming. Prepare your men."

Hoofbeats approached. A single horseman thundered past, glancing only briefly at the hills and the forest. A moment later a second horseman rode by, paying no more attention than the first had. They seemed more concerned with speed than safety, scouting for fallen trees or washed-out sections of road, anything that might slow the march.

Fools, Morgoth thought. *They still think they're chasing fugitives.*

The main column straggled into view, forced into a thin line by the narrowness of the road. The soldiers dragged their feet and stooped under the weight of their packs, strained by days of forced marching. Tired enough to give all their attention to putting one foot in front of the other but not tired enough to stop and rest.

Morgoth waited for the head of the column to march out of sight down the road then lifted a piece of polished brass to flash a signal to the archers waiting in the hills. The first arrows lifted out of the rocks, aimed upward at an angle that would bring them down on the road from almost directly overhead. What they lost in accuracy they made up for in confusion. When the arrows began to fall out of the sky, Devin's soldiers panicked and ran in every direction, unable to tell which way the attack had come from. Half the men ran north to the hills, half ran south to take cover in the forest. The archers leveled their bows and fired directly at the closest soldiers, and the crossbows opened fire as well. The first lines of men running toward the hills died without ever knowing who attacked them. The soldiers behind them turned to run back toward the south side of the road and fell with arrows in their backs.

The soldiers who ran into the forest made it several yards into the trees before they were ambushed by the men hiding in the brush. An entire division fell before the waves of panic rippled out to the ends of the column. The attack split the Storvian troops in half before most of them noticed it. Tired, caught off guard, and reeling from the first strike, still they responded with the discipline of a trained army. Archers returned the fire from the hills, while infantry made their way up the slopes holding their shields high. Spearmen from each end of the column swept into the forest. They plunged their spears into the brush ahead of them to flush out anyone waiting in ambush. A line of knights stayed on the road to run down any enemies that left the tree line.

Morgoth nodded and forced Erick's tortured lips into a smile. "Just as I expected. Perfect."

He flashed the signal to release the next wave of his attack. Shadow-weavers charged out from the forest, spread at regular intervals, each supported by a dozen infantry. Hints of black claws and reptilian tails moved in clouds of thick darkness. Morgoth's infantry dodged in and out, moving around the flanks and swiping clumsily at the Storvian infantry before pulling back out of range. They harried the soldiers, drawing them out of formation. Any time the line faltered the Shadow-weavers closed in and took them down in moments.

Three Storvian knights banded together to charge at one of the Shadow-weavers. A crossbow hit the first one, punching through a weak spot in his armor. He crashed to the ground and didn't rise. A steady-handed spearman, braced against solid rock, connected with a second knight and brought him down. The third knight managed to drive his lance through the creature, but the shock of the blow knocked him out of his saddle. His horse kept running, its battle training overwhelmed by fear at being so close to the demon. The knight fell on his back and struggled to sit up in his heavy armor.

Before he could regain his footing one of the brigands guarding the Shadow-weaver ran up and laid a short sword against his throat.

The Shadow-weaver reeled from the impact of the lance and let out a piercing shriek that froze the hearts of every man within half a mile. It swayed for a moment, then grasped the lance and pulled it out. It sniffed at the weapon the way a dog would sniff at a thorn stuck in its paw, then threw it aside and looked around for someone to kill.

The last of their morale shattered by the Shadow-weaver's cry, the Storvian soldiers broke and ran. Morgoth flashed one final signal. Two more Shadow-weavers and their support teams moved out of the woods, one far north and the other far south, to cut off the men trying to flee. The bravest men stopped, heads lowered, and sank to their knees in surrender. Many collapsed on the ground, either curled up in a ball or stretched out in a dead faint. Some managed to escape, but Morgoth smiled at the number of prisoners taken. Now they could settle into the forest for a while and gather their strength for battles to come.

Back at camp Morgoth sat outside his tent and wrote a short note. *Victory in the south. Expect all Devin's reinforcements to be called out from castle. Be ready.*

He added no signature but used Erick's signet ring to seal the message. At his summoning wave, a messenger stepped up to take the slip of paper.

"Deliver this as quickly as you can to Devin's castle," Morgoth said. "Give it to our man on the inside, then stay there with him. I can't risk you being followed back here just yet."

CHAPTER TWENTY-SIX

Three days of bouncing on cushions in the back of a wagon had failed to waken Master Deborah from her unnatural slumber. After so many long nights searching for life inside her friend's head, for Master Lenore it had become like walking through a dark room in your own house. It felt familiar even though she couldn't see. Except that here the darkness didn't hide anything. There simply wasn't anything, only a sense of space and direction as she glided forward into the emptiness.

She floated toward the center of Deborah's dream zone, searching for some sign of activity. Every night she came, and every night she searched in vain. She could feel Deborah there but couldn't make contact. She reached out with her mind, focusing on an image of her friend. The gloom began to take on shape, thickening in one area. Lenore held her breath as the murky outline condensed into the shape of a person.

"Deborah?" Lenore spoke softly, hardly daring to hope.

A faint voice answered, distorted like an echo down a long hallway. "Who is there?"

If Lenore had been in her body, she would have trembled. "Deborah! Thank God! I am Lenore. I've been trying to reach you for some time now."

"Lenore? What are you doing here? Why are you calling me Deborah? I am Jabal. I expected to find Deborah here, not you."

Lenore's mind staggered. "What do you mean, *you are Jabal*? I know who you are. I am sitting right beside you. You've been badly wounded, Deborah. I fear there might be some damage to your mind. You are confused—"

"I'm not confused. I am Jabal, and you are definitely not sitting beside me. My body is back at the city, in the library. I've been trying to reach you through your dreams. When I couldn't do that, I came here to see if I could contact Deborah."

As unbelievable as it seemed the manner of speaking did, in fact, belong to Master Jabal. She tried to push her worry for Master Deborah to the back of her mind far enough to focus on Jabal. "Have you learned something new, then?"

"I managed to speak to Prince Kenan, long enough to verify that he and two of his friends are tracking Erick."

Lenore gasped. "But why? They're children chasing a wolf! He could kill them in his sleep. What do they expect to accomplish?"

"I fear you are right, my friend. Even worse, their plan, such as it is, is for personal vengeance. They mean to attack him when they find him. Our contact was short, but it terrifies me that Kenan has no idea of the danger he's in. You know the legends as well as I do. If Erick is familiar at all with the legends of Anglachel—and I'm certain he is—he'll be doing everything he can to find one of the princes so he can kill them with it and transfer ownership of the sword to himself. Our best hope was to keep the two princes safe, and now Kenan is running straight into his hands."

Lenore felt someone shaking her physical body. "Someone is waking me. Meet me here again when you can. I need your counsel—"

"I will try." Jabal's faint reply came as she withdrew back into her own body.

A young soldier stood next to her. "Master Lenore, you must come to King Devin's tent at once. He has called an emergency meeting of the council."

Lenore nodded and rose, saving her breath for the short run to the king's tent. She pulled her hood up against the persistent rain that had been falling since they left the castle, splashing through thick mud. The other members of the war council had already arrived.

King Devin spoke as soon as Lenore entered. "The commanders of our southern forces sent us a message. They were ambushed while passing the forest. Erick's relatively small army has grown in strength since the attack on the castle. They have more Shadow-weavers with them, perhaps as many as a dozen. They killed or captured more than half our men."

Lenore flinched like she'd been kicked in the stomach. "A *dozen* Shadow-weavers?"

Devin nodded. "We're lucky our losses were as small as half. Those who escaped have joined with our search parties at the southern end of the valley and are moving to join us. Clearly the blockades failed. Erick's forces avoided them and have multiplied their numbers. We need a new strategy. But what can we do against so many Shadow-weavers?"

"I can tell you what I know," Master Lenore said. "But I don't think it will help. By the grace of God and a memory of a legend, I've killed one myself."

One of the other council members started to speak. Devin stopped him with an upraised hand. "They seem unbeatable. How did you do it?"

"The Shadow-weaver with Erick's strike force came after the king. None of the guards could hurt it. Those who tried reacted as if they'd been burned when they touched it. That's what reminded me of the legend. They have something like a shield of darkness around them that normal light cannot pierce, but if you focus a beam of light tightly enough it will cut through like a lance. While Master Deborah distracted it, I hit it with a beam of focused light. That killed it."

Devin rubbed his chin. "So, is that possible here, the next time we encounter them? Can we beat them?"

Master Lenore sighed. "I am doubtful. It requires more than Biomancy. It is one of the spiritual Arts, known only to Messengers of the Light with years of special preparation. I'm the only one here with that training, and I don't think I could kill them all myself. Focusing that much energy drains me too quickly. That one beam of light sapped my strength far more than my entire struggle against Erick in the king's chamber. I would have to rest for some time between each blast."

"You say this beam hits them like a lance?" Devin said. "Could an actual lance have the same effect?"

Lenore nodded. "It is possible a lance could do as much if driven with enough force. Or perhaps a crossbow. But it would have to be a very lucky hit. These creatures are incredibly resistant to physical wounds even after you breach their shield of darkness. I expect with a physical object like a wooden lance or an arrow you would have to hit them in the heart or in the brain to kill them. Neither of those is a very big target. With that shroud of darkness around them, you can't even see what you're aiming at."

"If we hit them enough times," Devin said, "we should get a lucky hit on them sooner or later, right?"

Lenore raised her eyebrows. "True. But a knight only carries one lance. Against those creatures his first miss will likely be his last."

Devin looked at each council member in turn. "Then we need crossbows. We need whole teams of crossbows. With good mobility. Maybe on horseback, to move to wherever the Shadow-weavers are and fire massive volleys at them, then get away quickly to reload."

The council members all nodded. One of them spoke. "That's good. That's very good. It sounds to me like it should work. What do you say, Master Lenore?"

"I think it might work," Lenore said. "We'll still need all the soldiers we can get, to defend the crossbows and fight the enemy's other troops. But yes, it is the best chance we have."

"Good. If we hurry, we should meet up with what's left of our southern armies in a few days. Our western forces will arrive about the same time, or soon after. We'll send word back to our reserves at the castle to come join us, and also to instruct Duke Arnould to hold the castle against attack should the enemy get around us. Erick's forces have proven quite adept at stealthy maneuvering. Gather all the crossbowmen as soon as it is light. We need to find them horses and organize them into fighting groups." Devin paced as he spoke, as far as he could within the walls of the tent. He paused in front of the council to give his final orders. "Put together as many groups as you can, with six or seven men in each. If they can flank each Shadow-weaver the creatures will have a harder time avoiding the attack. Master Lenore, you'll be in charge of training them to fight Shadow-weavers. Most of the instruction will have to be done as we move, we can't afford to lose more time. Let the men rest tonight. They'll march better tomorrow if rested. And get some rest yourselves. We'll all need our strength."

CHAPTER TWENTY-SEVEN

Kenan strode ahead at a steady pace, canteen in one hand and reins in the other. Peristra had insisted they alternate between riding and walking with the horses. She approached him, jogging to catch up, and pushed a strip of dried meat into his hand.

"It's time for supper," she said. "If you won't stop walking at least you should eat something."

He lifted the meat and bit a piece off without looking at it or turning around. His eyes remained as they'd been, fixed on an imaginary point in the distance.

"When are we going to stop?" Timothy walked behind them, leading both his and Peristra's horses. "My feet are almost as sore as my backside."

"It's not even getting dark yet." Kenan pointed to a line of trees in the distance. "If we push hard, we can make it to that forest before we camp for the night. It looks like a good place to make camp if you're trying to stay out of sight. We may find signs of the enemy having passed through. They might even be hiding nearby."

Peristra sighed and walked back to her horse. She dug through her pack, pulling out a strip of meat for herself. "If we aren't stopping yet, then we might as well ride while we still can. Once we leave the road and enter the forest, we might have to lead the horses again, or even leave them behind if it gets too thick."

Kenan stopped long enough to climb back into his saddle. He urged his horse into a slow trot, the fastest he could make it move after a long day of travel. They continued in silence until they came close to the edge of the forest. The thick undergrowth forced them to leave the horses and continue on foot.

The sun dipped closer to the foothills, and the insects began warming up for their evening song, welcoming the travelers to the forest. *Or giving thanks for their next meal,* Kenan thought, slapping at his arm.

The trees here grew thicker, a different type than the trees that grew in the mountains around the castle. They smelled of moss and damp earth. They also looked older and more secretive. The brush grew dense at the edge of the forest where more sunlight reached it and thinned as they moved deeper in among the trees. Lengthening shadows played with the old trees, giving them faces, while a soft wind gave them a whispering voice.

Peristra pushed forward to catch up to Kenan. She wore a mask of something that resembled composure, but her grip on his arm and the tremor in her voice betrayed her nervousness.

"Kenan, I know you feel this is urgent, but what will you accomplish by blundering through a forest in the dark? Even if they're here, you're likely to be shot by a sentry before you even see the camp. We should set up camp for the night, and decide in the morning—"

"Who goes there?"

Peristra and Timothy stopped and looked around to see who had spoken. Kenan looked up but kept moving forward until the voice spoke again.

"Stop where you are, or I'll shoot you. Tell me your name and what you're doing here, wandering in the woods so late in the evening."

"I am—" Kenan paused and tried to gather his thoughts. "I am

Brian, of Humac, here on a scouting mission for the king. These are my companions, Tom and uh—Sheri."

Peristra and Timothy stopped behind Kenan and waited, letting him do the talking.

"Humac, eh? Isn't that the city around King Devin's castle? You're a long way from home." A man stepped out from behind a tree, crossbow leveled. "Come with me then, and we'll decide what to do with you."

Kenan took a step forward then stopped again. "You're not part of the group that attacked the castle, are you?"

The man belted out a rough laugh. "No, I'm not one of them, whoever they might be. I am one of a band of free men, you might say. We wander where we will, but we've had no cause to wander up that far north. Nor would we set foot inside a city of that size will-ingly. City folk tend to not trust us much. I can't imagine why not."

He laughed his harsh laugh again and winked at Peristra. "Come on then, let's get to know each other a bit over supper."

The man spoke with a light tone, but the point of his crossbow didn't waver. He motioned for them to come past and walk ahead of him. Kenan leaned over toward Peristra and whispered, "If there's any trouble, I can handle him. I don't think he's lying about who he is."

Peristra gave him a doubtful look, and whispered back, "We don't know how many there are. Maybe you should go ahead and take care of him now."

Kenan shook his head. "They could be innocent. I can't kill him just because he *might* be dangerous. Let's just go with him and see what happens."

"You don't have to kill him; you only have to take his crossbow."

Kenan walked away without responding to her again. The sentry had been standing patiently, waiting for them to move, but once Kenan started walking, he turned his crossbow toward Peristra. "Stay together. Come on."

She followed Kenan, with Timothy close behind her. The sentry let them pass and then fell in behind them. "Keep moving, straight ahead."

Peristra elbowed Kenan in the ribs. Her voice an angry hiss barely soft enough to keep their captor from hearing. "What are you doing? He's not exactly being friendly. You don't have to kill him, just overpower him so we can get away."

"No. If I use the Art on him and leave him alive, and he *is* one of the enemy, they'll know we're here and start hunting us. Better to come in among them seeming helpless and take them by surprise. They might lead us right to the assassin."

Her mouth twisted in a way that had become too familiar. Kenan could almost see the sarcasm dripping off her lips as she spoke. "Well, you might have told me that was your plan. I would've let you try your own brilliant ideas while Timothy and I waited at the road to see how it turns out. You didn't have to get us all captured."

He blushed. "Sorry, I hadn't thought of it before. It was kind of a last-minute plan."

"Great," she snorted. "Very gracious, Your Highness."

A campfire glowed through the trees ahead. Kenan tried to clear his mind in preparation for whatever might happen. A strange bird-like cry from behind him startled him for a moment before he realized it was the sentry sending the camp some prearranged signal.

Relax, you can do this. Just focus.

The trees opened up into a clearing lit by a campfire, with about a dozen men sitting around it. Several patchwork tents had been set up around the fire in a loose circle. Judging by the number of tents and the size of the supper pot hanging above the fire, the men around the fire made up the entire group. And judging by the sloppy construction of the tents and the lack of uniforms they probably had no affiliation with any kind of army. Kenan's heartbeat slowed back down to its normal pace. A little smooth talk should get them out of this. Even if it didn't, a dozen normal men wouldn't be much of a challenge for him to take out.

The sentry prodded them out into the firelight, then stepped around to the side and called to one of the men sitting across the fire. "Hey Rolf, look what I found wandering in the woods. They claim to be on a mission from the king."

Rolf laughed as he stood, brushing the dirt off his tattered leggings. He ran his fingers through his short scruffy beard as he examined them with obvious amusement. "Oh really? You seem a bit young and ill-equipped for a war party. What is this mission, exactly?"

Kenan thought fast, trying to figure out how much truth he needed to mix into his story to make it believable. He decided that something simple would work best. "A small band of raiders attacked the castle. We're tracking them to their hideout, and then we'll report back to the king so he can send the army. We followed them to this forest and believe they're nearby. You should be careful. They may have demons helping them, and I don't think they'd hesitate to kill you all just to keep their hideout a secret."

Rolf threw his hands up in the air, eyes wide. "Oh dear. Lads, did ya hear that? Our lives could be in danger. Not to worry young master, we will certainly take all precautions. Are they very close, do ya think?"

Kenan didn't like the man's tone but figured he should answer as if he considered it a serious question. "Yes. They headed south not too long ago. This forest would be a better place to hide than the swamp on the other side of it. I'm certain they will be hiding in here somewhere. They might know you're here already."

Rolf put one hand against the side of his face and glanced around. "Oh my, isn't that a terribly frightening thought? Maybe it would be, if it weren't for the little fact that we are here by their personal invitation."

He looked around at his companions. "What do ya think, lads? Think we'll get an extra prize for bringing in some prisoners with us?"

The men all laughed, and a few of them cheered. Kenan felt fear and excitement at the same time. *So, they are with the enemy. All we have to do now is let them take us to the main camp. I can break free at night while they're sleeping and get the sword, then kill Lord Erick with it.*

Rolf motioned to the sentry. "Take the two boys, tie them up and keep them out of the way. Bring the girl to my tent. I could use a new maidservant and personal assistant."

He winked at Peristra. "Come on sweetie. I'll find you a pretty dress and you can provide my evening entertainment."

The color drained from Peristra's face, and she stumbled back a step. "Don't you dare touch me, you filthy brute." Fear touched her voice, but it also held fire.

Rolf gave a patronizing laugh. "Ah, look at the cute puppy baring her teeth. That's why I like the redheads. They're feisty."

She surged forward, pulling a dagger from her belt as she ran. Her right hand drew out the dagger and held it back, ready to strike, while her left hand balled into a fist. Kenan felt anger hit him between the eyes, turning the edges of his vision red. Through the rage he heard the voice of his teacher. *Focus, Kenan. Distract the anger, don't let it cloud your mind.*

Peristra sprinted across the clearing toward Rolf. The sentry had been watching for this reaction. He stood between her and Rolf, so he only had to take one step to block her path. He reached out and casually backhanded her as she ran by. The blow knocked her head back while her feet kept moving forward. She landed on her back with a strangled "Oomph!" In spite of the tension and his need to focus, Kenan couldn't help noticing the way her thick red curls spilled around her shoulders like flames.

Concentrate, you idiot, Kenan chided himself as he forced his eyes back to the enemy. He belted out a yell, but not in anger or fear. He'd cleared his mind of everything except the fight. He yelled as a distraction, drawing attention away from Peristra and onto himself. He surveyed the battlefield with a quick glance and launched himself into a run.

He centered on the sentry first. The man had held his crossbow slack in his left hand while he struck Peristra, but now he started to swing around, his hands tightening in preparation to fire. Kenan knew he had to reach it before the bolt launched. He used Biomancy to enhance his speed, but he couldn't move as fast as his teacher. He couldn't stop a bolt in flight. Even to dodge it would be difficult at this range. As he came within reach of the crossbow the man tightened his finger on the trigger, pulling it back.

Too late, it's going to fire.

Hands already outstretched to grab the crossbow, Kenan just changed the motion of grabbing into one of pushing and forced the crossbow around to point toward one of the men beside the fire. The bolt flew free, and the man crumpled, sword half drawn.

As soon as the bolt flew clear Kenan twisted the crossbow loose and hit the sentry in the head with it hard enough to crack the stock. The crossbowman collapsed, permanently out of the fight.

With the most urgent threat neutralized, Kenan scanned the area to find his next target. Peristra lay on her back, stunned by the double blow of a fist and of hitting the ground. Timothy sat in a heap, conscious and untouched but looking faint and not about to move anywhere. Three men ran away in different directions. The rest had begun to draw their weapons. Rolf stood with his sword drawn, reacting more quickly than the others. He was also the closest.

The leader is top priority, Kenan thought as he charged at Rolf.

Rolf reached a defensive position before Kenan got to him. Seasoned fighter or not, he couldn't match the speed and strength Kenan gained through the Art. Swinging the broken crossbow like a club, he first knocked Rolf's guard aside, sending his weapon flying into the brush. His return stroke caught the bandit chief in the head, putting him out of the fight.

Kenan allowed himself to feel a bit smug. *Not bad so far. Just a few more to clean up.*

Timothy still hadn't moved far. He'd managed to rise to his knees but looked ready to fall again at the slightest touch. Peristra had pushed herself up off the ground and picked up the knife she'd dropped. Kenan sprinted in among the small knot of men next to the fire, planning to take out as many as possible with just a few hits.

Efficiency is essential. He smiled to himself, silently thanking Master Jabal for drilling those lessons into him. *Don't lose focus,* he reminded himself as he picked his next target. The men clumped too close together, getting in each other's way as they all rushed to draw their weapons. Kenan dodged between them and used the energy of his blow bouncing off the first man to spin and hit the next.

Two men dropped in quick succession, and then a third. The three that remained now stood slightly farther apart. But now they had their weapons drawn. Kenan ducked under a sword, using the opportunity to pick up a dagger in his left hand. As he straightened back up, he saw the three who had run away, coming back into the clearing.

They must've gone for weapons, he thought as he grabbed a wrist and twisted it. The man whose arm Kenan was twisting dropped his sword, and Kenan swung him around to collide with one of the others. Those two went down in a heap, pushing at each other as they both tried to get clear.

He glanced at the men running back into the camp. The first man waved a sword, flailing it around like he'd never held a weapon before. Kenan discounted him immediately. The second man hefted a spear and looked for a moment as if he might throw it. But seemed to change his mind and charged instead. Kenan twisted to one side to dodge a strike, then looked over at the third man. He held a loaded crossbow. He froze, caught off guard, as the man raised it to take aim.

He can't shoot at me, Kenan thought, *he'll hit his companions.* He traced a straight line in the direction the crossbow pointed. Peristra stood there looking toward Kenan, unaware of the crossbow pointed at her back.

He started running again, trying to reach the crossbow before it could fire. He took one step before a heavy blow caught him in the shoulder. The force of it knocked him sprawling in the dirt.

In a moment he jumped to his feet again, but that moment

changed everything. The man had found his aim and begun to draw back the trigger. Knowing he wouldn't arrive in time to stop the bolt's release; he switched targets and ran for Peristra. Racing at full speed, he'd never felt so slow in his life.

The crossbow twanged as it released its missile. Peristra's head started to turn in response to the sound, but far too slow. At the rate she moved she wouldn't even see the man who shot her before the bolt struck home. Kenan said a prayer and jumped as hard as he could, hands stretched out toward her. He grabbed her shoulders and pulled her straight down, the momentum of his jump sending him over her head. The shaft scraped past her neck. He felt an instant of relief before pain stabbed his chest as the bolt struck him instead.

CHAPTER TWENTY-EIGHT

Queen Havilah pressed her right hand against her temple while she listened to the messenger describe the ambush. He told her about King Devin's request for reinforcements and his instructions for Duke Lukas. She did her best to maintain eye contact with the man while her left hand felt around clumsily for her medicine bottle, which she'd taken to keeping in her bag. Even with the medicine her headaches came more frequently, and with greater intensity each time. *As soon as I'm done here,* she thought, *I'll summon Master Jabal and have him examine me.*

Her hand found the bottle at the same time the messenger finished speaking. She gripped it tightly while she replied. "Thank you. I will relay the king's orders to the duke. You may rest here as long as you need before you leave. When you return, tell the king that everything is well. He shouldn't worry about anything."

She waited until the messenger had bowed and left the room before she pulled the bottle out of the bag and pried it open. She pressed it against her lips, tilting her head back, uncaring that she probably looked like a hungry baby suckling. She sucked so hard her cheeks hurt but could not pull a single drop from the empty bottle.

The dreaded and familiar pressure pulsed behind her eyes. She squeezed them shut and doubled over, dropping the empty bottle on the floor. She groped along the table next her until she found the bell sitting there. The sound of the bell ringing stabbed like a knife into her ears. Immediately the door opened, and a servant came in.

"Go and find Kris for me," she said. "Tell him to come here right away."

She watched the servant leave then squeezed her eyes shut again and pressed the heels of her hands against her eyelids. Even though she knew it would do no good she found it difficult to stop herself from getting up and trying to find him on her own. Once the headache reached its peak, she would hardly be able to stand, much less walk.

It felt like an eternity sitting there with the waves of pain crashing against her and through her, each one stronger than the one before. The pain rose like the tide, and she wished she could drown in it and be finished. By the time she heard the door she couldn't even open her eyes anymore, but just reached out her hand in the direction of the sound.

"Kris. It hurts, and I'm out of medicine. I feel like I'm dying. Give me more, please. Make it stop."

"Of course, my queen. Here, I brought some with me."

She felt him put a bottle in her hand and pulled out the stopper with trembling fingers. She drank so quickly that some of the medicine ran down her chin, and she swallowed twice as much as she normally took. She grimaced at the bitter aftertaste. It seemed worse than usual. It reminded her of something, but she couldn't think of what. The agony in her head left little room for curiosity about such details.

She carefully set the bottle on the table and waited for the pain to subside. It lessened, but it didn't fade away gently as it always had before. Instead, every muscle in her body cramped as if she were being squeezed by a giant fist. She opened her mouth to tell Kris, but before she could speak, darkness swallowed her.

THE WORLD SPUN AROUND KENAN, AND HE TASTED DIRT AND blood. He felt a helpless rage at the shooter that had nothing to do with his injury, but at what would happen to his friends, and his kingdom, if he couldn't stop these assassins. *There are still six of them,* he told himself. *I have to do something.*

He tried to focus his energy, but the pain and nausea overwhelmed him. He barely managed to focus his eyes, and when he did, he realized he'd fallen on the ground. It took all his strength just to raise his head. The two men he'd thrown into each other stood and picked up their weapons. The man with the crossbow set it against his foot, getting ready to pull back the cable and reload. The other three closed in from different directions. He tried to raise himself, to get to his feet, but his muscles refused to respond.

A shadow covered him. Peristra stood over him with her knife held ready, glaring at each of their attackers in turn. The one with the spear lifted it over his head and pulled it back as if to throw it. "Don't be stupid, girl," he shouted. "If you drop the knife and come quietly, we won't hurt you much. Try to fight us and you'll pay for it like your friend there did."

She pressed her lips together and crouched lower. She leaned her head back a little and shook it firmly, partly in negation, and partly to get her hair out of her face. A loud roar sounded from the woods behind her. She flinched but didn't turn around.

Good decision, Kenan thought. *Whatever's behind you might or might not be dangerous, but the men in front of you certainly are.*

Something crashed in the underbrush. All six men stared into the forest behind Peristra, the color draining from their faces.

Kenan strained his neck, twisting to get a glimpse of what they saw. A bear stood at the edge of the woods on its hind legs, so huge it cast a shadow over the entire camp. Its eyes glowed red. Timothy, who'd just managed to regain his feet, fell onto his face in a dead faint. Peristra whirled around long enough to identify what had happened, then returned to her defensive stance, knife out and ready, hair red and wild around her shoulders, eyes blazing.

Five of the men fled in panic, the sound of their footsteps fading into the forest. The one with the crossbow finished reloading and took aim, but he shook so badly the bolt flew several feet to the bear's left. The beast dropped back onto all fours and charged. The man threw down his crossbow and sprinted into the woods with the bear on his heels.

"That was entirely too convenient." Peristra swept her gaze across the clearing. "And a minute too late—Kenan!"

She ran over and knelt beside him to examine his wound. "You boneheaded fool! What were you thinking? Oh yes, you weren't thinking! Kenan, if you die, I'm never speaking to you again."

He managed a weak smile. "Promise?"

Seeing the hurt in her face he added, "You're right, I was stupid. I'm sorry."

She wrinkled her nose at him. "You were really good. Right up to the point where you let yourself get shot. Stupid boy."

Her smile twisted into a frown. "I don't understand how that bear happened to attack just now, but I wish it had come a bit sooner."

"I'm sorry," said a voice behind her. "I panicked. I never could work very well under pressure."

Peristra jumped and twisted, one hand groping for the knife she'd dropped.

Kenan flinched as she bumped him with her knee, but then reached up to rest a hand on her arm. "Put the knife down. I'd know that voice anywhere."

CHAPTER TWENTY-NINE

Morgoth waved a hand toward the lines of prisoners that filled the clearing. "Suddenly we have over three thousand new mouths to feed. I can summon spirits to possess several hundred of them per day, but even so it will be more than a week before we're ready to march. See if you can find any local villages to raid for supplies."

Commander Brach turned his head to spit in the dirt. "Why bother? Prisoners can go a few days without food. If you're just gonna feed their bodies to those black spirits of yours, why should we waste supplies on them?"

"If I'd wanted an advisor," Morgoth said, "I wouldn't have chosen a stupid slab of meat like you. Stick to what you know, little as it is. I have to feed them if I want them to be able to fight for us later. Even when possessed, the body runs on energy from food. I'm not going to starve my army just before an important battle."

Brach crossed his arms and scowled. "Fine. I don't care how it works, as long as they can fight and follow orders. Will possessed soldiers follow my direction?"

"They will obey me," Morgoth said. "because I summoned the

spirits that control them. They will follow your directions as long as I want them to. If you ever disobey me, or if you become more annoying than you are useful, I will make you one of them. So, I suggest you stop wasting my time with questions and go gather supplies like I told you to."

Brach blanched and backed away.

Morgoth returned to the line of men who waited to speak with him. A commotion at the back of the line caught his attention. Three men shoved their way toward the front, followed by a trail of angry protests. The men, like most of the newcomers who presented themselves, came dressed only in rags and mud. Weariness etched their faces and dragged behind them like weighted chains, no different from the rest of these men. But this group wore fresh bloodstains on their shirts.

Morgoth motioned for the others to let them pass. They reached the front of the line then stopped and looked at each other. Each of them pushed one of the others forward, arguing among themselves about who should be the one to speak.

Morgoth pointed to the one in the middle. "You. Report."

The man took a step forward and fell to one knee. "Sir, we were on our way to join you, with a dozen men, when our camp was attacked. Three travelers, brought in as prisoners. One of the travelers, a young man, he was harmless. Didn't even try to do nothin'. The girl tried to fight, but we handled her easy enough. The third..."

The man ducked his head and twisted his hands together. His ears, already reddened, deepened to crimson. The man's lips continued moving, but his voice grew too soft to make out the words.

"Speak up, man!" Morgoth growled. "Go on. The third?"

"It's like he wasn't human, my lord. He moved so fast! And he threw us around like we was straw men. Dropped Rolf with one blow —sorry my lord, Rolf was our leader. Then he came after me. Twisted the sword right out of my hand. I think he could've twisted my arm clean off if he'd wanted to. Seemed like he was everywhere at once.

Knocked down eight or nine of us before I even knew what happened."

Morgoth frowned and rubbed his chin. "I find myself wondering why you have brought me such a fantastic story. You're claiming that one prisoner whipped twelve armed men by himself?"

The man raised his head and waved a hand back over his shoulder. His voice regained some confidence. "Not quite, my lord. My brother here got him with a crossbow. Hit him good. Don't know if he survived it or not. A rabid bear attacked the camp just as we closed in to finish them off. A monster of a bear, the biggest I ever seen. Six of us got away and found our way here. The beast prob'ly killed those prisoners, but we thought we should let you know."

Morgoth looked out over the treetops and spoke as if to himself. "A man who fights like ten, and a rabid bear that appears out of nowhere to help him. I think we might have found a member of the royal court. Nobody else has the time or the resources to train in the Art like that. Perhaps one or two of his servants as well, from the sound of it."

He looked back at the man in front of him. "If you come across him again, don't kill him. I would rather see you dead than him. Bring him to me. I have a special use for him. Bring him in and you will be rewarded. If you kill him, or let him get away again, I'll feed you to the Shadow-weavers one piece at a time, starting with your filthy toes and working my way up."

CHAPTER THIRTY

Master Lenore watched the horses run back and forth in the failing light, wondering whether any preparation would ever be enough. It had been an exhausting four days for everyone since they'd left the castle. Every time they made camp; she would mark off an area fifty yards across with a large tree on one end. The horses started on one end and ran to within a few yards of the tree. The riders fired their crossbows at a circle cut into the bark, then turned and rode back to the other end of the area to exchange their spent weapons with fresh ones from the support team. The support team reloaded as the horses charged again.

They rotated the groups, so the same horses didn't run every time, but the extra activity still wore them down over time. Lenore paid special attention today to Ephron, their newest recruit. His marksmanship proved as excellent as he'd promised. His horsemanship, on the other hand, did not inspire confidence. He learned quickly, but he'd never ridden before a few days ago. It would take some time for him to be ready for battle.

Master Othniel stood nearby at Lenore's request. The Adoël had considerable skill both with horses and treating injuries. Today she would have to leave early to meet with Jabal and she didn't want to leave the training unattended. Seriam leaned against the boundary rope near the makeshift training grounds, watching her fiancé practice. Lenore pretended not to notice the proud looks she gave him every time Ephron hit the target, or the way she bit her lip when his horse stumbled or made an awkward turn. Pure adoration glowed in that young woman's face, and Master Lenore took pleasure in seeing it.

One of the Adoël approached Seriam and touched her on the arm. "Seriam? You are supposed to be in the training class with the other nurses. They said it's your turn to demonstrate the stitching of a wound. I was sent to find you."

Seriam sighed. "Ah, I was hoping to skip that class today. I can do the stitching all right, but I don't like it. I'd much rather be fighting alongside the men. I bet I could outshoot half the men in that company right there."

Lenore pressed her lips together to stop them from smiling. She leaned forward and pretended to focus on the crossbowmen, but her ears tuned in on the conversation next to her.

The Adoël replied, soft but clear. "I know what you mean. I wish I could do more too, but I won't even get to take care of the wounded except as a last resort. For me it's all cleaning and washing and fetching. I'm a bit jealous of Raendel. He went chasing after Prince Kenan. I wish he'd told me he was leaving. I would have gone with him."

"What's your name?"

"Aeriel."

"It's good to meet you, Aeriel," Seriam said. "Not many of the Adoël will talk so openly. I heard they won't let any of you fight, even the men. That seems strange to me. Why is that? Do they not trust you? Or do they think you can't learn how to fight?"

Lenore swallowed hard to suppress a laugh. She wondered whether either of them had noticed Master Othniel standing nearby. Probably not, from the way they were talking. The Adoël had a talent

for not being noticed. Seriam at least must be aware that Master
Lenore stood close enough to hear them. Which meant she didn't
care if someone overheard.

Aeriel looked at the ground, twisting her hair in her hands. "Why
don't we fight? Why do we act only as servants? I keep forgetting
you're not from the castle. Still, you lived close enough that I'm
surprised you don't know about the curse. Didn't your parents tell
you the stories?"

"Curse? No, I haven't heard anything about a curse. What is it?"

Aeriel glanced in Master Othniel's direction, then leaned over to
whisper in Seriam's ear. Curious, Lenore slid a bit closer and used
her small talent in Biomancy to enhance her hearing.

"Our people committed a great sin several generations ago," Aeriel
said. "Since then, we have carried the curse. We're not supposed to talk
about it. I can't risk telling you much, but at least I can tell you the part
so many others already know. The curse isn't the reason we cannot
fight, it's because of our sin. The Necromancer cursed us for our failures, and we don't know what will happen if we do it again. We could
lose the little bit of power we have left. Master Othniel doesn't even
want us to talk about doing anything wrong, but especially not killing."

Seriam shook her head like someone who understood what they
just heard but refuses to accept it. She answered in a normal tone, not
bothering to whisper. "What sin is so bad that you're all cursed just
for being related to the one who committed it?"

The sudden change in volume made Lenore flinch away. She
glanced at Master Othniel to see his reaction. Othniel's eyes
remained fixed on the horses, but a twitch in his cheek said he had
heard enough, and he wasn't happy about it.

"I can't tell you about the sin," Aeriel said. "I'm sorry. We're not
allowed—"

"Who doesn't allow you? Who has that authority? Isn't it God's
job to punish sin?"

The twitch in Othniel's cheek doubled in speed. Lenore found that fascinating, and slightly amusing. She'd never seen Master Othniel lose his temper before.

Aeriel took even longer to answer this time. Lenore snuck a glance at her. The servant girl shifted from foot to foot, staring at the ground.

"I don't know who forbade us first," she said. "That's just the way it is. Personally, I think our fathers made up that rule for themselves, because they were so ashamed. They didn't want anyone else to know what they'd done."

"That's silly," Seriam said. "Why wouldn't they—?"

"Aeriel!" Othniel cut in.

Aeriel started and jumped back a step.

"What are you doing there?" Othniel said, his voice cutting like a whip. "There is work to be done. We need water for the horses."

"I'm sorry, Seriam," Aeriel said. "I have to go. It was nice talking to you."

Seriam watched her hurry away then wandered off in the direction of the nurses' tent. Othniel glared at Aeriel until she was out of sight. "That girl talks too much."

Lenore shrugged. "People will talk, there's nothing we can do about that. Most of it isn't too bad."

Othniel shook his head. "It's not just that she was talking, it's what she was talking about. I didn't even have to hear it. I recognized the look on her face. That sneaky, shamefaced look people get when they're speaking of something they shouldn't."

This time Lenore couldn't hold back a chuckle. "Othniel, it's not so terrible. I have a hard enough time controlling my own wagging tongue. I gave up a long time ago on trying to control anyone else's. I know men who only stop talking long enough to eat and sleep. It's human nature. Shouting won't change it."

Othniel's face twisted. "I cannot deny that, but I'm not happy about it."

Lenore decided this would be a good time to change the subject.

"What do you think of our crossbows? Do you feel they are ready for battle?"

Othniel turned to the training area. "Of course, I would like for them to be more ready, but I can't say with certainty. The training has yielded results, just not enough to encourage me. The only way to know is to try it, and there's a high price to pay if we try too soon."

"Yes, there is," Lenore said. "But I fear the longer we wait the stronger our enemy becomes. And the timing might not be up to us."

Othniel's eyes narrowed. "You have news?"

Lenore nodded. "There are reports of an army coming out of the southern forest. In the next few days, we'll be choosing a battlefield and preparing to meet them."

"We will find out soon then, whether we are ready or not." His voice dragged like an overloaded packhorse trudging up a mountain.

Lenore had nothing to offer to counter his unease. She felt the same way.

They watched the training in silence until Aeriel arrived, along with several others, pulling a barrel of water in a cart. Lenore signaled a break and turned to Othniel. "I have an appointment to keep. Can you keep an eye on them until the training is finished?"

Othniel nodded. "Where can I find you if there is a problem?"

Lenore pointed back toward the center of the camp. "I'll be in the tent with Master Deborah."

Othniel laid a pale hand on her arm. "All right then. I'm sure it will be fine. I'm sure it will all be fine."

Lenore patted his hand and nodded, then turned and walked away without speaking. She tried to organize her thoughts as well as she could before she reached the tent. She never knew how much time she would have with Jabal, so she wanted to have a clear idea of the things they needed to talk about before their meeting.

She pushed through the tent flap. Deborah's chest rose and fell under the pile of furs. After a moment she edged toward the cot and studied Deborah's eyes, looking for any flicker behind the closed lids. She found none.

Sorrow twisted her heart into knots as she whispered, "It would be nice if you could join our discussions, old friend. Meanwhile, I hope you don't mind us borrowing your head as a meeting place."

She sat next to the bed and placed her hands against Deborah's temples, focused her thoughts and let her consciousness slide down into Deborah's mind. She made her way to the dream area where she would meet Jabal. Once there she settled in to wait for Jabal's summons. While she waited, she searched for some sign of Deborah's consciousness. Nothing disturbed the silent darkness. Every chance she got, she came early and used the time to search for signs of life in Deborah's mind. So far, her efforts only managed to magnify the feeling of emptiness. By the time Jabal arrived she had resigned herself to failure once again.

Jabal's first words did nothing to make her feel better. "The queen has been confined to her bed. Her brother Duke Arnould is managing the castle. He tells me the sickness is caused by stress, that she only needs to rest, and he will let nobody see her. I have a bad feeling about this, but we cannot interfere without either the queen's express permission or hard evidence of treason. The castle guard answer to the duke until one of the royal family tells them otherwise. Is there any news of Prince Kenan? I haven't been able to reach him since that single time."

"No, there is no sign of him," Lenore replied. "We haven't given up searching, though. The enemy is on the move. Erick has gathered quite an army and is coming this way."

"Do you think King Devin will be able to stop them?"

"It will be difficult," Lenore said. Stating her fear out loud lightened it somehow. "I wish you were here to help. They have an entire company of Shadow-weavers. I don't know how many exactly, about a dozen they said, but they routed four thousand of our men with only light support. Devin came up with a plan to fight them however, and I think it might work. It won't be easy still, but with the grace of God we might yet come through this."

"The search here is slow," Jabal said. "There is an entire section of the library devoted to books about magical creatures. Most of it reads like myth, but I'm sure I will locate something useful."

"Do it soon, or not at all. I fear in the next few days we will be tested hard."

A familiar exhaustion welled up in Lenore. Thinking of future troubles drained her strength almost as much as facing them when they came. "I should rest now while I still can. I will meet you tomorrow at this same time."

CHAPTER THIRTY-ONE

Peristra gazed into the small campfire as it painted its living art on the night air. The flames usually calmed her mind, helped her focus. Tonight, she sought a distraction from things that bothered her. Watching the fire didn't help. Neither did the rhythmic pounding of Timothy grinding herbs for a compress to put on Kenan's wound. In fact, that sound drew her thoughts back to the very thing she wanted distraction from.

Everything about Prince Kenan aggravated her. His insufferable arrogance had pulled them all into this trouble. He thought he could take on the assassin alone and treated everyone else like a burden he was forced to bear. Then he couldn't even defeat a few regular soldiers. He'd gotten himself wounded trying. Somehow the thought that he'd only done that to protect her made it even more aggravating.

His rank as a prince made her feel helpless. He represented everything she rebelled against, the whole system of superiority by birth and male dominance. Whenever he tried to talk to her as an equal it felt fake. It had to be some kind of veiled condescension. He pretended to be nice, but he always had a superior tone.

Worst of all, his naïveté compounded everything. How did he

think he would be able to win that fight? He should have known better. But he tried anyway. And nearly got himself killed doing it. What did he want from her? Couldn't he see the distance between them? One time she'd made an effort to bridge the gap, before she understood how wide it was, and he'd refused. Now she showed him, every way she knew how, that she understood the distance between them could never be crossed. But he tried anyway. And he had the nerve to look hurt when she shut him down. As if she had a choice.

With nothing else to distract herself, she finally gave up and listened in on the conversation between Prince Kenan and Timothy.

"You're going to put those on me?"

"Yes. It's a dressing for your wound."

"Dressing? Sounds like you're planning to cook me over the fire and serve me for breakfast!"

"This is hookroot. It will lessen the pain and help you sleep."

"Thank you. You've been a real help to us."

Peristra's stomach clenched, pressed between conflicting emotions. On the one hand, she never thought she'd hear him say those words to anyone, least of all to Timothy. On the other hand, she'd saved his life on the first day of their journey, and he'd never even mentioned it.

"I should've done more," Timothy said.

"More? You've done more than I have. You tracked the enemy for us when we would've lost them. You found us fresh supplies when we would've gone hungry. And now you're treating a wound I might have died from without you."

"If I had helped you in the fight, you might never have been wounded. I should have done something. But I didn't know what to do. I just—"

"It's all right. I've been trained all my life to fight. It's not your fault you haven't had the teaching I had."

"It's not just the training. I was terrified. My father was born a peasant. He earned his title in battle by being brave and strong. His actions proved that he had a right to be called noble. I was born a noble, but I acted like a peasant. Worse, I acted like a coward. I came on this journey to prove I'm good enough. Instead, I proved just the opposite. I failed to protect you."

The fire popped and threw a shower of sparks into the air, then it shifted, collapsing into itself. Peristra reached behind her and grabbed a handful of sticks, fed them into the fire one at a time, and enjoying the hissing they made as they burned. For a long time no other sounds broke the stillness. Then Kenan's voice spoke so softly she could barely make out the words.

"Do you know where I was when my father was killed?"

The silence felt longer this time because it waited for an answer that didn't come.

"I was hiding in the library," Kenan said. "Hiding. While my father fought demons, and my brother led the counterattack, I was hiding in the dark because I was afraid of a little scolding. That's why I decided to chase the attackers. I felt so guilty."

"You shouldn't—"

"Well, I do. But that's not my point. The point is that everyone feels afraid sometimes. That doesn't mean you're a coward. Everyone makes mistakes, misses their chance to do right. That doesn't matter. Being noble isn't only about fighting and being brave. Anyway, you were brave just to come this far. And you're still here. Honestly, back at the castle I didn't like you much. I hated it when I found out you'd come along. Now I'm glad you're here. When we get home, I'll make sure you have a place of honor in the court. You've earned it."

"Thanks, Kenan. It's nice of you to try to make me feel better. I don't know. Maybe I'm just tired. There. That should hold until morning, if you don't roll around too much in your sleep. Wake me if you need anything."

Blankets rustled in the darkness, and soon the sound of snoring blended with the sounds of burning wood. Peristra shook her head in amazement at how fast they could drop off to sleep. She let her eyes wander away from the flames.

Raendel sat with his back to the fire, keeping watch as he'd been doing since they made camp. The orange glow of the firelight on the back of his neck and in his hair gave him almost normal coloring. The Adoël intimidated her a little but cover of darkness and the warmth of the fire made her feel bold.

"Raendel?"

He turned his head. The firelight reflected in his eyes glowed red, and Peristra had to swallow hard to fight back fear. She took a deep breath. "How did you manage to find us? Have you been following us?"

He nodded. "I left the castle as soon as I heard that Prince Kenan had vanished. I caught up to you just after the village, and I've been following you since then. I thought about showing myself sooner, but I didn't know how Kenan would react. When you hid in that cave, I covered the entrance with an illusion to keep the scouts from finding you. I had to stay awake for two days to maintain it. By the time it was safe to stop I was so exhausted, I slept for a day. I caught up to you again just in time to see Kenan fighting with those men. It happened so fast; I couldn't think of what to do. Then Kenan got hit and I just projected an image of the first thing that came to mind."

"What's it like to make an illusion?" said Peristra, taking advantage of his talkative mood. "Do you have to sing certain words, like a spell?"

"No." Raendel closed his eyes and tilted his head back. "It's not like that. It's hard to explain. That's like asking someone how to sing. You just do it. You make a sound and see what comes out, and then you change it and see what happens. Learning to make images is like learning to make notes, only with pictures. There aren't really any words, just the sounds we use to shape the light."

"Shape the light? What do you mean?"

"I'm not supposed to talk about it, really. But I'm sick of keeping their stupid secrets for them." He frowned briefly, then opened his eyes again but didn't focus them on anything. He lifted one hand as if trying to catch the smoke from the fire and wring words out of it. "The images don't really come from our voices. Not directly. It's more like we use the sounds to shape light. Sorry, those are the only words I can think of to describe it. It's like painting on the air. We split light to make different colors and bend it into shapes."

She leaned forward. "Show me something."

He blinked at her. "Show you what?"

She shrugged. "I don't know. Whatever you want. I want to see you make an illusion."

He cleared his throat and shifted his attention to a spot in the air near the fire. He started with a hum, then parted his lips. His voice rose to a crescendo and leveled off. It faded out of her hearing. Not as if it were getting quieter, but as if changing to something her ears couldn't interpret into sound. Yet still, it captivated her in a way that she couldn't describe.

The air that Raendel focused on shimmered and blurred. The figure of a person appeared, growing brighter and clearer until a woman stood in the air above the fire. She had the white eyes and hair of the Adoël and appeared to be young.

The woman turned to look at Peristra and lifted one hand in greeting. Peristra smiled, and the woman smiled in return. The features of her face stretched and became smooth, her body shrinking while her head grew and changed. Peristra caught her breath, entranced, as the image of the woman transformed into a white rose.

The rose bloomed, opening to reveal the miniature figure of a woman sitting in the center of the petals. The woman stood and was in turn transformed into a smaller rose inside the first one. A soft rain fell all around. Peristra could feel the drops hitting her face. She reached up and stroke her cheek, but found it dry. Every place a raindrop touched the rose it left a spot of redness, painting it crimson in random splashes.

She continued to gaze into the air even after the vision faded, longing for the vision to return. After a while, she drew her eyes back to Raendel. "That was beautiful. You really are an artist. You say you do that by shaping the light? But how do you make the sounds? Surely you can't make sounds with light. The roar of that bear couldn't have come from your voice alone. How did I feel the rain-drops just now if they were illusion?"

Raendel glanced at her. When their eyes met, he flinched and turned his face toward the ground. He shook his head and said noth-ing. He seemed to have forgotten her questions.

"Raendel?" Peristra asked. "What is it?"

He raised his head, trembling as if it hurt him to look in her eyes. "I'm sorry."

"Sorry for what? You've done nothing to apologize for."

"Yes, I have," he said. "I've wronged you, and I hid it. I thought it would be better if you never knew, but it's killing me to keep quiet, and it's hurting you too even though you don't know it."

Peristra caught her lower lip between her teeth. She couldn't imagine what he might be talking about, but he sounded serious, so she waited for him to continue.

"The night you met Prince Kenan. When you had those, um, words with him."

She blushed but nodded for him to continue.

"You came back later to apologize."

Her blush faded into irritation. Of course, he would have told his servant about that. They probably had a good laugh about the whole thing. He should be the one apologizing, not Raendel.

He dropped his eyes and cleared his throat. His trembling grew worse. His words came out in a rush. "That wasn't Prince Kenan you apologized to. It was me. I disguised myself as him so he could leave the party without anyone knowing. I couldn't speak. Someone would've recognized my voice and the prince would've gotten in trou-ble. The longer I didn't speak, the harder it got to say anything. I didn't know how to tell Kenan, I thought it should come from you. Now I see how you look at him, and it's my fault. He still doesn't know you apologized, but I think he's forgiven you anyway. You didn't know that, because I didn't know how to say it. I'm sorry."

Peristra's emotions did a summersault inside her chest, knocking the air out of her lungs. Prince Kenan became a whole new person, even though he hadn't changed. Only her view of him changed. Everything he'd said to her, every look he'd given her, every little gesture, all replayed in her mind. She looked over to where the prince lay sleeping.

"We need to have a talk, Your Highness," she said, for once not salting the title with sarcasm. "As soon as you wake up."

Raendel made an urgent hushing motion and turned his head to the forest, listening. His mouth opened, and the light of the fire contracted. Though it still burned, its illumination now stopped after a few feet as if hitting a wall.

He looked at her and pointed to the woods, then touched his ear and made the hushing motion again. She peered into the trees where he had pointed, listening. A branch cracked somewhere in the darkness. The light from the fire withdrew into itself until she could no longer see its glow.

The moon cast a scant light around them, enough for her to see as her friends blended into the brush and disappeared. She looked down at herself and was startled to see only grass where her legs should have been.

A crashing sound made her look up. The figure of a man lurched toward them. His movements reminded her of the man who attacked them the first night away from the castle. His feet dragged along the ground with every step, scraping up piles of leaves and twigs. Vines trailed the ground behind him. Every two or three steps he paused, and his head swiveled as if he were looking for something. His eyes locked in a blank stare.

Peristra held her breath as the man passed within a few feet of them, turning his head back and forth.

His nostrils flared, smelling the air.

She turned to Raendel, lips pressed together in panic, but he had vanished as well.

The man sniffed, shuffled forward a few steps, then sniffed again.

She clenched her teeth to keep them from rattling. Her lungs burned with the strain of holding her breath, but she feared of making the slightest sound. She prayed Timothy and Kenan would stay asleep and that Kenan wouldn't start making those restless noises like he'd been doing recently.

She didn't move, but suddenly the man turned and looked directly at her. A shiver ran through her. She tensed, ready to flee.

He took a step in her direction, smelling the air, then stopped. The sound of voices drifted through the trees. The man turned, and Peristra followed his gaze. Firelight glimmered in the distance. The man sniffed one last time then shambled off in the direction of the voices. The sounds of his crashing through the brush faded, and she let her breath out slowly. The light of their own fire returned.

"They know we're in the area," Raendel said. "He'll be back, or others like him. If we try to travel in the dark, we're likely to run straight into them. I can't hide us while we move. Better to stay here and wait until they assume we're gone and give up. I'll stay up and keep watch for a while, but I'll need you to relieve me eventually so I can rest."

She nodded, still keeping her teeth firmly clamped until the nervousness passed. She pointed to her bedroll and raised an eyebrow.

He motioned for her to go ahead. "Yes, get some sleep. I'll wake you when I need a break."

She lay for a long time looking up at the stars. When she finally drifted off those dead eyes followed her into her dreams.

CHAPTER THIRTY-TWO

Havilah struggled into consciousness, then wished she could sink back into oblivion. Her whole body ached with an agony made worse by spasms that gripped her every few seconds. Her muscles felt like bags of wet sand, heavy and lethargic. She tried to raise her head and look around, to focus. The effort forced her to close her eyes and take a deep breath against the nausea sweeping through her. Sweat-soaked sheets clung to her limbs, and time felt as sluggish as her thoughts.

When she managed to open her eyes again, the first thing she saw was Kris standing over her. His expression showed no trace of concern, only triumph and a malevolence that terrified her. That look made her nausea resurge stronger than before, and she had to turn away. The sharp bitterness of the last drink of medicine he'd given her still lingered in her mouth. It reminded her of the strong aftertaste of the tea he'd made for her. The tea that had made her tired, just before the headaches began.

He poisoned me. The realization made her heart feel as sick as her stomach. *He's been poisoning me. How could I have been so blind?*

Somewhere deep inside her, anger smoldered. Her mind was so

detached from her body it felt like someone else's anger. Looking back at Kris, she forced out a single word. "Why?"

He laughed. An oily, sickening sound in her ears. "Why, my dear aunt? Because the old king is dead. The new king soon will be, along with his brother. You are all that stands between my family and the empire your husband stole from us."

He sat on the foot of her bed. She wanted to throw him off, but weakness held her down.

"But my dear queen, what do we do about you?" He patted her leg through the blanket. "The people love you. If they thought we'd killed you there would be a revolt. If you died too quickly there would surely be questions. We don't want Devin coming home early to investigate his mother's death, but we can't have you meddling in our plans either. So, you had a breakdown, poor thing. But there's nothing to worry about. I am here. I'll take good care of you, and I'll make sure the castle is properly managed."

Her anger surged, and she struggled to sit up. "You spineless, backstabbing, underhanded... you would do this to your own family? I'll make sure you hang for this treason!"

Kris clucked his tongue at her and shook his head. He reached out and, with a single finger, pressed her back against the bed. "Now, now. Take it easy, Your Majesty. You're not well. The harder you fight the worse it will get. I'm only thinking of you."

He stood and placed a small bottle on the bedside table.

"Here. I can see you've already run out, so I'll leave this for you. I told you it was my own special blend. A touch of blood-thorn, a pinch of heartsbane. A few other helpful things. You may suffer some minor side effects, but it will at least ease the pain. When it gets too bad you can take this and get some relief. And oh, I hope you don't mind. When that annoying Jabal called for nurses, I insisted that your ladies-in-waiting would be enough to assist me." He flashed his teeth at her in horrible amusement. "They were quite concerned, but I told them not to worry, that I would see to your needs if they only stay out of the way. So, I am your only caretaker. I am the only one who can help you feel better. If Jabal gets too inquisitive he might fall victim to a tragic accident."

Havilah shuddered, disgusted by Kris and what he was doing to her, afraid of the sudden urge that rose inside her to snatch up the bottle and drink it even knowing it was poison. "Stop it. I don't want your poison. Take it and leave."

"Oh, I think you'll be changing your mind soon," he said. "I'll just sit here for a while in case you need anything. I wouldn't want it to be said that I neglected you in your hour of need."

She fought to sit, but only managed to rise a few inches before her muscles gave up and dropped her back to the mattress. She lay still, exhausted by the effort. The throbbing in the back of her head signaled a headache coming.

The medicine bottle on the table drew her eyes the way a low spot in the ground draws water. *No.* She forced herself to look away. *I can get through this. It's that poison that's doing this to me, and I won't take any more.*

The first waves of pain hit her. They weren't strong yet, but she knew what was coming and broke out in a heavy sweat at the mere thought. She clenched her hands into fists to stop them from trembling and tried to think of something else.

Devin. She'd just sent him a message saying everything was fine. *That's all right. I don't want him to be distracted by worry for me. I will take care of this myself.*

But how? She closed her eyes, concentrated on slow, deep breaths. No good. The pressure built in her head, throbbing with the rhythm of her heartbeat. Focusing on anything else became more difficult with each pulse. *Think of something pleasant,* she told herself.

A memory of her husband rose up in her mind. That memory carried its own kind of pain, and she reached for something safer. *The beach. The sun rising over the water. Walking barefoot in the sand, looking for...medicine...looking for pretty shells. Writing in the sand, watching the tide come in to wash it away...it hurts, daddy, make it stop!*

Reality shifted, blending with old memories. She felt like a little girl again, in bed with fever. Every muscle in her body ached. Blankets heavy with sweat scratched like nettles against her raw skin. Her father sat beside her and held her hand, wiping her forehead with a damp cloth. It was a bitter memory but also beautiful, and it gave her comfort. Her hand clutched at one of the pillows and squeezed it. The pain washed over her, through her, trying to drag her under. She couldn't fight it anymore. She surrendered to it and let it pass over her. *I can get through this,* she thought. *Stay with me father, lend me your strength. It will burn itself out. I just have to hold on.*

Yet this burned hotter than any childhood fever. It hurt until she thought her head would burst, then it hurt even more. Random colors flashed in front of her eyes, so bright she could no longer tell if her eyelids were open or shut. It didn't seem to make any difference. She twisted, flailing her arms around. If her hands had found a knife, she thought she would stab herself between the eyes with it. Surely God would forgive her, he knew she could only take so much. *I'm in hell already. It couldn't hurt any worse than this.*

Another wave hit, drowning all coherent thought. Nothing remained but pain, flashing lights, and a horrible tearing sound she didn't even recognize as the sound of her own screams. Her hand hit the table next to her hard enough to leave a bruise, and blindly slid along it. She touched something cool and smooth and grabbed it out of reflex. The pain subsided, and she was already sinking into the darkness before she realized that she had snatched up the medicine bottle and taken a drink from it.

CHAPTER THIRTY-THREE

Seriam rubbed her hands together behind her and clamped her jaw down on a yawn. She savored the heat of the campfire soaking into the backs of her legs as the first rays of the sun transformed the frost on the tops of the trees into patterns of sparkling fire.

She basked in these rare moments of quiet whenever she could find them. Even in the darkest time of the night the sentries paced back and forth in their clanking armor. Already the troops awakened and prepared for another day of marching and training. Soon the camp would be filled with buzzing conversations and clattering of weapons. But for now, the sky and the forest filled her with peace.

A gust of wind worked its way under her collar, and she pulled her wool scarf a little tighter around her neck. As she tugged on the bright yellow material, she remembered her mother's hand wrapping it around her for the first time. It was the last gift her mother had given her. An early wedding present, she'd said that day. As hard as she fought to keep her mind off of tragedy, at times like this the memories would sweep her away with thoughts of home and fill her with warmth. She closed her eyes and felt her sorrow leave streaks of moisture down each cheek.

The wailing of a horn interrupted her reverie, and she quickly dried her cheeks with the scarf. Three short blasts cried a warning to the soldiers who still slept in their tents. This was not the standard wake-up call. This was a call to battle.

Seriam flew past half-dressed men tumbling out of their tents with weapons in hand. Knights stood with their arms straight out to the sides, looking much like scarecrows on duty, while sleepy-eyed squires fluttered around them like birds, tying their armor in place. Near the center of the camp, she heard pieces of a message shouted by heralds from the clearing around the King's tent.

"...to the field. Report to your commanders for instructions on where..."

The icy morning air stabbed into her side like an arrow, but her steps never slowed until she found Ephron packing a quiver full of crossbow bolts into his saddlebags.

At her call he turned and caught her in his arms. She buried her face in his chest and breathed in his warmth. One of his hands moved up to stroke her hair, while the other pressed against the small of her back. His head bent down; his breath tickled her ear. "Seri, my love. I have to go now. I have to fight. I'll come back to you; I promise."

She kissed his arm and pushed herself back far enough to unwind her scarf. "Wear this for me. Bring it back safe."

Ephron laid his hand on the thick yellow scarf and traced her fingers through the rough wool, pulled it up to his face and inhaled deeply, then rubbed it against his cheek. "My heart and my thoughts will be here with you."

She snatched the scarf away from him and looped it around his waist. "They'd better not be. You'd best keep your thoughts on what you're doing. This isn't a hunting party. People are going to die out there. I'd prefer you keep your thoughts on the battle today and have you with me tonight, rather than you dead on the battlefield because you were daydreaming."

She stepped behind him to tie the scarf in place, lifting the end of it to dab away the moisture from the corners of her eyes. That finished, she put her arms around him and pressed against his back. "You're all I have left in the world. Please come back to me."

He clasped his hands around hers and held them against his chest. "I love you, Seri. I have to go now."

He pulled her hands apart gently, kissed each of them, and then stepped away from her. She looked up and saw that the rest of his company was standing around them, feet shuffling, impatient to leave. They all turned away, pretending not to have been watching.

She straightened her skirt until she had composed herself, then lifted a steady gaze to watch them leave the camp. Once they were out of sight she looked back toward the nurses' tents and reviewed in her mind the assignment she'd been given during training. They had put her on the last shift, to be called only after the battle's end, during the greatest need. She would probably be up all evening and through the night — searching for wounded men on the field until dark and then caring for them by lamplight. She ought to return to her tent and rest while she still could. But as long as Ephron faced danger, her heart wouldn't let her rest. Fear had already sunk deep roots in her gut, and she couldn't weed out the feeling that if she let him out of her sight, she would never see him again.

Yesterday, searching for a private place to relax, she'd discovered a shelf of rock that jutted out past the trees far enough to offer a clear view of the valley below. It would be a good place to watch the battle. She hurried to the edge of the camp with her head down, hoping that nobody would take notice or ask where she was going. As soon as she passed the first line of trees, she picked up her skirts and ran to the place she'd found.

Gasping out puffs of steam into the morning air, she fell on her knees at the edge of the rock shelf and gazed down at the field below. From this vantage point she had a perfect view of the clearing where the crossbow teams loaded their weapons and prepared their horses. A line of infantry formed at the edge of the trees. She could just make out bits of movement far to the south that had the look of large groups of people. She strained to get a better look at what she felt must be the enemy army but could make out nothing more than a blur.

A trumpet sounded as the Storvian army marched out into the field. Before they reached its middle, a trumpet sounded from the other side and the spots of motion across the valley grew into a solid line. The Storvian infantry stopped to dig in. The men in front carried shields large enough to cover two men, and light swords. They stood close together, shields locked in an unbroken wall all the way down the line. Just behind them stood a line of men with long spears. They planted the butts of their spears in the ground and tilted them forward over the tops of the shields held by the men in front of them. A third row of infantry stood behind them ready to step forward and fill gaps in defense or charge through for a counterattack. The teams of mounted crossbowmen waited at strategic places behind the lines.

The enemy advanced until the individual figures of men and horses became clear. Interspersed among the enemy ranks, the Shadow-weavers appeared as dark smudges on the field.

The gap between the two armies diminished. A volley of arrows flew from each side, only to bounce off the shields and plate armor of the Storvians. Among the poorly equipped men of the enemy army the missiles found softer targets. Their light infantry moved in quickly and pressed in close against the Storvian line, trusting that King Devin wouldn't risk shooting his own men in the back. Many of the enemy soldiers fought with odd motions, stiff and jerky. Seriam couldn't quite make out enough details to figure out why.

The weight of metal that protected the Storvian defenders from attack also slowed their reactions. The leather-clad enemy struck, and then leaped back to dodge return strokes. The two lines flirted and touched each other like shy lovers before they committed to a full embrace.

Patches of darkness drifted across the battlefield where the Shadow-weavers fought. A chill slid through Seriam from neck to tailbone. The band of ruffians guarding the Shadow-weavers stepped forward to knock the Storvians' spears aside, trying to make an opening for the demons to break through. The spearmen held their ground. They snapped their spears back in line quickly for a counterattack.

Near the middle of the line a Storvian spearman lost his grip and his weapon clattered to the ground. The man beside him bent down to help him recover it and the point of his own spear wavered. A Shadow-weaver surged into the gap.

One of the Storvians in the back rank broke out through the line of shields and plunged a sword into the center of the darkness with the weight of his body behind his thrust. His back arched, his head flew back, and he screamed loud enough for Seriam to hear it from her seat on the hillside. Her stomach churned in horror as she watched a black arm shoot out from the darkness and choke off the scream, then toss the heavily armored soldier like a man tosses an apple core over his shoulder.

Seriam clutched her stomach and doubled over, but her eyes remained locked on the battlefield. A team of crossbows tore up the ground coming to a stop, fired their bolts, and turned to ride away again before they had time to judge the success of their strike. The Shadow-weaver staggered but didn't fall. While it recovered, the Storvian army fell back a few steps and regrouped.

Another link in their chain buckled, and another Shadow-weaver pressed against it. A crossbow team galloped into position. The Shadow-weaver stopped. The cloud of darkness around it billowed outward, expanding to double its previous size. The strike team waited for a clear target; weapons held level. Seriam leaned forward and yelled at them, not caring that they had no chance of hearing her. "Aim for the center. Don't just stand there!"

Two of Devin's infantry vanished into the expanding cloud. A bloody helmet flew out of the darkness and struck one of the crossbowmen, nearly knocking him off his horse. Still, they waited, searching for a shot. Seriam lifted a hand to her mouth and bit down on her fingers in frustration.

While the crossbowmen stalled, the enemy pressed forward, pouring in around the Shadow-weaver to attack the vulnerable horses. The team fired into the cloud and fled, leaving the infantry to fall back and try to close the hole torn in the fabric of their defense. Morgoth's army punched into the breach with the Shadow-weaver leading the way. A beam of light shot out from the hillside to Seriam's right, piercing the center of the darkness. The demon fell, its defensive cloud disintegrating. The enemy attack sputtered out in confusion, and a strong counterattack closed the break.

The beam of light left a trail across Seriam's vision. She followed it back to the source and saw Master Lenore on another shelf of rock like the one she'd found. She knelt on the rock, hunched over like someone who has eaten week-old meat and is moments away from spewing it all back out on the ground. For a long time, she didn't move. After several minutes, she finally staggered to her feet. She raised her arm and pointed. A ray of light streaked out from her finger, barely missing a second Shadow-weaver. This time she took even longer to recover.

The Storvian army struggled and fell back all through the morning. The Shadow-weavers continued to respond to the threat of crossbows by spewing out billowing clouds of darkness. Seriam grew hoarse from shouting at them, and at times had to restrain herself from running down to the battlefield to fight with her bare hands. After that first kill, Master Lenore fired her ray of light half a dozen times but only managed to take down one more Shadow-weaver.

A few wounded soldiers crawled back far enough from the active fighting for the Adoël to reach them and carry them back to the camp. Ten times as many lay where they fell, paralyzed by wounds or by fear. Most would bleed to death on the field, dying of wounds that could have been treated if they'd been able to reach safety. The cries of the wounded mingled with the noise of battle.

She knew she ought to go back to the camp and help if she didn't intend to rest anyway, but the intensity of the battle held her captive. Part of what held her there was worry, a feeling that if she let Ephron out of her sight again something would happen to him. A large part of it was anger at the enemy. How could men be this way, fighting alongside demons, serving an evil master for nothing more than the pleasure of killing? What right did they have to destroy her home, her family, and now threaten to destroy the last good thing she had left?

Her forehead burning with the heat of her anger. She glared across the battlefield, wishing her glare alone had the power to strike men down. *If it did, the battle would be over now—*

A flash of yellow caught her eye, and her hand went to her throat as she recognized her scarf on the battlefield. "Ephron," she whispered. Her knees buckled. She sank to the ground.

Ephron's crossbow team rode into position, targeting a Shadow-weaver. The cloud of darkness expanded as the demon prepared for their attack. The team fired into the cloud. A piercing cry echoed through the valley, throwing everyone who heard it into a blind panic. Ephron's company, close to the source of the sound, felt its grip more than the others. Their horses scattered in terror. Ephron's horse reared and step backward. Its hoof caught on a dead body, and it lost its balance. Seriam's forehead burned as if with fever.

Ephron hit the ground and rolled clear an instant before his horse came crashing down after him.

"No!" Seriam screamed, stretching out her arms as if to catch her beloved and lift him up.

He tried to rise. His leg folded under him, and he collapsed. The enemy infantry near him crouched, their hands over their ears, as panicked by the cry of the Shadow-weaver as the Storvians. They paid no attention to Ephron lying nearby.

Seriam clenched her fists and leaned forward, willing him to get up, to get away. Again, he tried to stand and failed. While he struggled, the cloud of darkness dissipated. The Shadow-weaver crouched low and clutched its shoulder. Ephron rose up on one knee and swayed as if trying to find his balance in a strong wind. The demon straightened and turned in his direction, its reptilian snout twitching.

No! It's not fair! You can't have him!

"Leave him alone!" Seriam cried. The heat in her forehead focused into a single white-hot point between her eyes.

The Shadow-weaver stretched its claws toward Ephron. Seriam's vision turned red, and she lashed out with her mind. Light flashed. A cracking sound reverberated across the battlefield. The Shadow-weaver collapsed in a smoking heap. Seriam fell back against a rock, dazed.

A buzzing noise filled her ears, her vision marred by the ghost of the flash that had struck the Shadow-weaver. Ephron still hadn't managed to stand, but at least his condition didn't seem to be worse than it had been a moment ago. The ghostly streak across Seriam's vision reminded her of a thunderstorm.

Lightning? She looked up at the clear blue sky. *How?*

She remembered the heat in her forehead, the feeling of lashing out. And then she knew.

I did that! It's impossible, but I did it! I know I did.

She recalled the night outside the village when she'd lashed out at the boulder and lightning struck it. She'd thought nothing of it at the time. This time she knew it was no ordinary lightning. Somehow, she had summoned it.

I've done it twice. I could do it again.

She scanned the battle, picked out a Shadow-weaver, and concentrated. She willed as hard as she could, trying to recreate that sensation of lashing out. Nothing happened. She tried harder, squinting her eyes and straining until she thought she would faint from the effort, but still nothing happened.

What am I missing? She rubbed her forehead. *There was a heat, a burning. I was angry, and then I just lashed out—I was angry! That must be it.*

She concentrated again, trying to work herself up into anger. It felt like trying to build a fire out of soggy wood. Exhaustion smothered her best efforts.

She closed her eyes. *I need to build up to it slowly. Think angry thoughts.*

She had plenty of angry thoughts to choose from. The warmth blossomed in her forehead, and she felt a surge of triumph. That feeling of elation snuffed out the scant anger she had built up and the warmth in her head vanished.

Curse it! She clenched her hands into fists. *I have to stay focused!*

She turned the train of her thoughts back to the destruction of her home, the death of her family. She thought of Ephron lying on the field, wounded. A spark of warmth flashed between her eyebrows, and she fought to not be distracted by it. She imagined Ephron being captured alive by the enemy. The enemy infecting his mind, using him as a spy and assassin. Torturing him and sending him in to be killed by his friends. Rage built up inside her. She looked out over the battlefield and chose her target.

A trumpet sounded the retreat. King Devin's army fell back toward the hills. Her anger faded again; this time smothered by disappointment. She trudged back to the nurses' tents. With each step, the thought of Ephron lying wounded on the field spurred her faster until she nearly flew down the hillside into the camp.

CHAPTER THIRTY-FOUR

Queen Havilah blinked to clear the blurriness from her eyes. She wished she could do the same for her brain. Her brother's bearded face came into focus beside the bed, watching her with eyes void of any concern or worry. Her right arm twitched with the effort of reaching out to him, her voice strained with desperate weakness.

"Lukas. Lukas, help me. Kris. The medicine. Poisoned."

Duke Arnould answered with a face that advertised his guilt by showing no emotion at all. "I know. He sent me with your refill. I put it here on the table for you."

Bile rose in the back of her throat. She shook her head. "No! How could you? Our father—"

Duke Arnould surged up out of his chair, his face twisted. "Our father tossed you to the dogs to save his own neck. He surrendered our birthright, your nephews' birthrights—"

"No, Lukas." She fought back tears. "Don't you remember how it was? We had nothing. Trying to fight Edward's army would've been like spitting on a bonfire. They wouldn't have even noticed. Father's diplomacy *gave* us the throne. He saved our family. We gained an empire without a fight."

The fury drained out of Arnould's expression, leaving it cold and hard as a stone wall. "We? No. Y*ou* gained a throne, you and those two pups you whelped. All he gave me was a pile of moldy fishing nets and a life of servitude."

"We—my sons and I are family, Lukas. We love you. How can you do this to us?" Her whimpering devolved into outright sobs. "If you're not happy, I— I'll talk to Devin. We'll find a place for you in the court. Talk to us. We can work something out. There's no need for this—"

He sneered. "You think diplomacy is better than war? Mere words? You think I should be happy with scraps tossed down to me from the king's table? Can your words stop arrows in flight? Can they break down walls of stone? Will your pretty speeches destroy armies? Win kingdoms? Go ahead, lie there and talk philosophy and politics while I seize the throne by force of arms. We'll see which is more effective in the end."

Duke Arnould stormed out of the room, slamming the door behind him. Havilah gazed after him, tears gushing down her cheeks. When the sobbing subsided, she wiped her face and looked over at the table. She lifted the bowl of water and drained it in one long gulp. As she set the bowl back on the table the medicine bottle caught her eye, and she trembled. It glittered on the table, pulling at her.

I have to get rid of it. If I leave it there, I'll drink it when the pain comes. I have to do it now while I still can.

She grasped the bottle and lifted it as high as she could, ready to throw it against the floor. Another thought stopped her hand.

If Kris or Lukas come back and see it smashed, they'll just bring more. And they'll stay to watch me drink it. She lowered the bottle. The pressure of her urgency masked the pressure building inside her head. *I could pour it out on the floor. No, they might see that too.*

Her brain struggled to form thoughts like a tongue numb with cold struggles to form words. The numbness faded, but as it did the pain crept in to take its place. *They only bring me one dose at a time. If they come back and it's gone, they'll assume I drank it. I have to pour it out somewhere they won't see it.*

The stench of old sweat mixed with urine rose from the mattress, making her head spin.

Into the mattress! The sheets will cover it, and it will blend in with the sweat...

She worked the stopper loose, then pushed the bottle as far under the sheets as she could reach and tapped it against the bed to make it drain faster. She placed the empty bottle back on the table and tried to relax. Her heart raced; each beat echoed by a throbbing in her head. *Now it will come. One more time and I'll be done with it. All I have to do is endure it.*

The pain rose in waves that swelled from bad, to worse, to unbearable. Sweat poured from her body until she wondered how there could be any fluid left in her at all. Her muscles spasmed and twisted, making her twitch like a dying snake. Hallucinations seized her, horrific scenes where toxic beasts with the face of her brother stabbed her with barbed spears and cooked her over open flames.

The madness ebbed for a few seconds, and she realized she was sucking on the empty bottle. She'd expected this but hadn't expected to hate herself so intensely for pouring out the medicine.

I don't care if it's bad, she thought. *I need it. It hurts. Oh, why did I waste it?*

The nightmares engulfed her again. Ceaseless agony stretched each moment into eternity. She couldn't dredge up enough energy to open her eyes. The smell of sweat assaulted her with the strength of twenty horses, and her mouth tasted like salty cotton. Her jaw ached so terribly, she wondered whether it might be broken, yet still her muscles went through the motions of convulsive sucking. Something felt wrong, something in addition to the pain that still pounded in her head.

She couldn't make her mind work well enough to figure the problem, until she tried to move her arm up to wipe her forehead. Her forearm met firm resistance, and she finally opened her eyes to see filthy sheets less than an inch away. Her face pressed against the mattress where she'd poured the medicine, sucking with all her strength. Her stomach heaved and bile rose in the back of her throat. Her muscles trembled and strained as she tore herself away from that spot and inched her way back up the mattress. Her head felt as though it were split down the middle, and her stomach cramped so badly she wanted to curl into a ball and whimper. And yet in spite of it all, her mind felt clear.

Well, at least I finally feel better.

For the first time in weeks, Queen Havilah smiled.

CHAPTER THIRTY-FIVE

Peristra laid a hand on Kenan's forehead, willing him to recover. "His fever's getting worse. He keeps opening his eyes, but I don't think he sees anything or understands what I'm saying."

Timothy dumped a handful of herbs into a stone bowl and pounded them vigorously with a rock. "We'll have to mix these with water and make him drink it. The lucinor should bring his fever down. I found more hookroot to make a new dressing for his wound. I don't like the way it looks. I think that's what's causing the fever."

He glanced at Peristra. "It's not bad, though. I'm sure this will take care of it."

She turned away, rubbing her eye with the heel of her hand. "What can I do to help?"

Timothy waved in the direction of his saddlebags. "Get my big cooking pot and heat some water. Make sure it boils, then let it cool a bit. We'll use some to make him a drink and the rest to wash the wound when we change the bandage."

"All right," she said. "If you hear anything while I'm gone to fetch the water, wake Raendel."

"He looks exhausted," Timothy said. "Maybe we should let him sleep a little longer."

Peristra considered the tuft of white hair sticking out of Raendel's bedroll. "That would be nice. He's been looking kind of rough. But he'll look even worse if we get caught. We can't take any chances. If there's even a hint of trouble, we wake him at once."

"All right," Timothy said. "But next time I go gathering herbs I'm going to find something for him too, to help him sleep."

"If you think you can trick him into drinking it, go right ahead. You know how hard it was just to get him to eat. I can imagine what he'll say if you try to give him medicine."

Timothy chuckled. "Yeah. I'll have to find something bitter to mix in it. Then I can tell him I'm trying to help him pay his penance."

"Ha! That would be about right. Poor Raendel." Her initial feeling of intimidation had faded, leaving in its place a vague urge to protect him from himself. "He's really a good person, if he'd just stop feeling sorry for himself long enough to see it. Oh, here's the pot! I won't be long."

They'd set up camp near a stream and she'd already walked back and forth to it several times. Even in the dark it didn't take her long to find the way. The rhythmic pounding of Timothy grinding herbs followed her all the way to the water.

Peristra filled the pot then crept back toward the campsite, testing each step carefully before putting her weight down. She wanted to avoid tripping and spilling the water, and also to avoid making any noise that might attract attention. By the time she reached the fire her arms burned with the weight of the water. She couldn't hold back a small sigh of relief as she set it down.

Timothy set aside the batch of herbs he'd been working on and opened his mouth to say something. A branch snapped in the woods behind him. He froze, mouth hanging open. Peristra waved a hand at him urgently, straining her eyes and ears for any sign of trouble.

Timothy whispered, "Do you think we should wake—"

Ten men jumped out of the surrounding woods; weapons drawn.

They grabbed Timothy and Peristra and held knives against their throats.

Raendel sat up.

Two men in dirty uniforms pounced on him. One of them clapped a hand over his mouth while the other held his arms. "Bring the gag," the man called to one of the others. "This is the one he told us to watch out for. Look at his hair."

Kenan stirred and groaned in his sleep but didn't wake up until one of the men dragged him out of his bedroll and held him against a tree. Even then he looked only half awake, squinting at the man holding him with a dazed expression.

The man holding Timothy looked back and forth between him and Kenan. "There are two boys. Which is the one we want?"

One of the others sneered at him. "You want to live a long life doin' this kinda work you better learn to pay attention. The wounded one is the prince. Probably can't do much in his condition, but we'll drug him anyway. Might as well drug that one too, just'ta make sure. The girl don't matter, we can do what we want with her."

The man holding Peristra reached around her waist with his free hand and pulled her against him. "I caught her; I get her first."

"Leave her alone!" Timothy shouted.

Peristra stared. She'd never heard him raise his voice before.

Timothy grabbed the wrist that held the knife against his throat. He pushed the blade far enough to duck under it. The man's arm twisted in Timothy's grasp. The knife fell. Timothy scooped it up and drove it into the man's stomach just under his rib cage.

Five men converged on him, two with short swords and three with knives. He shrieked and barreled into them, spinning and slashing like a wild boar. One man fell clutching his leg. Another jumped back to avoid a blow, then staggered to keep from falling over backward. Timothy lashed out at everything that came close, until a flying tackle from behind pinned him to the ground. He twisted to cut at the man who held him. Another man grabbed him by the hair and pressed a knife against his throat.

Fury boiled up inside Peristra. She screamed, projecting her rage toward the attackers. The campfire flared to double its previous size and threw sparks twenty feet in every direction. The man holding her shouted a gargled curse and hurled his knife to the ground. The grass blackened and smoked where the knife touched it.

Peristra swept her glare over the group of men across the fire. An arm of flame leaped out of the fire and struck the man holding Timothy. His shirt burst into flames. He fell over backward, shrieking. The man nearest him ran to help. Peristra focused her anger on that man, and a ball of fire engulfed him.

Metal scraped against leather as a sword slid out of its sheathe behind her. Pain exploded in the back of her head and her legs buckled. Strong arms squeezed her from behind. A gruff voice spoke near her head. "I think we gotta drug this one too."

CHAPTER THIRTY-SIX

Queen Havilah opened her eyes and tasted the familiar ache in her bones. Sleep dragged her down in random bursts, but the pain followed her even into her dreams. Kris or Lucas brought several more bottles of the medicine. Whenever they entered, she would pretend to be asleep until they left. As soon as they left the room, the new medicine followed the previous bottles into the mattress. The routine of waking and sleeping blurred together until she lost track of how long she had been here. The overwhelming flood of pain she'd endured left her feeling battered and numb. Her nerves still tingled from the experience, making everything else feel distorted. Even hunger had faded to nothing more than a vague sick churning in her stomach.

Door hinges creaked. She closed her eyes to feign sleep. No heavy footsteps broke the silence, only the whisper of bare feet against the stone floor. She couldn't imagine Kris or Lukas coming in without the heavy boots they always wore, and they weren't likely to be afraid to wake her. She cracked her eyes open.

One of the Adoël stood next to the bed, setting a new medicine bottle on the table. He dropped into a bow as soon as he noticed the Queen looking at him. "Forgive me Your Majesty, I didn't mean to wake you. Lord Kris sent me with a new bottle of medicine for you. Do you require anything else?"

"Many things, most of which you can do nothing about." The warble that had replaced her voice startled her, but she cleared her throat and pressed on. "For now, some water, a little fruit, and clean sheets for the bed would be very nice. What's your name?"

"I am called Joel, Your Majesty."

"Thank you, Joel. Is there any news from King Devin?"

Joel looked down and picked a piece of lint off his shirt. He bit his lip and glanced toward the door. Havilah worried that perhaps he had been sent by Kris or her brother to spy on her, but she tried to keep her worry from showing on her face. "You can tell me about the king, Joel. I am well enough to handle it, and I need to know what's going on. What is it?"

The young servant kept his head lowered as he spoke, running his hand nervously up and down the rough white fabric of his robe. "I heard that a message came from King Devin two days ago by pigeon. Our army suffered defeat and have fallen back to the hills. Part of the enemy army split off and are headed this way. He said to prepare the castle for a long siege. He doesn't know whether he will be able to help us."

Havilah knew the character of the Adoël. They would die before betraying her or the king. She hated to deceive someone so trusting. But others in the castle could not be trusted. The less he knew, the safer they both would be. She rubbed her forehead. "Send a message to Master Jabal in the library, tell him what's happening. Tell him I am recovering, but that he shouldn't come back into the castle for a while. Say that because of—because of certain things we discussed it might not be safe for him, but I have the situation under control. Tell him I'll keep passing him information as I can."

"Yes, Your Majesty." Joel bowed and took a step toward the door.

"Joel? One more thing. If anyone asks you, tell them I never woke. I wouldn't want them to worry about me."

"As you wish, Your Majesty. Do you still want the things you asked for?"

She debated with herself. After so long lying in these filthy sheets with no proper food, she craved those little touches of comfort. But she did have to be careful. The water wouldn't arouse suspicion. She had drained the bowl dry. But clean sheets and fruit might be too much risk. Most servants wouldn't go so far without being told.

"No," she said. "Just the water. If anyone asks, just tell them that you noticed the empty water bowl."

He smiled, and bowed. "Yes, Your Majesty."

She waited a few seconds after the door closed before she opened the medicine bottle and poured it into the mattress.

MASTER LENORE STRUGGLED TO QUELL HER UNEASE AND desperation. She focused on breathing. Her steady heartbeat pulsed, giving her a connection back to her own body. She pressed deeper into the darkness of Master Deborah's mind.

She'd learned, over the course of the last dozen meetings, to recognize the arrival of another person by a change in the atmosphere. A warm puff, like a breath, stirred. She began to speak even before Jabal's image took shape in the darkness.

"Jabal! Have you found anything at all on the Shadow-weavers? They have decimated our army. I fear we won't last another battle without some kind of miracle. King Devin's forces have withdrawn to the hills. They no longer have the strength to meet the enemy on the open field. They've had us pinned here for three days. Meanwhile, part of the enemy army is moving north toward the castle. I don't think they carried much with them, they may be trying to move quickly enough for a surprise attack. Queen Havilah holds a strong position with months of supply. I know she can withstand a siege for a long time, but unless we can break free and help her the castle will eventually fall."

"I'm afraid it's worse than you know," Jabal said. "The queen sent me a message this morning through one of the Adoël. Duke Arnould has revealed himself to be as traitorous as his son. I don't think I can stop him on my own. His soldiers control the castle."

"What?" A surge of panic shook Lenore so badly that her connection to her body wavered. Her vision blurred and her footing slipped like a person trying to stand in an earthquake. "If that is true, the queen must have been forced to tell King Devin that everything is all right. Is she held captive? Can you reach her?"

"I'm afraid I cannot reach the queen myself. I'm staying hidden for fear of assassination by the duke's men. She cannot leave her chambers but sent word through the servants that she is well enough under the circumstances. As for the Shadow-weavers, all my research has turned up only one weakness, the one of which we are already aware—they are vulnerable to focused light."

Lenore fought off the despair that threatened to overwhelm her. "That is hard news, and the worst possible timing. King Devin just sent a message to the castle calling the last of his reserves to come and help us. That leaves Duke Arnould in total control of the castle with the queen trapped inside, in danger of assassination at any moment. If it is true—if Arnould and Erick are working together—we have already lost. The information about the Shadow-weavers doesn't really help us at all. I am the only one who can focus light, and I can't defeat all the Shadow-weavers alone—"

"Take heart, my old friend," Jabal said. "The queen lives and has found a way to pass information to me. She has a few people on the inside to help her. And while there doesn't seem to be any more information on Shadow-weavers, I *have* found references to the Adoël that intrigue me. I discovered one old manuscript that suggests the power of the Adoël to work illusions is related to the Art of Light-Bending. If that is true, then you aren't the only one who can focus light. You must speak to Master Othniel and convince him to allow the Adoël to help you."

"That is the thinnest of hope," Lenore said. "The Adoël will refuse to fight, as they always have. What could I tell them that might convince them to break a hundred years of tradition?"

"They must. It's as simple as that. The Adoël are our last hope. Faced with the choice of fighting or seeing the kingdom fall into the hands of evil, surely they will fight."

"If we have no other options, then I will try," Lenore said. "I'll meet you again here next time I can get away. If things go poorly, I will meet you in eternity. Farewell, my friend."

Lenore retreated into her own body. She sent a messenger asking Master Othniel to meet her outside the cave where the Adoël slept. They stood close together in the darkness, neither of them carrying a light for fear of attracting the attention of the enemy camped in the valley below.

Master Othniel responded exactly as she had feared. "Never! What you ask is impossible. You know our laws."

Lenore put a hand on his arm. "Please Othniel, we have no other chance. You know I wouldn't ask this of you if there were any other way. You must help us, or we'll all die here."

Othniel pulled his arm away. "Better to die than to break our oath again."

Lenore clasped her hands together. "Why, Othniel? If you will condemn us all to death for the sake of your tradition, at least tell us what we are dying for."

Othniel's eyes flashed. "It is not just a tradition. The sin of our ancestors weighs on us every day. Killing is a mortal sin. We will not jeopardize our souls to save our bodies from death."

"Very well then, you leave me no choice," Lenore said. "I didn't want to put you in this position. If it were only your own lives in danger, I would applaud your decision, but thousands of innocent lives depend on you. I'll call a meeting with all the Adoël and present my case before the king. Gather your people and meet me outside King Devin's cave."

Lenore turned away without waiting for a response. She needed to send messages to the king and the other members of the war council. All the commanders of the army should be there as witnesses, no matter the outcome. She prayed the Adoël could be persuaded, by whatever means. If they could not, the kingdom would fall.

CHAPTER THIRTY-SEVEN

Between the Adoël, the commanders, and an assortment of soldiers and other staff who somehow got word of the meeting and came to watch, a crowd of several hundred pressed around Master Lenore and Master Othniel while they presented their arguments to King Devin.

The king looked from one to the other, his thoughts betrayed only by the steady clenching and unclenching of his left hand. When they all finished speaking, his breathing slowed, and the fingers of his left hand uncurled.

"Master Othniel, you are bound by the laws of your people," Devin said. "You are also bound to my service. I have always tried to treat you with respect and have never before asked of you anything you were not willing to give. But as you are bound to your laws, so I am bound to mine. I am king, and that means I must do whatever I have to do to save this kingdom. As your king and your master, I command you to speak. The time for secrets has passed. I must make a decision, and to do that properly I must have all the facts. Tell us why you won't fight."

Othniel set his jaw and remained silent. A cloud of despair

settled over Master Lenore's heart. Even the king's command wouldn't compel Othniel to reveal a reason for his refusal.

Some of the younger Adoël began to murmur, and from somewhere in the group a voice said, "Tell him." Other voices sounded in agreement. The waves of murmuring grew louder until at last Othniel turned to Devin and bowed stiffly. "Very well, I will speak."

He lowered his head, refusing to look King Devin in the eye as he spoke. His voice carried, clear and strong, and held an uncommon note of pride. "My king, we were once the same as you in appearance and in strength. We labored as servants to a Messenger of the Light who went by the name of Ophis. Few could match his skills in the Spiritual Arts, or as a blacksmith. His mastery of the Art of Crafting has not been seen again since his time. His passion for knowledge knew no limit, and no fear. Then something happened to him. He lost someone he loved. His quest for vengeance led him down dark paths. In his lust for revenge, he gave himself over to evil, and became a Messenger of the Dark. The darkness transformed him into a different man. He even took a new name. From that day, he's been known by the name of Morgoth."

Master Lenore's head jerked back. She knew that name. Every apprentice to the Spiritual Arts learned the name Morgoth as one of their first lessons. It served as the prime example of what can happen when a Master of the Arts gives in to selfish ambition. In all her years of study she'd never heard that name associated with the Adoël before.

"Our first, and probably the worst, of our sins was this," Othniel said. "We saw the change in Ophis and did nothing. When our master first allowed himself to be seduced by the Dark, we should have tried to stop him. If we could not stop him, we should have left his service. We did neither. We stayed and followed him into the darkness. We didn't intend to give ourselves to evil, but we made no effort to stop it from happening. We tried to close our eyes, to avoid choosing, and in doing so we made the wrong choice."

Master Othniel fixed his eyes on King Devin. "That was our first and greatest sin, but it was not our last. Morgoth became obsessed with power. He spent all his energy finding new ways of gaining control over others. At his personal forge, he began work on what would be his last and greatest creation. A sword that steals the power of its victims."

King Devin's face turned as white as the Adoël.

Othniel nodded. "Yes, Morgoth is the one who forged Anglachel."

"That can't be right!" King Devin held up his hands in denial. "Everyone knows that Arkos, who founded our dynasty, forged Anglachel. All the record books agree that the sword was passed from father to son, straight down the line from the time it was created. How could this Morgoth have forged it? I don't remember any Morgoth in my family tree, so if he forged it, then how did it get from there to my father's hand?"

Othniel waited for Devin's tirade to finish, then answered him with calm dignity. "You will find, Your Majesty, that the men who write history books can be deceived as easily as any other man. Especially when they are eager to be deceived. It is true that Anglachel has been in your family since the time of Arkos. But Arkos did not forge the sword. He took it from Morgoth, once known as Ophis. Just as Morgoth finished his work, Master Arkos broke into the smithy and attacked Morgoth. Morgoth called on his servants to help him, to distract his attacker long enough for him to strike him once. One cut from Anglachel would have ended the fight. And so, for the second time, our ancestors betrayed their master. He called on them for help and they ignored his commands. They hid in the shadows watching his fall. Once again, they failed either to protect their master or to leave him as they should have. This was our second sin."

Master Othniel's defiant tone and stiff posture exuded pride, in contrast with the shame he talked about. Most of the gathered Adoël held their hands clasped together in front of their waists, eyes downcast. They accepted the burden of shame without protest. A few, however, showed a touch of defiance. One in particular, near the front of the group, wore a thoughtful expression.

"Morgoth drove away the Messenger," Master Othniel continued. "But he suffered a mortal wound in the process. When Arkos returned to kill Morgoth and take the sword, the first Adoël begged him to allow them to redeem themselves in his service. Our ancestors, Morgoth's servants, once had the same potential to learn and grow in the Physical Arts as any other man or woman today."

Master Othniel ran his fingers through his white hair, pulling it away from his head, drawing attention to its unnatural hue. "These obvious traits that mark us are merely incidental. The primary effect of the curse blocks our ability to use Biomancy or Pathomancy. Our bizarre appearance sparked fear in the general population. At that time, we had no skill with illusions. Without magic to protect ourselves, our people faced death at the hands of frightened mobs. With no other options, they offered to make themselves servants to Arkos and his family for life. They only asked that he keep their past a secret. Arkos agreed, not only for their sakes, but also so he could claim the sword as his own. His secret hid behind ours. He conquered kingdoms using power drawn from Anglachel, and then passed it to his son. He always kept its true origin a secret, not even telling his family. We, the Adoël, have served faithfully the penance laid on us by our fathers. A penance our fathers deserved. Twice they failed their master—"

"But I don't understand," Devin interrupted. "They failed Morgoth, who was evil, not Arkos. You said yourself that they only became his servants because they had no other option. Why should you have to serve anybody? Why should you continue to suffer for their actions? Their choices don't seem like failure to me, only self-preservation. Why should you carry guilt for that?"

Master Othniel frowned. "Morgoth turned to evil in the end, but he did not begin that way. They had sworn to serve him. They should have either obeyed him or left him, but they did neither. They betrayed their oath. They willfully refused to submit to his commands, and yet they refused to leave his service. And then, while still bound to his service, they failed to protect him. Many people died because of their actions, and we bear that burden. The value of a life cannot be measured. How could that debt be paid in one generation? We continue to make small payments against what we owe, by dedicating our lives as servants of the God of Light. We will do anything to serve our master, except commit another sin. We have quite enough to atone for already, too much blood on our hands. We will not add to our sins by shedding more blood. That is why war is the one thing we cannot be part of. You cannot ask this of us. You must not ask it of us. Not ever. Not for any reason."

Devin lowered his head. His lips twisted as if tasting something bitter. "Thank you for sharing this. Although I don't fully agree with the reasoning behind your belief, at least I now understand that your people carry a heavy burden. Even so, the time has come to set aside your own burdens for the sake of the Kingdom. You must help us. If you do not, we will all die together."

Othniel crossed his arms on his chest. "We cannot."

"Help us."

"No."

Devin and Othniel stared into each other's eyes. Lenore fought the urge to grab Othniel by the throat and shake him. *How can someone who claims to be dedicated to the king's service display such open rebellion?*

Something about Othniel's attitude struck Lenore as wrong. His face displayed too much pride for one who claimed to be so humble. The rest of the Adoël shrank into themselves, as if trying to avoid being pulled into the confrontation. They knew the story already, but this was the first time their duty to the king had come in direct conflict to their duty to Master Othniel. Every one of them stood with their head lowered and their eyes fixed on the ground. They shifted their feet and seemed to be trying to avoid notice even more than usual.

The Adoël that Lenore had noticed before, standing near the

front of the group, scowled at the ground with more anger than timidity. She trembled and muttered, biting her lip and shaking her head. Her private struggle seemed to reach a conclusion. She pressed her lips together and stepped forward. "Master Othniel, I have something to say."

"Hold your tongue, Aeriel." Othniel shifted his glare from Devin to her. "If you have something to say you can tell me later, in private. Remember your place."

Aeriel flinched but didn't step back. "No. I will speak here. Now. What I have to say is for everyone. The time for false humility and self-imposed shame has gone, if there ever was such a time. We have become too proud of our humility, and our shame causes us to act in ways we should be ashamed of."

Othniel's mouth opened and then snapped closed again without speaking. His hand rose as if demanding Aeriel to stop or shielding himself from her words. The other Adoël stared, wide-eyed. They glanced at each other, but otherwise none of them moved or spoke.

"Our fathers committed one sin," Aeriel said. "Only one, although they let it shape their actions at least twice. Their sin was cowardice. Cowardice stopped them from confronting Ophis when he first turned to darkness, and cowardice stopped them from leaving his service. Cowardice stopped them from acting at the end when he was killed. We sinned by failing to act when we knew we should. How can we ever atone for our sin if we willfully commit the same sin over and over again? How can we break the curse if we go on repeating the same actions that brought the curse on our heads to begin with?"

"For the last time, be silent!" Othniel's voice trembled. "You don't know what you're saying. Our sin was indecision and failure to protect the life of our master."

"I say again, our sin was cowardice. Standing by and doing nothing when we should have fought. Like you are doing now."

A collective gasp escaped the watching Adoël. Master Othniel's jaw hung slack.

"Master Singer," Aeriel said. "You may choose to go on wallowing in self-pity and cowardice if that is how you want to live, but I will live that way *no longer*. I hate violence. I detest killing. I wish that nobody would ever hurt anyone else. But I am not so foolish as to think it will go away just because I want it to. As long as there is evil in the world there will come a time when there is no other way to stop it. To refuse to stand against evil is as bad as to commit it yourself. Our enemies will not stop simply because we ask them nicely. There is no reasoning with that kind of evil. If we do not want evil to control our world, we must fight. If we ever want to atone for our sin, we must fight. If we wish to lay claim to any amount of mercy or human dignity, we must fight."

Master Othniel's face grew darker with each word she spoke. As soon as she finished, he opened his mouth to answer.

Master Lenore broke in before he could speak. "Peace, old friend. There may be a grain of truth to what she says, even if her attitude leaves something to be desired."

She held up her hand against Othniel's protest. "There is truth in your words as well. Choosing peace is not cowardice, and fighting is not bravery. You make hard choices and stand by them in the face of opposition. I respect your beliefs, and your courage. We aren't asking you to kill men. We only ask that you help us destroy the demons. Surely killing demons is not a sin."

Othniel's breathing slowed, his face slowly returning to its normal color. The stiff muscles of his back relaxed. "You speak wisdom, my friend. And your timing is impeccable, as always. Thank you for taking the part of a peacemaker and showing me the way. Your Majesty, I will not kill men. Killing men is still a product of evil, and not less so for being made necessary by evil men. But I can offer you this much—I will fight demons. I will help to destroy evil spirits. If there is some way, we can help stop these Shadow-weavers, we will do it."

Aeriel blinked and shook herself, a smile twitching at the corners of her mouth. Master Othniel frowned at her, his eyes promising consequences later. She managed to look both chastised and pleased with herself at the same time.

Lenore laid a hand on Master Othniel's arm. "Dear friend, you are a good man. I wouldn't dream of asking you to violate your conscience. Come with me, and I will tell you what I know about Shadow-weavers."

CHAPTER THIRTY-EIGHT

The door creaked. Queen Havilah peeked out between her eyelids. The young Adoël slipped into the room. Havilah opened her eyes and sat up. "Joel? You're early today. What's going on?"

Joel spoke in a hurried whisper. "We have to go, Your Majesty. Duke Arnould and Lord Kris are no longer trying to hide their treachery. The enemy arrived, walked through the city unopposed, and have been welcomed into the castle without a fight. I fear your life is in danger now that they have shown their hand. Come with me quickly."

She threw back the blankets and pulled on her sandals. "So, they *have* been working with Erick all this time. Where are we going?"

He cracked open the door and peered out into the hall. "I'll take you to the kitchens for now. We can hide you there disguised as one of us. But, Your Majesty, there is something you should know. I saw Lord Erick as he arrived at the castle. Something about him seemed not quite right. He stumbled as he walked through the gates, for no apparent reason. No external reason, at least. It seemed as though he were fighting with something inside himself to stay upright. His eyes didn't match his face somehow. Judging by his face I would have said he feels confident, triumphant, even arrogant. But his eyes looked tortured. I didn't speak to him myself, but I asked the other servants who did. They believe that isn't really Lord Erick."

"What do you mean?" said Havilah. She stopped walking to give Joel time to check the next cross-corridor. "Describe him."

He looked around the corner, then waved the Queen forward. "A thin man, almost unnaturally so. He had dark, sunken eyes, and his nose was bent to the side as if smashed. Twisted lips, though I couldn't tell if that was their natural condition or just his bitter expression."

Havilah nodded. "Yes, that's Erick. My nephew has a quite distinct look about him. I've only seen him a few times, but his image is burned in my mind from the day of the attack."

"Still, I can't get over the feeling that it was not really him in that body." Joel hurried down the corridor toward the next intersection. "I don't know how to explain it any better than that, but of course you might be right. Duke Arnould thought it was Lord Erick too, and I would expect him to know his own son. Duke Arnould and Lord Kris met him at the gate. But there's more to it than only my imagination. When others called him Erick, he told them that's no longer his name. He said his name is Morgoth."

He emphasized the name, both with his tone of voice and with a significant look. He seemed to expect some response. The name did sound familiar, but she had to think about it for a moment before she remembered.

"I heard a story," she said. "About a Messenger of the Light who fell into darkness. I think he called himself by that name. The rest escapes me at the moment. Do you know that story?"

"Yes, Your Highness," Joel said. "To my shame, I do. He died generations ago, but his name is well known to all the Adoël. He is the one who cursed us. It's been said he turned to Necromancy, that he made contact with creatures from the shadow world. That some of them served him. Things like Shadow-weavers. Other things with no name, but creatures that look a great deal like what I saw in the court-yard today."

A shadow crossed Joel's face. He turned and continued down the hall toward the kitchens.

"What things?" Havilah asked. "What did you see?"

"The man who called himself Morgoth gave orders to Duke Arnould," Joel said. "The duke lost his temper, yelling about how he was in charge of this operation and wasn't going to take orders from his own son. Morgoth's soldiers grabbed the duke and Lord Kris from behind. Morgoth pulled a small box out of his robes and opened it. Things came out of it. I'm not sure what manner of creature. They looked like black snakes, but they floated in the air like smoke."

He stopped in front of the door to the kitchen and took several deep breaths, as if steeling himself to continue. "The duke yelled for his guards. A few responded, from near the gate, but not nearly enough to overpower Morgoth's soldiers. His men moved with inhuman speed, and incredible strength. They held the duke's guards captive as these creatures floated across to the duke and Kris and slid up into their noses. They screamed, then fell limp and quiet. When Morgoth's soldiers released them, they moved like men who are walking in their sleep. That's when I left to come find you. I thought he might come for you next."

"They will pay for this." Havilah clenched her fists. "As soon as you leave me, go to Master Jabal and tell him everything you've seen."

They entered the kitchens. Joel nodded to two Adoël working there. The lack of surprise on their faces made Havilah think they expected her. Joel led her to the back corner near the cupboards.

"You'll have to stay here all the time, Your Majesty," he said. "You can eat and sleep here. There's a closet for personal business. As long as you stay nearby, we can keep you disguised as one of us. If anyone comes looking for you, just keep your eyes down and don't speak. We cannot disguise your voice."

Havilah laid a hand on his arm. "Thank you, Joel. I will remember your kindness."

"I am only doing my duty, Your Majesty," Joel said, bowing. "We have sworn to serve you and your family until death, and that is what we will do."

CHAPTER THIRTY-NINE

Peristra drifted on the edge of consciousness, her dreams merging with reality. She dreamed of a hunt, riding through thick brush. Only instead of her chasing prey, something chased her. Her horse crashed through the overgrowth in a mad panic. She tried to pull in the reins to guide it but somehow her arms wouldn't respond. Something pushed against her back. Everything else faded, but whatever had pushed her continued to press and shake her.

She opened her eyes, but her brain couldn't sort out what she saw. Was that a wall? Why was it so close to her face? Her bed felt unusually hard, and it vibrated as if someone were jumping on it. It felt far too early for the maid to be waking her.

"Leave me alone," she said. "I'm tired."

The scent of old urine hit her, making her stomach clench. She closed her eyes. She had no hope of going back to sleep, but she didn't feel like waking up yet either. Someone pressed against her back again, shaking her insistently.

"Five more minutes," she said. "I promise I won't be late."

She couldn't remember why she would need to wake up this

morning, but it must have been something urgent. The next push hit her between the shoulder blades, hard enough to hurt.

"Ow," she said. "I'm up!"

She tried to sit up, but her arms wouldn't move. The bed dropped away, then slammed into her hard enough to bruise. Her eyes snapped open, and this time she made slightly more sense of what she saw.

"Why am I sleeping in the back of a wagon?" she said. "What's going on?"

A muffled sound came from behind her, like someone trying to talk around a mouthful of food. She tried to roll over, and realized her hands were tied behind her back. She bumped against something soft. She twisted herself far enough to see, and recognized Prince Kenan lying next to her. Memory flooded back.

"Kenan!" she said. "Are you alright?"

He didn't respond. The noises she'd been hearing continued from her other side. She pushed with her feet and finally managed to rotate far enough to see Raendel, bound and gagged. Her most recent memories came back to her, foggy and distant.

"They drugged us, didn't they?" she said. "Why are you awake already? Didn't they drug you too?"

Raendel rolled his eyes and worked his jaw, muffled sounds coming out around the gag.

"Oh," Peristra said. "I guess I won't get many answers out of you that way. Maybe I should try to take that gag off."

He nodded emphatically. She rolled over to get her knees underneath her then pushed herself up into a sitting position. She turned sideways to Raendel and stretched her fingers out as far as she could. "Roll over here, let me see what I can do with that thing."

He scooted over next to her then rolled on his side and lifted his head as high as he could. It took quite a bit of twisting and blind reaching, but finally got her hands on the knot. She tugged on it a couple of times. "It would help if I could see it while I work on it. I'm afraid if I pull on the wrong part, I'll only make it tighter."

Raendel stayed quiet, trying to hold as still as possible. She found a good grip and pulled as hard as she could.

"It's no good," she said. "I can't get any leverage with my wrists tied together. Then again, I guess we don't have anything better to do."

The wagon jolted, knocking her sideways into Timothy. He mumbled something incoherent, pushed her away, and opened his eyes. He blinked a couple of times and licked his lips. "What—? Tastes like tea made from bloodthorn leaves. Mother used to give me that when I was a kid to help me sleep. She never made it this strong."

"Whatever it was," Peristra said, "it's wearing off. Which means they'll probably give us another dose soon. Come on, help me get Raendel's gag loose. Maybe he can help us get out of here."

Timothy started to roll over to them, then stopped. "I've been thinking about something. That fire that burned up the guard just before we were captured? They talked like they thought you made that happen. Did you? If you did, how? And if you didn't, then who did?"

She shrugged. "It might have been me. Something like that happened before. I didn't do it on purpose, I was just angry. There was a burning feeling, then I lashed out and things caught on fire."

"Could you do it again? You could kill the guards and get us out yourself."

"No, I don't think so. I'm too tired to feel angry right now. Whatever they gave us affects my mind some way. I feel kind of numb. Anyway, I think it only works on things I can see. What could I do? Set the wagon on fire with us tied up in the back of it?"

"I don't know," Timothy said. "Maybe you'll think of something. Until then, I'll do what I can to help Raendel loose."

The wagon lurched to a stop, and all three of them fell over. In unspoken agreement, they all stayed quiet, pretending to be asleep. The flap opened and two guards climbed inside. They grabbed Timothy and shook him.

"Wake up now," one of them said. "Time for your evenin' medicine. Give us any trouble and we'll knock you over the head again."

Another guard gestured toward Raendel. "Boss said to drug that one too, now that we're close to the castle. We don't want any accidents."

Timothy groaned dramatically, "I need a rest stop."

"You can water the side of the wagon," the guard said. "No fancy chamber pots around here."

"No." Timothy doubled over, shaking. "I think I ate something bad. It's giving me cramps. Last time this happened we had to bury the chamber pot because we couldn't get rid of the stink. I should go into the woods at least, maybe find a stream to wash in. Do you really want to be smelling me for the rest of this journey?"

The guard's mouth twisted, and he turned slightly green. "Wait here. Don't move until I get back."

He walked off a few paces and conferred with the other guards. The remaining guard pressed the water skin against Raendel's mouth, pulling at the gag with his other hand to move it out of the way without untying it. With the guard distracted, Timothy leaned over and whispered to Peristra. "If I can find some ashberries, those should counteract the drug they're giving us. If I give you something when I come back, just eat it."

The guard returned with a long rope. "All right, then. I'm going to untie your feet, but I'm going to tie one end of this rope around your wrists, and I'll be holding on to the other end of it. If you try to run, I'll kill you. If you do somehow manage to get away, I'll kill the girl instead. So don't try anything. Got it?"

Timothy dropped his eyes and nodded. "Yes, sir."

While that guard led Timothy off into the trees, two other guards approached the back of the wagon. One of them carried a water skin. He poured some into Raendel's mouth through the gag. Then he turned to Peristra.

"Wait." She glanced toward the trees where Timothy had gone. "I have to relieve myself too."

The guard's eyes narrowed. "Don't tell me you have the same problem as that other one. We can't take you all off into the woods."

"No, I can just squat beside the wagon." She stretched her eyes as wide as she could, tilting her head to give him her best innocent child look. "It won't take any extra time since we're waiting for Timothy anyway. Please?"

The guard drew his sword. "All right, but don't think I've forgotten what happened when we first caught you. If anything catches on fire, the first thing I'll do is cut off your head. And don't try to play shy. I'm going to stand next to you with my sword ready. If anything funny happens, you die first. Then your Adoël friend here. We're only keeping you alive because the boss wanted to know more about you, but it's not worth our lives. Give us any trouble and you die."

She nodded meekly, and mentally pleaded with Timothy to hurry. The guard cut her ankles loose and pulled her out of the wagon. He loosed her hands and retied them in front. She made a great show of trying to pull down her undergarments while keeping herself covered with her long riding jacket. She took as long as she dared. It helped that she really did have to relieve herself. Even so, once she got her undergarments clear and squatted, she held it in. She glanced at the guard and then looked away as if embarrassed. "It's hard to do this with you watching."

"Too bad," the guard said. "Do it now or wet yourself later, whatever suits you. I'm not leaving you alone. You're lucky I'm allowing you this much. Hurry up. We're leaving as soon as that other one gets back."

She finished her business, then took her time pulling up her stockings. Going slow didn't require much pretending. It took long enough with her wrists tied together and a man standing over her with a sword. As soon as she finished, the guard led her to the back of the wagon and tied her feet together again.

Timothy stepped out of the trees.

The guard pushed the water skin against her mouth. "Drink now.

Don't make me force it down you again. Last one before we reach the castle."

She took a few reluctant swallows, hoping it wasn't too much. *Just a little longer,* she thought. *Maybe he found those berries.* The guard lifted her into the wagon. By the time Timothy climbed in next to her, she couldn't keep her eyes open any longer.

Timothy pushed something into her hand. "I told the guard if he let me collect these, they wouldn't have to feed us from their own rations. He doesn't know what they are. Eat them as soon as you can."

CHAPTER FORTY

Seriam dangled her feet over the edge of the rock shelf overlooking the valley. The morning sun beat against her back, casting her silhouette out among the other long shadows that stretched across the valley.

The enemy camp had grown depressingly visible. It spread out across the entire width of the valley floor and bustled with morning activities. The days had been hard on the besiegers but even harder on the besieged. Morgoth's army kept their vigil with full stomachs. King Devin's army stood watch night and day, fearing an attack, but they did it on siege rations. A few more days and they would be starved out.

King Devin's original army of ten thousand had shrunk to half that number. The enemy camp had grown enough that it outnumbered them by almost two to one. Worst of all, soldiers had been reporting sightings of familiar faces among the enemy. Comrades taken prisoner in a skirmish might show up the next day on the other side of the battle. These transformed prisoners wielded unnatural strength, and eyes that lacked any spark of recognition or mercy when confronted by old friends. Master Lenore said those men must have been possessed by some kind of spirits, like Ephron had been. With that fate in mind, surrender was not an option.

Seriam watched with mixed feelings as the crossbow teams prepared to ride out. Ephron would spend this day in the relative safety of the nurses' tents recovering from his broken leg, out of reach of the fighting unless things went badly. But that also meant she had to leave him to come watch the battle. She wanted to stay beside him, but she also wanted to help protect him. Perhaps it was only a silly fantasy, but she kept feeling that if she could kill even one more Shadow-weaver it could be the difference that turned the battle in their favor.

An alarm sounded from the enemy camp as the front lines of the Storvian army marched onto the field. The enemy's infantry formed ranks to meet the attackers. She counted nearly thirty Shadow-weavers spread across the enemy line, more than they'd started with. Only ten crossbow teams remained to face them. Several Adoël now accompanied each of the remaining team. Seriam held her breath, hands clasped together in front of her. Tension and worry swept through her, smothering any chance she had of building up anger.

A volley of arrows lifted from the enemy archers, falling among the Storvian soldiers with small effect. The Shadow-weavers charged. The Storvian infantry settled into defensive formations. The demons, shrouded in life-draining blackness, crashed into the Storvian infantry. The crossbow teams charged. The infantry dodged and fell back before the Shadow-weavers, just trying to hold them off long enough for a crossbow team to arrive.

The first of the crossbows moved into position. The Shadow-weaver spat out its cloud of darkness. A brilliant light flared around the Shadow-weaver, tearing the cloud of darkness apart like smoke in a strong wind. The demon staggered and covered its eyes. The crossbows fired, half of them targeting the Shadow-weaver and the other half firing into its supporting infantry. The creature fell, bristling with shafts. The Storvian infantry stepped in to finish off the enemy support team while the crossbows turned to ride away. Cheers rose from the battle lines, and King Devin's men attacked with renewed vigor.

Seriam's hands relaxed and fell back to her sides as hope rose up inside her to replace the tension. Her excitement grew as lights flared all along the line and more Shadow-weavers fell.

The enemy archers fired a few shots at the crossbow teams, but the mounted crossbows never stopped long enough to present a good target. The enemy arrows fell into mud churned up by the hooves of the horses as they rode out of range. The first wave of crossbow teams withdrew to the clearing behind friendly lines to reload.

A unit of enemy cavalry charged out of the trees on the far side of the clearing.

Seriam cried out a warning, knowing even as she did it that they would never hear her. The crossbowmen spotted the danger too late. Their weapons not yet loaded and only lightly armored, they scattered. The enemy pursued and cut them down as they fled.

A trumpet sounded, and the knights King Devin had been holding in reserve drove into the enemy cavalry. The enemy horsemen retreated; their mission accomplished. Two crossbow teams destroyed. The remaining eight teams continued strikes at the Shadow-weavers all morning, cutting them down one at a time. The Storvian line fell back, then held steady.

Near midday, the injustice of seeing the Storvians fighting so bravely without success built up Seriam's anger. Lightning struck down another Shadow-weaver. Several more fell to the crossbows. At last, the momentum shifted and the Storvian army pressed forward. Through the afternoon the enemy lost ground. The crossbow teams, supported by the Adoël, destroyed them one by one until only a few remained.

A trumpet sounded from the enemy camp. The few surviving Shadow-weaver units pulled away from the front lines. As the demons withdrew, a new wave of infantry charged in from Morgoth's camp. The enemy reserves and night watchmen swelled their numbers until the Storvian line fell back again under the sheer number of attackers.

I have to help them. Seriam clenched her hands into fists, consciously building up the rage inside her. *But who do I target?* The Shadow-weavers had all either fallen to crossbow teams or withdrawn, effectively out of the battle. The rest of the enemy line had merged into a seething mass of infantry that offered no clear individual targets.

A fresh squad of infantry marched in to reinforce the enemy's right flank. Polished armor winked in the sunlight. Brightly colored banners waved in the breeze, marking them as some kind of special unit.

Seriam focused her anger on one of that group who seemed to be giving orders. Heat burned between her eyes. Lightning flashed, and the enemy officer collapsed in a pile of smoldering armor. The others in the unit stopped and stared, weapons hanging slack in their hands. The Storvian soldiers also reacted with shock, wasting their brief advantage by hesitating.

The enemy recovered first. They pressed their attack, and the Storvian right flank began to buckle and fold in on itself. Seriam slumped back against a rock. That strike had burned all the energy out of her and accomplished nothing.

A rumble on the horizon drew her eyes north. An idea formed in her mind. *Maybe if we have a thunderstorm, I can guide the lighting from it. That should be easier than making my own.*

But no storm clouds appeared on the horizon. Instead, a cloud of dust rose in the distance. A line of knights charged out of that cloud at full gallop, with a column of infantry close behind. Seriam lifted a hand to her mouth and bit down on her knuckle in excitement. The reinforcements from the castle had arrived.

The enemy had already committed their reserves to the battle line. They had nothing left to face this new threat. Fifty knights plowed into the enemy archers, trampled them into the ground, then turned to hit the enemy infantry from behind. The Storvian army surged forward in a renewed attack. The newly arrived Storvian infantry advanced with their spears lowered, threatening to cut off a large pocket of the enemy army. A trumpet in the enemy camp sounded retreat. As the enemy withdrew, more of them noticed the wave of soldiers coming at them from the north. The clatter of dropped weapons spread down the line from one end to the other. In moments the enemy army fled in full rout.

Elation lifted Seriam to her feet and sent her racing back to the camp. The wounded being carried in from the field slowed her steps and her smile slipped a little. They had paid a heavy price for their victory, and the war wasn't over yet.

She wanted to run to Ephron and tell him the news, but first she wanted to make sure she had all the news herself. She held herself back long enough to listen to the proclamations being made around the camp before rushing to his side.

He looked up with concern as she doubled over, gasping for breath. "Seri, darling, what's wrong?"

"Nothing," she said. "At least not yet."

She sat beside him and clasped his hand in hers. It took a few more deep breaths before she managed to continue. "The army's headed back toward the castle today to attack the enemy as he tries to lay siege. Some of the nurses are going with them, and some will stay here with the wounded who can't yet be moved."

She squeezed his hands. "I did it, Ephron. At least, I helped. I don't know how, but I called down lightning out of the clear sky. Two of the Shadow-weavers fell to my lightning. I know I could help them break the siege at the castle, too. I want to go with them, but I don't want to leave you."

He pulled a hand free, reached up and caressed her face. "Go, my love. I'll be fine. It's only a scratch. Seeing your expression when you came in, I know you won't be happy unless you're near the fighting."

She held his hand against her cheek. "I won't be happy unless I'm near you. Looks like either way I go I won't be happy."

He smiled. "I'll be with you in spirit. There's nothing more you can do for me, but you can help in the fighting. There are plenty of other nurses here who can look after me."

She clenched his hand hard enough to make him wince. "Those other nurses had best keep their hands to themselves. And so should you, if you know what's good for you."

He laid his free hand over his heart. His attempt at an innocent expression was spoiled by the grin that kept breaking free of his efforts to control it. "Consort with anyone but my favorite nurse? May I be struck by lightning if I even think of doing such a thing."

She did her best to look stern, but the corner of her mouth twitched into a smile. "That's exactly what would happen, and don't you forget it."

He laughed and pulled her down for a kiss. "I promise to behave. I'll be too scared not to. Now go on and smite another one of those creatures for me."

She pressed her lips together and nodded, overwhelmed by conflicting emotions. She stood and made her way out of the tent, stopping every two or three steps to look back at Ephron. Once she couldn't see him anymore, she set her shoulders firmly and went to collect her belongings.

CHAPTER FORTY-ONE

Peristra hung slack against the chains that bound her to the wall. The last dose of the drug had worn off, so she could have moved, but she didn't want to draw the guards' attention. Another dose of that drug would overwhelm the last of the ashberries she'd eaten just before being brought into the castle. So far, she hadn't come up with a plan. Burning one of the guards would only end up getting her killed. She had no way to free herself or her companions. This would be her last opportunity, and she had no idea what to do. She needed time to think. She couldn't let the guards standing outside the door know the drug hadn't affected her or they would give her another dose and end her last chance.

She eased her head around just far enough to look at her companions. Raendel stood chained to the wall on her left, alert but still gagged to keep him from singing. Kenan moaned in his sleep on the other side of Timothy. He still hadn't regained consciousness since the first night. She worried about him, but she couldn't afford to let it distract her now. Timothy slumped against his chains on her right, sleeping off the latest round of drugs. She hadn't known it at the time, but he'd given her all the ashberries, trusting their lives to her untrained talent. Even now the realization made her stomach twist in fear.

I didn't want to risk burning us to death in that wagon and now we're chained to a dungeon wall. They'll be coming with another dose of that potion soon. Even if I kill a few guards, we still couldn't get away. What can I do?

Boots thudded against the flagstones outside the cell. Peristra closed her eyes and feigned unconsciousness. A voice on the other side of the door said, "Open the cell. I want to examine the prisoners."

"Yes, Lord Morgoth," the guard's voice replied.

At the sound of that name Raendel's chains rattled, and he made a faint hissing sound. She cracked her eye open far enough to look at him. He pulled against his chains, shaking his head and biting the gag as if he wanted to chew through it. He froze the moment the cell door creaked open. Fear radiated off him in waves so strong she could smell it. His head shook back and forth in a gesture of denial, his eyes locked on the man who entered the cell.

The man nodded toward Raendel. "Yes, it is me. The face is new, but it's me inside. You recognize the name Morgoth don't you, little servant boy? Little Adoël. Are you here to help your master? Look in my eyes. This is the face of your true master. This is the new face of Morgoth."

Ignoring Raendel's desperate struggles, Morgoth drew a sword from the sheath at his waist and held it up toward Kenan. "At last, son of Arkos, I will have my revenge."

Kenan stirred. He lifted his head, eyes still closed. Morgoth waved the sword lazily back and forth and watched Kenan's face move to follow it.

"You want this, don't you?" Morgoth's lips twisted with grim amusement. "Is it calling to you, dear prince? Do you want to touch it? Your wish is granted."

The blade hissed through the air. Kenan's head rocked back, and Peristra clenched her teeth against a scream. A cut opened on

Kenan's cheek like a pair of tiny red lips, drooling blood. His eyes opened. He drew a deep breath, and with that breath the air returned to Peristra's lungs.

Morgoth reached out with the flat of the blade to wipe the blood into a streak of red across Kenan's chin. A flash of light rippled through the sword and then through Morgoth. His eyes rolled back in his head for a moment, and he sighed like a man laying down a hundred-year burden. "At last, Anglachel belongs to me again, as it always should have. Arkos stole it from me, and for that I will destroy his family. Soon you will die on its blade. But before you do, I will use you to capture your brother."

Kenan shook his head. He didn't seem fully alert, but he clearly recognized the threat. "Devin. Never."

Morgoth laughed. "You have no choice. Soon your brother will be laying siege outside these walls. Your brother is just like you. Your childish idealism makes you weak. It led you right into my hands, and it will do the same for your brother. When he sees you with my sword at your throat, he will do anything to save you. He'll surrender his army in exchange for your life. And without an army he won't be able to stop me from killing you both. Just like the spawn of Arkos deserves."

Anger surged in Peristra, starting in her gut and rising in a wave all the way up to her forehead until it burned in a focused point between her eyes. Her chance had come. The one they'd been looking for stood before her. The source of their pain. The head of the snake. She focused her rage on Morgoth, lashing out at him with her mind.

Morgoth turned and waved a finger at her. "That's not very polite, you know. You can't just go around setting people on fire. The guards warned me about your little trick. Don't you know I was around when the physical Arts were first discovered? I know more about it than you ever will. Whatever energy you throw at me becomes mine, and I can convert it for my own use. You can't hurt me that way. But you'd better keep that temper under control, or you'll just end up hurting yourself, and killing your friends. My guards' arrows can reach farther than your fire, and they have orders to kill you at the first sight of flame."

His mockery only made her anger burn hotter, but she held it back in frustration. It couldn't touch him. All the anger she threw at him only made him stronger. She had nothing else to try. Kenan had given everything to save her life, and now he would die, and she couldn't stop it. She fought to hold back tears. *Oh, Kenan, I'm so sorry!*

"I will give you one warning, little girl," Morgoth held up a finger, waving it under Peristra's nose. "And one warning only. If anyone in my service happens to fall victim to an unexplained fire, under any circumstances, I will come back here and kill you for it, whether you did it or not. So be nice."

Whether you did it or not. One uncontrolled burst of anger and I'll only destroy any chance I might have had to get us out of here. But there's nothing else I can do. Is there? She thought back to the night they left the castle. Kenan hiding in the straw, and the flames that had brought him out. Her anger hadn't been focused on any specific target then, not one she could see. She'd been focusing on a thought, and her eyes had just landed on the straw by chance.

I'm lucky I didn't cook Kenan alive that night, she realized. *And when that straw caught fire and he came flailing at me, I was so shocked I forgot my anger for a moment.*

Something about that memory felt significant. That night her actions had been different from the uncontrolled lashing out she'd been doing lately. More focused. The beginnings of an idea tickled the back of her mind.

Morgoth turned back to Kenan. "Where were we? Oh yes, I was explaining to you how you'll convince Devin to surrender. So, I can kill you both at once. What do you think? Do you like my plan?"

Kenan struggled weakly against his chains, his legs trying to straighten but failing. "Devin. Never. Surrender. I'd rather die."

Morgoth shrugged. "Then I'll kill you while he watches. It

doesn't matter. Regardless, the power of Anglachel is mine again. Using that power, I will defeat him anyway. It will require a bit more work that way, but the result will be the same. The idea of killing you in front of his eyes pleases me. Either way I cannot lose."

He wiped the blood off Anglachel with the corner of his cloak before sliding it back into its sheath, then turned his back on Kenan's glare. He gave instructions to the guards on his way out. "Keep the prisoners well drugged. I don't want them causing trouble before Devin arrives. Kill anybody who approaches this dungeon except me. Give a hundred gold coins each to the scouts who brought them in and tell them they have two days to spend it before they report back to me for duty."

The cell door clanged shut. Peristra looked at Kenan. "I won't let this happen. Don't worry Kenan, I'll get us out of this. I have a plan. Just hang on."

She turned to Raendel. "Turn your face away from me and brace yourself. This is going to hurt. A lot."

He stared at her for a moment, uncomprehending. At last, he shrugged, and nodded. He squeezed his eyes shut and turned his head. She focused on the knot that held his gag in place. Holding on to her anger with a tight rein, she poured a thin stream of it into that one spot.

The skin of Raendel's neck reddened. His teeth clenched and beads of sweat popped out on his throat. A wisp of smoke rose from the cloth gag. The clank of the cell door broke her concentration. Her anger slipped away.

Two guards entered, the second one carrying a tray with four cups on it. The first guard picked up one of the cups and eyed the prisoners.

"Time for your evening dose, freaks. Extra strong from now on." He shot Peristra a sharp look. "He told me to do yours first."

She had no time to think how best to deflect him. He grabbed her nose with his left hand, squeezed it shut and slammed her head back against the wall. With his right hand he held the cup to her lips, waiting for them to open. She struggled as hard as she could, trying to sneak in a quick breath through the side of her mouth. The guard moved faster, tilting the cup to let the liquid trickle into her mouth as soon as it opened. She closed her mouth and spit it out. The guard held on and waited.

Her struggles made her even more desperate for air. Her chest heaved, and her mouth opened again. The liquid poured in. This time she swallowed until it was gone, and then drew a ragged breath.

The guard released her and moved on to Kenan while she coughed and spat and shook her head to keep it clear. She turned back to Raendel, no longer caring that the guard might notice her attempt. This might well be her last chance.

Numbness crept into the edges of her thoughts, dampening her anger. Raendel's gag slipped in and out of focus. The weight of her chains seemed to multiply until she couldn't stand up under them any longer. Her lips tingled and went numb. It took all of her remaining strength to lift her head and whisper, "I can't. I'm sorry."

CHAPTER FORTY-TWO

Master Lenore ducked through the doorway into the meeting tent pitched outside the ruins of the village. A good bit of daylight still lingered, but King Devin had called an early halt for an emergency meeting with his council. She knew what the meeting was about, because she was the one who'd brought the news to the king. Still, it pained her to hear it spoken aloud.

"A message arrived from the castle," King Devin leaned forward, resting his fists on the table. "My uncle has betrayed us and opened the gates to the enemy."

Shocked murmurs buzzed through the tent. Devin raised a hand, waiting for them to subside. "Most of Duke Arnould's soldiers have joined in his treachery and will fight with the enemy. The rest have been killed."

That caused another commotion. Several officers tried to ask questions at the same time, but one question came through above the others. "What about the queen? Is there news of her?"

Devin nodded. "My mother is alive, and in hiding. The Adoël are protecting her. She's the one who sent the message to us by way of Master Jabal, who is in hiding outside the castle. He can open the city gates for us from the inside but getting into the castle itself will be more difficult."

He stood quiet for a moment to allow the group to absorb the news. Once the murmurings died down, he continued. "Lord Erick knows we're coming. He's preparing for siege. There's no sign yet that he has used the sword, but there's little hope left that he's ignorant of its history and its potential for great harm. I fear he knows more about it than we do. For our enemy, our real enemy, isn't Erick. He goes by the name of Morgoth."

Othniel's face could hardly turn any paler than it already was, but it took on a green tinge and he staggered as if he'd been struck. Normally reluctant to speak even in the best of times, he hadn't spoken a word since his people had defied him and gone into battle. Now he broke his silence. "The man claims to be Morgoth? It can't be! Morgoth has been dead for generations. It must be some impostor, some arrogant fool taking on his name. Or coincidence, even. It's only his name, it can't be him."

Master Lenore shook her head. "This stretches happenstance further than I am willing to believe. Who would take the name Morgoth? It's not a name any mother would choose for her child. This man calls himself Morgoth, made a targeted raid for the purpose of stealing Anglachel, and is aided by creatures out of our darkest legends. I would say this is no coincidence. If it's not the same man, then at least it must be someone who knows much about him and perhaps is trying to become him."

Devin's brow furrowed. "That changes some things, but nothing that affects our decisions right now. Our options are either to lay siege to the castle, to find some other way in, or to get him to come out. I loathe the thought of laying siege to my own castle for several reasons. First because some of those inside are still loyal to me and are likely to be wounded, perhaps killed in the fighting. Second because I know how hard it will be to break that castle by siege. Father often showed me the extra fortifications inside it, some he had commissioned himself."

He paced back and forth across the tent as he spoke. "In other circumstances it might be possible to compel or trick this man who claims to be Morgoth—to draw him outside the castle's safety. I don't know of any way to accomplish this, however. What lure could we possibly use? He has what he wants in the castle with him already. He is intelligent, and he holds a position of strength. He's not likely to give that up willingly."

Devin stopped pacing. He clasped his hands together behind his back. "Our remaining option is to find another way in, and I know of none. Master Lenore, do you know any way into the castle? A hidden passage, perhaps a secret door? Father never mentioned anything like that, but I suppose he might have wanted to keep such knowledge limited."

Lenore shook her head. "Hidden passages and secret doors? None that I know of. Even if there were one, it would offer no entry. Those things are designed for getting out only, never for getting in. The exit would be built so that it can only be opened from the inside. No engineer in his right mind would build an impenetrable fortress and then punch holes in it like that. It's asking for trouble."

Devin raised his hands in a gesture of surrender. "All right then, no secret entrances. What about the Art? Can you break open the gate for us?"

Lenore sighed. "I can't. For one thing, my specialty is Dream-walking, which might be useful but can't get us inside. Jabal is the Master of Biomancy. I have so little skill that my greatest effort would accomplish nothing. But Master Jabal wouldn't be able to do it either. It's not a question of strength but of mass. He could push on that gate as hard as he wants, but it is quite a bit more solid than he is. He would break his own bones before he broke that gate."

Devin rubbed his chin. "What if he used something else? Besides just his bones, I mean. He could carry a good-sized battering ram and hit the gate with that. Or throw something at it."

Lenore nodded. "Yes, he could do that. But it would be no different from twenty soldiers carrying a ram up to the gate and hitting it or firing a mechanical catapult. The mass of the ram wouldn't change just because he's the one lifting it. And a series of small hits is more effective than one heavy one anyway. Again, it comes down to mass—if he hit the gate with too much force, he could shatter the ram and hurt himself in the process. Meanwhile he would expose himself to arrows and stones and hot oil from the walls, all to do something common soldiers could do just as well or better."

Devin frowned and turned to the others. "Do any of you have an idea?"

The nobles glanced at each other and dropped their eyes. After a moment of silence one of them cleared his throat and spoke. "King Devin, I realize you are looking for an easier way. And I agree it was worth considering other options. Yet it looks like we're in for a siege. We might as well come to grips with it now and start planning."

Another of the nobles nodded in agreement. "There's no use avoiding it. It has to be done, and delay will only make it harder. A siege will be long and difficult, but we do have some advantages. We have friends on the inside that our enemy has to worry about. Also, he has only one or two thousand men remaining with him to face our five thousand, depending on how many of Duke Arnould's soldiers joined him. Also, we know the layout of the castle, so we know best where and how to attack."

"Your fears hold merit, Your Majesty," Lenore said. "If we attack the castle, it's likely that innocent people will be hurt. But if we leave Morgoth in control of the castle, innocent people will certainly be hurt. From the beginning he has shown himself willing to cut down the unarmed when it suits him. It would be a small comfort to a grieving family to tell them 'At least it wasn't me who killed your children' if you could've stopped it from happening but chose not to out of fear."

Devin's sigh seemed to rise up from his boots. "I don't want to have to face any grieving families no matter who killed their children. But if that happens it will be in spite of my best efforts to save them. Do any of the rest of you disagree? Or have other ideas?"

He looked around at them one at a time. None of them looked happy, but none offered alternatives. "It's decided, then. Tomorrow we reach the castle and prepare to lay siege."

THIS IS WORSE THAN BEING SICK IN BED. HAVILAH POKED AT THE vegetables floating in her soup. She felt awake and energetic, but still couldn't do anything. As the days dragged past, hope drained from her body. Her appetite diminished along with the hope that had given her a reason to continue going through the motions of keeping herself alive. She forced herself to take a few bites then handed the bowl back to the cook. "Thank you. The soup is good, but I can't eat right now. Perhaps later I'll try a little."

After a moment she regretted giving back the soup. Not because she was hungry but because now, she had nothing to occupy her hands. *Perhaps I should ask for yarn and do some knitting. At least it would pass the time.* She looked around, trying to decide whose work she should interrupt to ask for a ball of yarn. The humor of the situation struck her. *I'm like a bored kitten, pestering the adults to play with me.* She smothered a laugh, and then broke off when she saw Joel enter the kitchen and approach her. She sat up straight, her hands clasped tightly in her lap. "Do you have any news?"

He knelt in front of her so she wouldn't have to look up at him as he spoke. "We sent a message to King Devin. There hasn't been time for a reply to come back, so we don't even know if he got it yet. Morgoth's scouts have brought in three prisoners. One of them is Prince Kenan."

Havilah sprang to her feet. "Kenan? Here? Then he's alive! Where are they keeping him? Can you take me to him?"

Joel raised a hand against her stream of questions. "He is here, and he is alive. I think he's wounded but I can't be sure. They've drugged him and locked him in the dungeons under Morgoth's own guards. No one can get close to him."

She leaned forward and gripped Joel by the shoulders. "You have to get me to him. Can't you disguise me?"

He shook his head. "I could, but what good would that do? Who could I disguise you as? They won't let anybody get close. Any disguise I could give you has limits. I could even make you blend in with the wall if you stood still against it, but that wouldn't get you through the door. As soon as you moved, they would see you. Even if we could get close, how would we open the door? Morgoth holds the only key."

She closed her eyes and made a conscious effort to slow her breathing. Emotions swirled in her head like a whirlwind, trying to scramble her thoughts. She shoved them aside. All the energy of her emotions blew away like dust in a windstorm, leaving her mind clear and calm. "If we can't get in then we have to find a way to help him get out. He could break himself out if he weren't being drugged. That must be why they're doing it. Could you tamper with the drugs they're giving him?"

Joel thought for a moment and then nodded slowly. "It shouldn't be too hard to find out who is mixing them. Perhaps we could substitute their herbs for some of our own. I'll see what I can do."

She let go of his shoulders and stepped back. "Do that. And God help them if anything happens to him."

The light coming through the windows dimmed, and thunder crashed outside.

CHAPTER FORTY-THREE

Morgoth stood on top of the wall, peering out into the dim light. The sun had risen, but thick iron-colored clouds blocked most of the light. Those clouds had been hanging over the castle for three days now without dropping any rain. Just thick clouds that refused to go away, lit by occasional flashes of lightning. Inconsistent breezes did nothing more than stir them up a bit. It felt unnatural, and that worried him.

Devin and his army had arrived the night before. Morgoth's scouts reported that the king's army had been busy all night with some kind of activity just out of sight of the castle. The veteran commanders agreed that they were probably constructing siege machinery, and maybe fortifications in case of counterattack. Those things didn't worry him at all. He knew how to handle siege machinery.

Morgoth nodded and dismissed the scouts. He questioned commander Brach, who assured him they were well prepared. The small defensive catapults spaced around the walls had been loaded with pitch. Teams stood beside them with torches. Near each catapult they'd piled stacks of stones and more pitch for reloads. Archers lined the walls all the way around, most of them on the front wall over the main gates. All of them had strips of cloth soaked in oil as well as their standard supply of arrows. Torch runners stood ready near each squad.

"My Lord, King Devin's army wasn't prepared to lay siege to a castle when they started this campaign," Brach said. "Though we haven't yet been able to observe it, I'll wager that any siege machinery they've managed to throw together isn't likely to have much protection against fire."

"Very well then," Morgoth said. "Return to your duties on the other side of the wall. For your sake, I hope you are right. Otherwise, if things go badly, your head will be the first to fall."

Brach bowed and left. Morgoth returned to his watching.

A siege tower rolled into view out of the forest. He'd seen this kind before, and already knew what it could do. Inside the tower would be a rough staircase, or perhaps just a ladder, to the door at the top. If they'd done their job correctly, the door would be exactly the height of the castle's wall. Men climbing it would have better cover than a ladder alone would provide, and a tower couldn't be easily pushed away from the wall.

As it edged closer, Morgoth's confidence returned. They'd built the tower in a rush, leaving gaps between the rough-cut planks that could be seen even from this distance. Dark streaks down the front showed where they'd poured water over it to make it more fire resistant. But large dry patches stood out between the streaks of water. Morgoth glanced up at the threatening sky, then back down, willing himself not to be concerned about what hadn't yet happened. If the weather turned against him, he'd just have to fall back on trying to knock it down with rocks.

The tower approached at a steady pace. Before long, the base of it rolled into view, with the dark form of a column of infantry trailing behind it like a line of ants. Beside it rolled the long, low shape of a battering ram. Disturbing, but to be able to use that ram they would have to come directly to the castle gates. Which he knew would never happen. They drew near the edge of catapult range, but he preferred to wait for a closer target. At this distance it would take a lucky shot to bring them down, and ammunition for the catapults had limits.

He looked down into the courtyard and drummed his fingers against the hilt of his sword. The prisoners should be brought up to the wall any time now. He debated waiting for them to arrive. The siege engines moved slowly enough that they probably wouldn't come close by then. On the other hand, he decided, it wouldn't hurt to shake their confidence a little. "South wall, stand ready to light."

Commander Brach had trained the soldiers well. Along the wall, archers wrapped their arrows in oil-soaked cloth and the torch runners stood at alert. Two mini catapults protected this wall, one on each side of the gate. Both had loaded pitch-covered shot and waited for the order to light it up.

"Light missiles and fire when ready."

Soldiers lit the catapults and prepared to launch, while the torch runners made their way down the row of archers. Two balls of fire streaked through the air and passed close on each side of the approaching tower. While the catapults reloaded and adjusted their aim, the archers loosed their first volley. A rainbow of fire traced an arc from the castle wall, curved down, and passed straight through the tower without any visible effect.

Illusions? The first tendril of alarm coiled around his spine. Somehow Devin must have convinced the Adoël to help him. *Is there no tower, or is it in a different place? I hear the sound of its wheels, there must actually be a tower out there somewhere. How do you stop an invisible tower?*

"Hold fire," he shouted. "Two runners!"

The command to hold fire came too late to stop the catapults from firing a second round. Their aim had been corrected, but like the arrows their shots passed through the tower with no visible effect.

Two runners raced toward Morgoth. Their report confirmed that Brach had observed the same thing he had and felt a similar quandary. There could be siege towers approaching from anywhere.

How can we possibly know which one is real? Morgoth thought. *We'll have to expend every bit of our weaponry on illusions! Best not to waste the catapults until we can be sure we have a physical target.*

"Instruct the archers to each fire straight ahead," he told the messengers. "At an angle that keeps the arrow within the height of a tower for as long as possible. Tell them to spread their fire across as much space as they can, but no farther apart than half the width of the tower. Watch for any arrows that seem to strike the air or simply vanish. I'll watch as well and mark the place. When they see that happen, archers and catapults are to target that spot. You go east, you go west around the walls, telling all the division commanders until you meet on the other side. Go!"

The runners sprinted away in opposite directions. A soldier stood nearby, waiting for his chance to speak. When the messengers had gone, he stepped up. "Sir, the prisoners are here."

"Keep them below for now," Morgoth said, smiling. "And keep them quiet. I'll call for them in a moment. I want to make sure Devin understands I'm not afraid of his little siege toys."

A volley of arrows lifted from the wall in a wide low arc. Instead of all targeting a single point, the arrows flew in a straight line stretching out in a sheet of fire. Two of the arrows hung frozen in the air for a moment before they continued on their paths.

Morgoth lifted his hands to point at that spot. A ray of light beamed from his fingers. It shot out in a straight line to the place where the arrows had paused, then splashed outward like a stream of water hitting a stone wall. He maintained the beam for several seconds. The spot where it spread out against the air drew slowly closer.

The catapults fired balls of burning pitch. Both hit the target, one striking just above Morgoth's beam of light and the other just below it. As soon as the pitch struck, the air wavered and the remains of a siege tower appeared, broken and burning. Water poured from the top of the tower down the sides, but it wasn't enough to quench the flames. A moment later flaming arrows struck the tower as well, and the soldiers abandoned it like fleas leaving a dead dog.

Morgoth shouted down the wall to the soldiers standing by the flagpole. "Parley!"

The parley flag rose over the castle gates. Now he had nothing to do but wait for Devin to respond to the signal. He examined the prisoners. The redheaded girl glared at him with malevolence but seemed to have given up trying to burn him for now. The Adoël slumped against the wall, eyes closed. Probably fainted from fear. The wounded Prince stood on his own power but with his head hanging, looking ready to collapse at any moment. The other young man stood wide-eyed and trembling. Morgoth considered draining him immediately just to get him out of the way but decided he might be useful alive later. Soon the young prince and his usurper brother would be dead, and the Kingdom would once more belong to its rightful owner.

The hair on his arms stood up. A blast of energy crashed against him, only to be absorbed by his power. He threw the girl a threatening stare but realized it hadn't come from her this time. He closed his eyes and traced the power back to its source. It flowed from a window in the tower behind him.

"So, there's another one in the castle," he said to himself. "Now I have that one's attention too. I had wondered where the queen has been hiding. No matter, soon your power will be mine. Your death will come at the hand of your own dear nephew. Fitting."

He looked at Raendel and frowned. The Adoël was the least responsive of the three, barely able to lift his head. "You, son of a dog, will not die on Anglachel. I wouldn't risk corrupting it on your cursed flesh. I wouldn't want to take what you have anyway. Making pretty pictures for others? It's a disease not a talent, eating away any real power you might otherwise possess. No. You can stand there and watch your friends die. Your people have always been good at doing that. Then if you beg for your life, I might let you live to serve me again."

Raendel's eyes remained tightly shut, but his whole body twitched. The muscles in his jaw worked as if trying to speak.

"What's that?" said Morgoth. "You can't beg because you're wearing a gag? What a shame. I guess I'll have to kill you after all. Just not with Anglachel. A long, slow death by torture perhaps. There will be plenty of other rodents left to serve me."

Kenan stood slightly apart from the others. A chain looped around his neck and stretched behind him like a leash, the end held by a burly guard.

"Your time is coming, son of Arkos," Morgoth said. "You will die first on the blade of Anglachel by the hand of its true master. I've waited long enough for this. I have only one thing left to do before I take my revenge. If I cannot make your brother yield, I'll make sure he watches you die. If you struggle at all, I will cut your throat instantly, but I'll make sure your brother dies much more slowly. If you keep quiet, I might be merciful and kill you both quickly."

Kenan didn't even raise his eyes. He only nodded in silent surrender.

"Morgoth!" A voice called from outside the wall.

Morgoth reached out to the guard and took the end of Kenan's chain, then pulled him to the edge of the wall and leaned out. The blurry forms of a half a dozen men stood below. *Still hiding behind the illusion of your servants? Pathetic.* Morgoth sneered down at them. "Devin? Is that you, son of Arkos?"

"It is me, son of Darkness. What do you want?"

"I would speak to you about terms of surrender."

"That is wise of you," Devin said. "I cannot guarantee your personal safety, you have caused too many deaths. But some of your men perhaps could be pardoned. I am willing to discuss it."

Morgoth laughed. "It's not my surrender I'm talking about. It's yours."

"Why are you wasting my time with this foolishness?" Devin said, sounding annoyed. "When I'm ready to give up, I have only to withdraw. Our reinforcements carried the castle siege supplies with them when they left to come join us. You are trapped inside the castle with a weaker force and a few weeks of supply at most. The snow will begin to fall at about the same time you run out of food. Winter will seal you in better even than my army can. When the cold and hunger begin to eat away at your soldiers, how many of them will remain loyal to you then? I have only to wait. What makes you think I'll surrender now on any terms?"

Morgoth jerked on the chain, pulling Kenan up to the edge of the wall where Devin could see him. "Why will you surrender? Because I have your brother. If you want him to live, you will send your army away and surrender your kingdom to me. If you refuse, he will die."

"Kenan!" Devin's voice shook with anger and grief. "If you dare to harm one hair on his head, I will cut you into a thousand pieces and feed you to pigs. You're a liar, and you always will be. It is the nature of evil. You've already proven yourself treacherous, and I know you would betray us again if I give you the chance. If I surrender, you'd kill him anyway. That's the kind of person you are. I will accept no bargain from you. Now hear my terms. Let Kenan go and surrender the castle, and I will let you live. Harm him and you will die. Those are your only choices. What will it be?"

In response, Morgoth drew Anglachel and laid the point against Kenan's heart.

CHAPTER FORTY-FOUR

Joel burst into the kitchen and ran over to where Havilah sat knitting. She looked up at him, her muscles tensing when she saw the strain in his face. "What is it, Joel?"

"King—" Joel swallowed and drew a few quick breaths, trying to slow his breathing enough to talk. "King Devin is attacking the castle. Morgoth is on the south wall near the gates. He's had Prince Kenan and the other prisoners brought to him there."

Her knitting flew out of her lap, and she was out the door before it hit the ground. She raced down hallways, around corners, and through doors, faster with each step. Joel followed a few paces behind her. She reached a flight of stairs and ran up them two at a time until she found the first window. Looking out, she saw the east courtyard. She slapped her hand against the stone and continued to climb until she found a window facing south toward the main gate.

The windows in this tower had a wide opening on the inside and narrowed toward the outside of the wall, designed for archers to be able to shoot through it easily while remaining as protected as possible. Panting from the unaccustomed running, she squeezed her head as far as she could into the narrow window slit, twisting until she found the angle where she could see her nephew standing on the wall.

No. Not my nephew, she thought, her heart sinking. *Not Erick, but the creature who has taken his body.* She fought to quash the anguish that rose within her. Her nephew was lost, and grieving wouldn't help anything. She wasn't quite high enough to see the ground just outside the castle wall, so she fixed her gaze on the main gates and murmured, "Be careful, Devin. Oh, my son, you know you can't trust any offer he makes!"

Morgoth stood on the wall. Behind him, four figures stood in chains.

Kenan! Havilah glared at Morgoth with the full intensity of her anger. He turned his head and looked directly at her. She jumped back from the window. *He couldn't have seen me. Could he?*

By the time she leaned forward to peek out again he'd turned back to the line of prisoners. He talked to them for a moment then turned and looked down toward the ground outside the wall. Her heart sank once more as she realized what he must be doing. *He's using Kenan as a pawn. He's bargaining with Devin for Kenan's life.*

The clouds hanging over the castle swirled wildly. She glanced up at them, then back down at Morgoth. He had drawn his sword and pointed it at Kenan's chest.

He won't keep his bargain. He'll make a deal and then kill Kenan anyway. You have to get in and stop him. Hurry, Devin!

Yet she knew that even if Devin breached the castle, it was likely that both her sons would be killed. *I need to find some way to distract him!*

She looked at the gates again, her heart breaking, desperate to save her beloved sons. She wished she could pull them open by force of will alone. The swirling of the clouds intensified over the gate. A funnel dropped from the clouds, touched the gates, and rose back into the sky. The gates rattled when the funnel touched them. As the whirlwind lifted away, the massive doors tore free of their hinges and flew off into the air.

MORGOTH GLANCED AROUND AS A CRASH SHOOK THE WALL. THE castle gates ripped free of their hinges, sucked into the sky by a funnel cloud. His alarm faded. *No matter, they are too late. With Anglachel under my control again, I can destroy his entire army myself.*

He stepped forward and plunged Anglachel through the center of the prince's chest. A bond formed between them the moment the sword's tip passed through Kenan's skin. He closed his eyes, savoring the flow of power through the sword into his body.

His eyes sprang open again. Even that small action took a shocking amount of effort. Something felt wrong. His legs trembled with the effort of holding him upright. Energy flowed into him. He ought to be growing stronger. The flow of energy felt corrupted. A twisted form of power filled him, suppressing his own strength instead of enhancing it. Desperate, he tried to drop the sword, but it remained fastened to his hand as if it had become part of him.

The skin of his fingers faded to a sickly shade of white. The sudden pallor spread rapidly up his arm. He stared in horror as Anglachel turned black, twisting and sliding out of Kenan's chest. Fire erupted from the air around him, engulfing his entire body. Paralyzed by sudden weakness, he was helpless even to slap at the flames. The last thing he saw was Kenan's face flickering, changing into the face of Raendel.

CHAPTER FORTY-FIVE

K enan leaned back against his pillows and watched Peristra's hands dance in the air as she spoke. His mother had already visited this morning and explained most of what had happened. But she had to go back to her duties, passing sentence on the traitors, her brother and his son Kris. They would be hung the next morning. Kenan wanted to hear Peristra tell the story again anyway. If nothing else, it made a good excuse to stare at her. He didn't really care what she said, as long as he could watch her say it. Her face flushed from excitement so that her freckles stood out clearly around her nose while she talked about their capture and the journey to the castle. When she came to the part where she burned the soldier, she grimaced and looked away.

"I knew it was you who caused that fire the day we left the castle," Kenan said. "I thought you were just keeping it a secret."

"No," she said. "That was the first time I'd seen it happen too. I didn't really believe I'd done that. It wasn't until we were captured that I finally realized I could control it. I just wish I'd been able to control it well enough to burn through Raendel's gag before they stuck us in the castle dungeon."

"Wait," Kenan said. "You skipped ahead. We were tied up in the back of the wagon. How did we get from there to the castle?"

She wrinkled her nose at him. He wondered if she knew how fetching that made her.

"I was going to tell you before you interrupted me," she said. "Duke Arnould and Lord Kris had been plotting treason the whole time. They drugged your mother and let Morgoth into the castle thinking he was Lord Erick. Once he got inside, he did something to them that made them like that man who attacked us our first day out. Once he had them under control, he held the castle uncontested. The men who captured us brought us straight here to the dungeon. Morgoth planned to use you to trick King Devin into surrendering."

Kenan nodded. "I kind of remember that. I'd recovered a little by then. What happened at the wall? That part's a blur."

"It's too bad you missed it. That was the best part! First, apparently there's a whole different kind of Art. It's similar to Biomancy, only instead of redirecting our energy on the inside, we push it out into nature. Your mother has a strong talent for it. She's the one who tore open the gates, just from wanting to! I don't know if she can light fires, but she creates storms."

He chuckled. "I could have predicted that one."

She wrinkled her nose at him again, then went on as if she hadn't heard him. "We're not the only ones with that kind of talent. Other people have been showing signs of power at least as strong as Biomancy, maybe more powerful, without even having any training. Apparently, it's a kind of magic that's been banned for ages, but now that we've used it to save the kingdom, they changed their minds. There's a woman with the army who summons lightning. She plans to open a school to train people in this new Art. As soon as she gets back from her honeymoon, anyway."

Peristra's voice trailed off. She gazed vacantly into the air. Kenan was debating with himself whether to poke her with his foot or just say something to start her talking again when she shook herself and started up again without any prompting. "I thought Raendel was going to use his illusion to hide us or get us free somehow. Instead, he disguised himself as you, and you as him. Master Lenore explained the next part to me but I'm still not sure how it works. The sword Anglachel apparently transfers energy from the person it cuts into the one holding it. Every kind of energy. Morgoth must have planned to use it to steal your strength for the fight against your brother. He stabbed Raendel, thinking he was you, and the sword transferred the curse of the Adoël into Morgoth."

She squinted, considering the idea. "Or maybe the curse was part of his energy. A corruption of it. Either way, when it entered Morgoth it corrupted his power. Whatever power he had to protect himself from me disappeared, and I burned him."

Kenan grinned at her. "Remind me to stay on your good side. Where's Raendel now?"

"He's in another sick room," she said. "But don't worry, he's recovering too. Master Jabal tended to him and said he should be back on his feet soon. And it's always a good idea to stay on my good side."

Her hand dropped onto the bed while she talked, resting a few inches away from his. He slid his hand over and rested it lightly on hers. "Every side of you is good, Peristra. I'd be honored if I could just stay at your side."

He made a mental note that her blush was even more charming than when she wrinkled her nose.

RAENDEL OPENED HIS EYES TO SEE A YOUNG WOMAN STANDING over him. She had a slim figure, with long dark hair and deep brown eyes. He felt like he should know her but couldn't quite figure out where he'd seen her before.

I don't even know where I'm seeing her now. He tried to lift his head to look around. It took two attempts, but on the second one he was able to swivel his head left, then right, then down. He wasn't in his own room, unless someone had recently furnished it with a feather bed and silk sheets. Wood paneling hung with bright tapestries covered the walls. It looked more similar to Prince Kenan's room than to his.

He tried to sit up so he could see more but didn't make it far before a sharp pain in his shoulder stopped him. The woman put a hand on his chest and pushed him back down.

"Take it easy," she said. "That wound goes straight through you. Master Jabal managed to seal it up, but you don't want to break it open again. Anglachel didn't leave much energy in you for him to work with, so it'll be a while before you're ready to walk around."

He stared in disbelief. He knew that voice. "Aeriel?"

She laughed. "Yes, it's me. I do look a bit different, don't I? So do you. So do all the Adoël."

His neck refused to hold his head up any longer. He dropped it back onto the soft pillow. "How?"

Aeriel grinned at him. "You did it. You broke the curse. You're a hero! Don't even try to be modest, you knew what you were doing."

He closed his eyes. "No, I didn't know. All I did was try to save Kenan. When Peristra burned through my gag...I'd heard Morgoth threaten Kenan, and I had to protect him somehow. All I could think to do was take his place. So, I made myself look like him, and him like me, then I shifted my image a little so the blade would miss my heart."

Aeriel raised her eyebrows.

"Not that I was scared of dying," Raendel said. "But if I died the illusion would be broken and Kenan would've been in danger again. Where is Kenan? Is he all right? And Timothy—?"

Aeriel laughed at him softly. "Prince Kenan is fine. Lord Timothy too. Lady Peristra is tending the prince in another room down the hall. He's still a little weak from that crossbow wound and the fever, but he'll recover now thanks to Lord Timothy's early treatment. And just so you know, I didn't think you were scared of dying. I just couldn't believe you really didn't think this would make you a hero."

She leaned forward and placed one hand on his shoulder. "As long as I've known you, you've underestimated yourself. I suppose we all did that to some degree, but I'll bet you still don't expect to get a reward."

"A reward? For what? I was only doing my duty. We are sworn to protect the royal family—"

"Well, you do deserve a reward, and you're going to get several. A hero—and you are a hero, Raendel—always deserves rewards. Here's your first one."

She bent down and stopped his protest by pressing her lips on his.

ABOUT THE AUTHOR

Kevin King grew up in south Louisiana, raised on a steady diet of gumbo and fiction novels. His hobbies include Renaissance Fairs, bookstores, fencing, and daydreaming. He lives outside of Seattle with his wife and their combined book collection.
Learn more about him on his website at -
www.kevinkingauthor.com .

f facebook.com/KevinKingAuthor
🐦 twitter.com/KevinKingAuthor
📷 instagram.com/KevinKingAuthor
📌 pinterest.com/KevinKingAuthor
g goodreads.com/KevinKingAuthor

Made in United States
Orlando, FL
23 February 2022